AIR AND ANGELS

AIR AND ANGELS

a novel by

Annie Bullen

An Alison Press Book
Secker & Warburg. London

First published in England 1987 by
The Alison Press/Martin Secker & Warburg Limited
54 Poland Street, London W1V 3DF

British Library Cataloguing in Publication Data
Bullen, Annie
    Air and angels : a novel.
    I. Title
    823'.914[F]   PR6052.U43/

    ISBN 0–436–07560–1

Photoset by Deltatype, Ellesmere Port, Cheshire
Printed and bound in Great Britain by
Biddles Limited, Guildford and King's Lynn

Twice or thrice had I loved thee
Before I knew thy face or name;
So in a voice, so in a shapeless flame,
Angels affect us oft, and worshipped be.

John Donne

Chapter One

'That's not the point,' said Philip, staring and sighing like a tired schoolmaster. 'They stay there for at least a day. You've got plenty of time to collect the swarm.'

'I know, I know – and that is just what he was doing. He asked me to help.'

'But I don't quite understand what he wanted you to do, dear. You mean you had to hit the bees?'

Petra stared across the table at her mother, not sure whether the powdery face behind the brightness of round silver-blue eyes was wrinkled in genuine perplexity, or if the questioning was deliberately obtuse.

She put down her knife and offered the cheese dish to the older woman, who sat looking at her, eyebrows raised in what Petra took to be quizzical amusement. Petra tried not to feel silly.

'No, not the bees. I had to hit the branch,' she said. 'The bees were on the branch in a swarm, like a sort of growth. They looked unreal, as if someone had just stuck them there, and what I found disturbing was that the surface of the swarm was shifting and moving all the time.'

Philip sighed. He had heard all this before. How the old man who lived in a little timber-planked bungalow just outside the village had run up to Petra one day, as she was walking past with the children, and had asked for her help in recovering his swarm.

Philip cut himself a large slice of cheese, gloomily ignoring

1

the Brie and the Camembert which Petra and her mother were eating with salad. He reached out for a piece of bread to go with his Cheddar. Petra heard the sigh and understood it. She carried on.

'There they were – a great crawling mass and he wanted to catch them. But the branch was at such an odd angle that he couldn't do it all by himself. So he asked me to give the branch a good knock and he scooped them up in his basket. I was stung on the knee.'

M's face lost its bright, polite gaze and she leant forward, elbows on the dark table. 'Caroline was allergic to bee stings when you were children,' she said. 'I remember once on the beach, Devon, I think, or perhaps Cornwall. Anyway, you were both playing in the dunes – so it must have been Cornwall – and she came running up to me and just held out her thumb. She was so pale and her eyes had gone very big and black. She didn't cry, though, and we pulled out the sting and your father took her down to the water to bathe her hand. But it didn't do the trick and she had a rash all up her arm – right the way up from her thumb to her shoulder. Don't you remember, we had to take her to the little hospital, and they gave her an injection? I don't think she was ever stung again after that, but the doctor said she was allergic to bees.'

Petra thought for a minute but she could not remember the incident, although she instantly had a vision of the sunny little hospital whose sandy-floored waiting room had been packed with holidaymakers suffering from sunburn. 'I thought we went to that hospital when I was stung by the jellyfish,' she said, but her mother shook her head vaguely and turned to Philip.

'How's business, Philip?' Philip Garlick did not dislike his mother-in-law; on the contrary, he admired her energy, but she made him feel inadequate, as if she were mocking him the whole time, ever so gently. Her constant interest in other people and their affairs, her genuine concern over even their trivial doings, put him on the defensive. The innocent 'How's business?', with the slight emphasis on the latter word, irritated him. He knew that she thought his job slight and the

2

books that he edited were not, he knew, what M would call real books, good solid ones with hard covers and authoritative prefaces. Flimsy guidebooks, designed to turn the most inept into an expert overnight, that was where his work lay now. It seemed to Philip that M was echoing Petra's patronizing attitude to his job.

His wife treated his career as if it were a step, a stage on the way to something better. But a year or so earlier, Philip had realized that he enjoyed his work; he liked producing guides to this, and step-by-step child's-play manuals to that, and the days when he dreamed first of becoming a top-flight journalist, then of guiding great works of literature through to publication, were times that he looked back on with some measure of incredulity.

He knew that he dared not admit his satisfaction to Petra, he would not say: 'I have lost that enthusiasm which you still possess; I am content, while I know that you are restless for me.' It was not, he supposed, out of any sort of respect for her feelings that he kept this contentment (stagnation, she would have said) to himself, using it as a wrap, a comforter, he realized, slightly ashamed. It was simply that he no longer had the mental energy to argue his case.

Perhaps he *was* stagnating, atrophying into the dry routine of middle age. He sighed again and looked across the oval table to his wife, who was, as usual, without repose. Her small hands were busy peeling an orange. She had used a knife to cut off a circular cap from the top of the loose jacket and was now levering the rest of the peel away with her thumb and her forefinger. She sat slightly sideways on the rush chair ('My God, we must get those chairs re-seated,' thought Philip, without resolution), aloof and absorbed in the task of just sitting and peeling. Philip felt a pang which he could not identify, as he looked at her small head with its shiny fall of almost-blonde hair tucked neatly behind her ears, and her unbelievably straight nose, which fitted her face perfectly, reminding him of the nose of a child, before adolescence has pulled the face into its adult shape.

The dark red corners of the Garlicks' draughty dining room

3

were vague and indistinctly defined in the flickering light of the candles that Petra insisted on using every time they ate in there, and M shivered. The room was very large and, like the rest of the old stone house, had an abandoned air. The walls were painted in a dull brick-red, which M liked. But why, she thought, had not they done something with the doors and the windows, which were shabby with peeling white gloss paint.

She rubbed at her ankle, which still tingled from when she had banged into an untidy pile of books as she came into the room. There seemed to be hopeless piles of things all over the house – bundles of clothes spilling out of cardboard boxes earmarked for jumble sales, but never sent once Petra's initial enthusiasm for clearing them out had waned. Books, old radios, were left in the same state of limbo and there were heaps of magazines and newspapers on chairs and on the floor. Windowsills and tables drooped with sad pots of moribund plants which Petra refused to throw out until she was completely satisfied that there was no chance at all of revival. On a previous visit, M had suggested that she do something to help tidy up, but Petra had seemed worried by the offer.

'I haven't the time to go through the magazines just now,' she had told her mother. 'I'll do it next week and then I can chuck them out.'

'You haven't read *any* of them?'

'Oh, yes. It's just that there are bits that I need to cut out. You know, recipes and decorating ideas, and plants. I'll do it soon.'

Perhaps she had a plan, some sort of a project, thought M. That was just like Petra. Full of ideas which could never be fulfilled, because then their perfection would be spoiled.

Petra was well aware that both her husband and her mother were thinking about her and it made her feel defensive. She tapped her foot on the rung of the chair as she divided her orange into segments. Luckily it was a loose-skinned fruit with little white pith, which split evenly. Petra hated orange juice to ooze between her fingers.

'Oh hell!' she thought. 'The bedside lamp in M's room doesn't work and she's noticed that these chairs are coming to pieces. I wonder if it costs a lot to get them done. Perhaps I can sneak the bulb out of here and get it up to her room, without her noticing. She made that up about Caroline. She wasn't allergic to bees or anything for that matter and she wouldn't have been brave if she was. She would have made a scene.'

'You won't forget to pick William up from Mrs Swann's tomorrow, will you, Philip?' she said. Her husband, who normally hated being reminded of anything he had to do, especially if he had forgotten about it, turned and smiled at her. She relaxed.

'Of course I won't. And Fiona's outing to the village hall. And Dan's flower.' Dan, their middle child, a gentle boy of six, had lately developed an obsession about flowers and had carefully set himself the task of taking one flower each morning, fixing its name in his head, and presenting it to his teacher.

'He's looking forward to being on his own with the children,' thought Petra, surprised. She said: 'You're looking forward to it!'

Philip peered at her so that the bright points of light from the candles reflected in the lenses of his dark-rimmed glasses and she could not see his eyes. He wondered if she was going to accuse him of being glad to be without her for a couple of days and he decided, with relief, that she was not. He suddenly loved her very much. 'I don't know how we're going to manage without you,' he joked. Petra smiled, M beamed and they each felt a flood of good will.

Petra's smile and the dissolution of Philip's aloof detachment brought warmth back into the room, thought M with amazement. She worried a lot about her elder daughter's marriage, well aware that Petra's hyper-critical attitude, to herself as much as to others, was a force capable of terrible destruction.

'I must not compare her with Caroline,' thought M, full of the dark perfection of her younger daughter.

'We're doing a beginner's guide to beekeeping,' Philip was telling Petra, his voice pedantic and precise, as it became when he spoke for any length of time. 'I'll bring you home a copy when it is completed. It might interest you.'

'Darling Elise,' Frederic wrote, wiping a thin age-blotched hand across his bony nose. 'Today I find that they have settled well in their new home. I have added more frames to two of the other hives, as the nectar is flowing well this year. I picked some of the little wild roses for you today, but the petals fall so quickly.' He sighed deeply, his watery eyes fixed on the pollen-dusted stamens of the roses whose heart-shaped petals lay crumpled sadly on the table. 'I cannot describe the beauty of these lanes at this time of year, but you will know what I mean when I say that they are full of the luxury of June – as you love them. I will try to tell you about them tomorrow.' He carefully folded the lined writing paper and put it in an envelope which he took from a large box.

He licked the flap, sealed it carefully, smoothed the edges down with his clenched fist and then, letter in hand, left the square wooden room which was cosy in the light of the oil lantern hanging from a strong hook on one of the plank-like beams. He returned briefly to pull an old brown cardigan round his sloping shoulders and, opening the other door, which led to the garden by way of three wooden steps, disappeared into the warm night.

Frederic was running, rushing, to meet Elise. His thin, clever Jewish face was sharp and keen, with no rounded edges to blur its strength. The plane of his cheeks made an angle with his long, bony nose, and his high flat forehead was a shelf, below which his yellow eyes sparkled. As he ran, he clutched at a piece of paper folded flat. The message, scribbled hastily on a page torn from a student's notebook, read: 'Must see you today. Usual place after lectures. E.'

It had been handed to him just before the last lecture of the day and he had fretted a little during the hour-long anatomy class, aware that the ease with which he usually lost himself in this subject was disturbed and gone. Elise, who normally divided her time happily and easily between her classical language studies at the university and her friendship with Frederic, had slowly become nervous and edgy over the last few troubled months and this tension had communicated itself to him.

He knew the situation as well as anyone in the university town, but even though his Jewish descent was plainly proclaimed by the cast of his features, he felt that the rumour and hatred which seemed to be growing against his race did not apply to him.

Frederic was a unit, alone, apart from Elise's astounding love which he had accepted, at first without recognition – (personal love had been a story, a fable, in the orphanage) – and then with a kind of fear, trembling at a gift that he felt he did not merit and did not know how to return.

He had never given his Jewishness much thought, and in fact he had not really been aware of it until he had left the orphanage as a prize pupil, a surprise success who had been chosen to go to medical school. Perhaps there had been other Jews among the parentless boys; he did not know. It was only when he started his studies that Frederic became aware of himself as an individual in relation to other people, to his place and time in history and to the fact that he, Frederic Mann, was a being who had some control over his own future.

Many years later, as conversant as he ever would be with conventional behaviour patterns, he realized, with a sense of shock, that Elise had picked him up – chosen him. Confronted by an outraged, delighted Frederic, Elise had laughed at him.

'Now you have grown up! Of course I chose you!'

Elise, the serious classical language student, had literally bumped into Frederic in a large, cobbled courtyard outside the main university buildings. He had not noticed her before – indeed he had not noticed any of the women students, as he was still too busy discovering himself. At the moment of collision, he was walking backwards, absorbed in the graceful aerobatics performed by a wheeling, arching cluster of birds.

A pile of notebooks fell, with a clatter, onto the cobbles and

Frederic immediately started to gabble apologies and bent down to gather everything up. The frowning dark-haired girl took no notice of his discomfort.

'Those,' she lectured, pointing skywards, 'the dark ones, with the curved wings, are swifts. They scream.' For the first time, the harsh yelling screech of the scrambling birds came into focus for Frederic. 'And those, the swooping ones with the forked tails and white patches, are swallows,' said the girl, calmly.

A year later, Frederic experienced a curious sensation as he hurried along the road which would take him abruptly out of the town, and he again heard the screeching of the swifts as they wheeled and turned in their never-ending quest for food. He knew that the pleasant year of friendship was over. That game was finished and, for the first time in his life, he was going to have to make a commitment. What it was to be he did not know, but he shivered at the thought of change, and hurried on to Elise.

The road, lined with precise rows of stone-built houses with scallop-shaped tiles on their roofs and cobbled paths up to the neat front doors, suddenly gave way to a dusty cart track which curved to a farmhouse in the distance on the left and branched off to the right in the form of a narrow lane, tunnelled beneath hawthorn and beech trees. Frederic followed the rutted path whose awkward ridges were softened by swathes of lush, sprawling grass. He sneezed as the pollen from the lacy flat heads of the cow parsley, which rampaged over the banks, tickled his nose. Easing his tie undone, he pulled it off over his head, and slipped his fingers into the open neck of his shirt to feel the perspiration running underneath his arms.

Sunlight sparkled on the high overgrown banks, where it filtered its way through the young green of the beech leaves and made jewels of the wild roses which studded the sides.

Elise was savagely pulling the soft pink petals from a wild rose which she held carefully between her thumb and forefinger. Her left hand was scratched and bleeding and Frederic saw that there was a heap of torn-off petals spread in the grass

8

by her sandalled foot. She was sitting in a hollow in the bank and, when she looked up at Frederic, he was frightened by the hard, blank look in her dark eyes, which fixed themselves on a point just above his head as she started speaking quickly.

'You've got to leave Germany, Frederic,' she started, her eyes becoming brighter with passion as she searched his uncomprehending face. She tried again, emotion clipping her words, so that they came out in a rapid staccato stutter.

'It is my father. I can't talk to him any more and now I don't feel for him any more. Since he came back from Berlin there is a madness in the way that he talks about your people. I know that terrible things are going to happen and I know that you won't be safe. He talks about it, to me and to my mother. I don't think that we can accept this,' she said in formal tones, and her face wrinkled, near to tears.

Frederic was speechless and did not know how to react. He had never met Elise's parents – her German-born, Army officer father and her French mother – but he had always sensed her worship for her father.

'You must apply, now, for that exchange to England, before anything does happen,' Elise said, coldly and rapidly. 'You said that Professor Lippisch told you that you were likely to be chosen and there is no reason at all why you should not finish your studies there.'

This was in fact quite true, Frederic knew, and if it had not been for the fact that he had shied away from leaving Elise to go to England, he would have put his name down for the exchange scheme, and spent his final year at a British medical school.

'No, Elise,' he said, looking gently at her small pale face with round, brown poodle eyes, spiked now with tears. 'No, I shan't go – how can I leave you?'

'Don't be stupid,' she shouted at him, the tears spilling out as she stood up, so that the dismembered bits of rose in her skirt fell to the ground. 'I shall come with you!'

'Philip?' asked Petra, in low tones as they lay side by side in

9

bed, each staring at the dark ceiling. Philip was thinking about taking the children to the village cricket match the day after tomorrow and Petra was still dwelling on her encounter with the thin old man who kept the bees. Philip grunted.

'Doesn't that old man live on his own in the wooden bungalow?' she asked.

'You mean the bee chap?'

'Yes.'

'I think so, yes. He moved in about five years ago, I think, and there was no one with him then. Why?'

'He said something after we'd got the swarm in the basket. Something about his wife.'

'Perhaps you got it wrong. I'm sure that there's no one else there.'

'No. But I thought he said: "I must go now, to write to my wife." '

🐝 🐝

'Come on Petra, let's put our stuff here – no, here, by these rocks. Help me spread the towels out now – *come on*!' shouted Caroline at her elder sister, who was looking anxiously up the length of the beach to the distant stile, to see if their parents, laden with all the equipment for a good day out at the seaside, were on the way.

The beach was perfect, with rolling, sloping farmland behind; only a fence and the stile stopped the big blundering Friesian cows from walking onto the sand. It was a long inlet, narrowing on the landward side, snuggling between two protecting headlands, with a sea that was today gentle and friendly, sidling and rolling slowly up over the enormous width of perfectly smooth sand between the headlands' tips.

Great blue-grey mounds of rounded rocks, mussel-covered and fringed with seaweed, cupping little pools, fortified the cliffs that were marked here and there with the damp slits of cave openings. A stream from a spring at the top of the beach – now a long way off from the two small girls in blue shorts and red jerseys – trickled down, widening as it spread to meet the sea and caused bumpy ridges in the sand on its way. The sea sparkled calmly in the sun and the sand was warm underfoot and Caroline accepted this perfection as her right.

'Let's get into our swimming costumes, Petra – come on, quickly, before they get here. Bet you can't!' she laughed at her elder sister who was standing uncertainly, a stripy towel over one arm and her little blue knapsack, with her bathing costume and a book tucked in it, still on her back.

Petra saw, with some relief, that M and Daddy were making their way to this side of the beach. They had crossed the stream at the top, where it was only a trickle, so that was all right and they would not have to paddle across it lower down, where it was quite deep. But would they like this place on the beach that she and Caroline had chosen? They were usually very fussy about where they sat; it must not be too near other people and they always wanted the right sort of rocks to lean against and dry towels on and put the picnic on, so that the food did not become gritty and sandy. And the sun must be just right. Petra tried to work out if the rocks that they had chosen were going to cast a shadow on their bit of sand before the day was out. She waved anxiously as M and Daddy came closer, and screwed her eyes in a squint to see if M was looking crossly at Caroline, who was standing stark naked on the beach, pulling on her navy blue swimming costume.

'That's a lovely spot, girls. Come on Petra, get your bathers on, slowcoach,' shouted Daddy. 'Look, Caro's halfway to the sea already!'

'I don't think I'll swim just yet,' said Petra, turning red and knowing that she badly wanted to get into the water.

'Well, get that stuffy jersey off, anyway. You'll bake.'

'I feel cold,' lied Petra, stiffly. 'I'm going to explore.' She wandered up the beach, keeping close to the cliff, where the sand was gritty with small stones which worked their way between her bare toes slipping sweatily inside her brown leather sandals.

At eleven, Petra was old enough to realize that Caroline, whose every action was made with natural grace, slipped through life, taking everything that came at face value and enjoying it accordingly. Petra, nearly two years older, was

11

suspicious of her own reactions, and watched.

It was all right for Caro, Petra thought grumpily, wriggling her toes to try to scrape away the gritty sand. She was slim and pretty and always looked right so that people never minded what she did. Petra gasped as she grazed her ankle against a jutting piece of barnacle-smothered rock and self-pity made her eyes prickle and her throat feel tight. She was hot and uncomfortable in that horrid red jersey – M had knitted them one each, and Caroline's looked perfect against her evenly browned skin and her long black hair. Petra felt red-cheeked and lumpy in hers and she pulled it over her head and deliberately dropped it in a rock pool.

Was it that day she had been stung by the jellyfish, Petra wondered sleepily as she lay in bed beside Philip, who was by now fast asleep, defenceless and soft-faced in the moonlight. She turned onto her right side, hands clenched into tight balls as she drifted in and out of dreams.

Caroline, sitting straight and easily on her pony, frozen in Petra's mind against the backdrop of a brightly berried holly bush. Her ginger jacket was neatly buttoned and her pale jodhpurs spotless. The bay pony's coat gleamed and shone as he fretted, stamping and chewing on his bit. Caro knew how to soothe him and stood no nonsense, while Petra, wearing that prickly red jersey again, still dripping from the rock pool, tried time and time again to clamber up onto her own mount, a dirty-looking grey, who infuriatingly swung away each time Petra heaved her left foot up to the stirrup.

Then, there she was, standing at the top step of a broken staircase, looking despairingly at the great gap gaping before her as the deep green steps mocked her down to a heaving mass of swelling water below. She would overbalance if she jumped.

'Come on, Petra – don't be wet – jump – jump – jump!' yelled Caroline, an alarming grown-up Caroline, beautiful as she linked arms with M and Daddy, standing on the flat unbroken shoreline across the water from the fractured staircase in the tower. They all turned away, laughing.

M never dreamed. She usually read a few pages of Jane Austen or Anthony Trollope, before she lay carefully on her back, ready for sleep. This had been her habit for the past twenty years and she felt she knew the Trollope and Austen characters intimately, although she had no idea of the complete pattern of the stories because she had never read one to the end. She picked out a little bit at random and read it to soothe herself and she knew that there would be nothing to upset her because she was sure that all would be well in the end. She knew that it was, in fact, because she enjoyed the last pages of the stories best of all, saving them up for really trying days. Any upset that she might stumble across in the pages was always neatly balanced, as she felt that life ought to be.

But tonight there was no bulb in her bedside light, and she did not want to get out of bed after being soothed to the point of sleep by Fanny Price or Doctor Thorne, in order to turn off the rather bright overhead light. Her thoughts drifted, as they always did, towards Caroline, and the sharp pain twisted inside her, so that she gave a little hiss, until the curtain came down between the bright image of her younger daughter and her own well trained mind. It was good, instead, to think of Petra being tender towards Philip tonight. The children, too, had all been perfectly happy and thrilled to see her when she had arrived at Coombe that afternoon. Fiona, pretty, self-confident and independent, was just like Caroline at that age, M allowed herself to think. Caroline, when she was young, had always known exactly what she could and could not do – she went to her limits but was contained by them and did not look for anything else. Petra on the other hand – M sighed to herself. There had always been a lack of self-confidence, although there was no doubt that, as a child, Petra's intelligence far outstripped her younger sister's, even if she had no common sense at all.

M was not a stupid woman and she cared deeply about her relationships with other people, but there was a self-conscious centre to Petra that she had never been able to melt or pierce. Petra had demanded more than love as a child, while Caroline, then open and undemanding emotionally, had given and received love in equal portions, thought M. Suddenly she tired of the mental burden of this analysis, folded her hands calmly on her stomach and instantly fell asleep.

Dan woke in the night and heard an owl hunting through the dark. He climbed out of bed and quietly stepped past the bundle that was his younger brother, William, blissfully asleep and curled up with a moth-eaten soft toy which had once resembled a lamb. Dan tiptoed to the window. The owl hooted again and the sound was loud and urgent as he peered round the curtain into the moonlight that transformed the safe apple trees in the garden into gaunt, twisted shapes. He stared, thrilled, as a great white shape etched itself into the night and swooped away, disappearing suddenly and quietly.

'Tomorrow,' thought Dan, 'I shall pick a piece of meadow-sweet from the field and take it in to Mrs Beckett.' He let the corner of the curtain drop and clambered back into bed, overwhelmed by the owl and by the cloying scent of the fragrant meadowsweet, already in his mind.

Chapter Two

'I often feel,' Tom Appleton said to his wife as he swallowed the last drop of his second gin and French that evening, 'that we got the children's names the wrong way round.'

M, sipping slowly at her first sherry, looked up sharply and cautiously asked 'Why?', knowing exactly what he was going to say. Petra, listening outside, crouched under the window-sill, stiffened and froze. She was not exactly eavesdropping, as she had been on her way into the house to filch some matches on Caroline's orders, and the air of secrecy which this mission engendered had persuaded her to creep softly, Red Indian style, crouched uncomfortably low and careful not to step on twigs or anything that would crunch or crackle underfoot. She had been planning a silent flit past the open french windows of the drawing room, which were mostly filled with Daddy's broad back and legs, straddled wide apart. She was then going to climb in at the dining room window which was always open in the summer.

It would not really have mattered if Daddy or M had seen her, as they took little notice of their daughters while they had their evening drinks and they could not possibly have guessed that she was going to steal matches. But staying hidden mattered now that she had overhead them talking about her. She liked her name and she knew that it was the only thing about her that made people take notice. They weren't going to give that to Caroline.

Tom, content now that the gin had done its usual soothing

work, did not want to enter into any argument with M, who tended, he thought, to be far too ready to shout down any criticism of the children.

He was a tall, fair-haired man with a face that always looked slightly sunburnt. His hair was not really thick enough to cover his scalp, so he always combed it carefully and the marks of the teeth of the comb traced a sharp, straight pattern across his head from the well defined parting. Petra liked it when he had just washed his hair and it was fluffy and wispy, softening his brick-like face. Tom was a large man and although his suits were made by the best tailor in the town, his clothes always seemed to be under some sort of a strain. His jackets stretched tensely across his back, the good cloth giving and pulling a little as he moved his arms, and when he sat down his trousers creased tightly across his thighs.

Petra, when very small, had seen a picture of a bullfrog, all puffed up, and had told M that it was like Daddy when he was cross. M, stifling a giggle, had told Petra, more sharply than was necessary, that she must never say that again.

'What I mean,' said Tom, waving his empty glass in one hand and clinking the coins in his trouser pocket with the other, 'is that Petra as a name would have suited Caroline better than it does Petra. It's an unusual name, romantic and all that – the pink city, you know – and Caroline is, well, less ordinary shall we say, more noticeable, than Petra.'

M didn't remind him that the naming of their elder daughter had been his idea entirely. She knew exactly what he meant and agreed with him, although she would not have admitted it. 'I don't know what you're talking about, Tom,' she said, deliberately sounding vague. 'They're both nice names. Petra's a much cleverer child than Caroline, anyway,' she added defensively.

Petra started to back away around the corner of the house, keeping close to the wall and feeling the warm, ugly pebbledash finish scraping against her bare upper arms and catching at her blue and white summer skirt. Her knees were stained green and brown from the sour mossy earth and she felt indignant that M and Daddy should discuss her behind her back.

16

When she reached the corner, she got up and rushed into the kitchen, banging the door as if she had walked across the gravel path and the lawn. No one took any notice and she opened the middle drawer where boxes of matches snuggled neatly into a paper packet. Luckily it was already open, and so no one would realize that she had taken a box. She stuffed the matchbox into the pocket of her skirt and noiselessly opened the larder door so that she could steal a few biscuits from the red tin with the Coronation picture on it. Petra always felt hungry.

She ran across the strip of grass and skirted the gravel driveway so that she would not be heard entering the little clump of elm trees that the children called their wood. She blinked and hung back by a straggling holly bush, spying on Caroline in the dim, tree-diffused light. A thick wooden plank had been laid across the stumps of two sawn-off saplings and the dry, dead holly leaves and brown elm leaves had been swept away in a little semicircle from this makeshift table.

Caroline was kneeling on the soft earth in the space, setting out long white candles, a small box and a large tin plate. Petra watched her curiously as she sat back on the ground, her legs still folded in a kneeling position. Petra could not do that because it hurt her legs too much, but it came naturally to Caroline, like standing on her head and doing steady handstands, going right over and landing on her feet and being able to do neat little cartwheels, right round the lawn.

'Have you got them?' asked Caroline, without looking up. Petra stepped forward, trying not to look silly, and put the matches down on the slab of wood.

'You melt the candles – upside-down, like this, so that they drip onto the plate – and I'll make it. Ouch! That hurt my finger.' Caroline sucked her burnt forefinger and looked doubtfully at the little heap of solidifying wax.

'How big does it have to be?'

'I don't know. It's silly, really, Caro – it's only something in a book. We shouldn't do it really.' Petra wished she had never told Caroline about the wax doll.

'Why not? I hate Mrs Macey. She said I'm stupid. She's

17

stupid. I don't see the point of working out all those sums and I'm not going to do them, even if she makes me stay at school all night. I don't like maths and I'm not doing them.'

'Don't be silly. She'll make you. I'll do them for you.' Petra, who was good at figures, knew that Caroline would refuse. Caroline certainly was not stupid – she was completely self-absorbed and, having made up her mind that she could not be bothered to do something, or that she could see no advantage in doing it, just turned her back.

The junior maths teacher, Mrs Macey, was one of the few people at their school who did not seem to have fallen under Caroline's spell. She was wrong to have called Caro stupid though, thought Petra, who also disliked Mrs Macey, although the woman had made something of a teacher's pet of her. Caroline, she guessed, had shown no emotion at the time, but was now planning to put her life back on a smooth course by removing the irritant.

'Don't worry. No one will do them. Mrs Macey won't be there tomorrow.' The lump of wax in Caroline's slender fingers was being rolled and moulded into a sausage shape and the child held it over the flame of the lighted candle to soften the point where she planned to add arms and legs. Petra, growing horrified at what they were doing, nevertheless carried on melting wax for her and hoped that she had forgotten about the fire. She watched as the doll took shape and Caroline poked in two tiny stones to make eyes.

'What's that?' she asked as Caroline opened the pin box to reveal a dark, matted tangle lying on top of the pins.

'Her hair. You said it worked better if there was something belonging to the person. I took her brush out of her desk at break and combed out the hair. It was disgusting, her brush, all greasy and black. Serves her right.' Caroline pressed the tangled hair on top of the doll's head and Petra squeaked in horror as the piece of wax took on a grotesque, human aspect. The thought of her sister stealing back into the classroom and going through Macey's desk, and the sight of her sticking the obscene straggle of greasy hair onto the doll, appalled her, but Caroline carried on with her pressing and shaping and moulding.

'What do we say when we stick the pins in? Did it say in the book? You make something up – you're good at that. I'll build the fire.'

'I don't think you – we – should put it in the fire. What if something happens to her? We shouldn't do it,' stammered Petra, turning pink and standing on one leg.

'Don't be weedy. Something's got to happen to her. That's the whole point. You make up the words.' Caroline gathered up dry twigs and leaves and built a small fire, making a wigwam shape with the wood and piling the leaves underneath so that it would catch quickly. She had already gathered another small heap of twigs and pine cones to feed the fire once it had caught.

'Well, what do I say? Haven't you thought yet? Do we do anything else? What else did it say in your book?'

'They took their clothes off and danced round the fire.' Petra regretted the words instantly.

'That's good! We'll do that and I'll say – I know! Come on – take your things off.'

'No, I'm not going to! What if they see the smoke and come out?'

'They won't. Come on!'

'It's wicked. I'm not going to.'

'Well shut up then. You're weedy and a big drip!' Petra, red-faced, watched Caroline put a match to the little fire and feed it with bits of leaf and bark until it started to make a good blaze.

'See – it's not smoking at all.' Caroline slipped off her summer smock and stood holding the doll, slim and pale with dark hair shading her face and shoulders. She picked up a handful of pins and then, displaying the doll over her head, she paced around the fire, wearing only her grey school knickers. She intoned: 'Sticking pins in Macey, sticking pins in Macey, sticking pins in Macey – Macey's going to *die*.' Then she stood still, intent on viciously jabbing pins at the wax body.

'Macey's going to *die*!' she repeated and held the thing over the fire, balancing it between her forefingers which she pressed against the two pin heads sticking out of the doll.

19

Petra stiffened as she heard footsteps scrunching across the gravel. 'Caroline! – someone's coming – quick!'

'Macey's going to *die*!' shrieked Caroline, as she pulled her hands apart, letting the misshapen doll topple into the flames, which crackled and flared up as the hair and dripping wax singed and burnt.

Daddy marched into the wood in the way that grown-ups had, looking straight ahead at Caroline and the fire and taking no notice of the path which the girls had carefully trodden. He ignored Petra altogether and she noticed even through her shame and embarrassment that he had trampled down the little patch of white round-headed flowers which she and Caroline were always careful to avoid in the hope that they would eventually spread over the floor of their wood. Petra covered her face with her sweaty fingers.

She stirred in a shallow, dream-filled sleep as the urgent night hooting of an owl swept through the images in her mind. She had been frightened by this sound as a child, the rawness and the basic urge for survival that it told making her bury her head under the sheets, or call across the room to Caroline, who was always fast asleep. Now she snuggled up to Philip, who grunted and shifted and, as the owl flitted, silent again, back and forth across the small garden, they rearranged arms and legs in neat, sleeping shapes and twisted and wriggled until once more their bodies were lost to the control of the secret, night-time part of their beings.

Frederic, on the other hand, liked owls. He knew all the night noises, as sleep came increasingly less easily to him. The songs of nightingales and nightjars and the unearthly howl of the vixen, bumps and gruntings and clangings as hedgehogs blundered around his garden and the awful yellings of predatory night-prowling cats, were sounds that Frederic marked with the same pleasure that welcomes the song of the thrush on its high branch at deepening evening.

He lay in his bed, next to the large wooden trunk, with the letters F M painted on the side in unsteady white capitals. The trunk was capacious and old-fashioned, blue with a domed top sectioned with strips of fraying leather. On the other side of this trunk was another bed, the twin of Frederic's own. An iron bedstead, a flat, thinnish mattress and a pillow. No sheets or blankets, but a thin linen coverlet, pulled up over the hump of the pillow and tucked neatly in at the bottom, so that a shape like that of the corner of an envelope was achieved.

Frederic's coverlet was much the same, except that Elise had embroidered a green and blue pattern of twining herbs and grasses on his, whilst in the centre of hers there were pink, purple and blue flowers and green leaves. The room was sparsely furnished; the prettily embroidered bed covers and the jar of wilting dog roses whose petals littered the desk that served as Frederic's dressing table were the only touches of colour.

Frederic had made no changes to his lifestyle after Elise died. They had settled carefully and then happily in England, made careers, a few, not too close, friends; they had worked hard and seriously and had taken their relaxation with the same sort of care and with perfect pleasure. As two young refugees they lived in that style, never buying or getting or hoarding. They collected nothing and their life was a continual process of discussion. They walked and talked over the sunset, the sunrise, the early morning, the evening. Elise had known the names of all the birds, the flowers, but Frederic did not remember these names, preferring to dwell with pleasure on the knowledge of their shapes and colours and the places where they flew or grew.

When they lived in the town they walked every day in the countryside, but also enjoyed what the town had to offer in the same simple way. They always rented apartments or small houses, and this wooden bungalow with its paddocks and garden was the first home they had owned. Now Frederic was its sole possessor.

It did not occur to him that the impermanence of its wooden frame was the very thing that had attracted them to it in the

21

first place. Books, and now the bees, had been their only possessions. In the last years Frederic had sometimes wondered whether if they had built up more things, made a sounder material base to their life, then perhaps Elise would not have gone so quickly, left everything so suddenly and easily.

In the steady stream of moonlight that made nonsense of the skinny white cotton curtains, Frederic gazed at the humpy outline of his old trunk and then stretched out a thin arm so that he could curve his hand over the lid.

He remembered arriving in England, bewildered and rather afraid, and standing stiffly beside his trunk, which was then brand-new and less than half full with his medical textbooks, his other suit of clothes and a few underclothes. He had gazed around the seaport, taking in the smells and the sounds, and thinking all the time that, somewhere in England, Elise was waiting for him. There had been no time to make definite plans. His exchange year had been fixed by his Professor and Elise had arranged to come to England to stay awhile with her aunt Bernadette, her mother's younger sister, who by that strange sort of coincidence that turns a chain of events into a preordained fact, lived just outside the southern town which harboured Frederic's medical school.

Elise, as far as Frederic knew, had been in England for just about a week. They had agreed not to contact each other after making their plans – or rather, Elise had decided that this was the wisest course. Frederic had agreed to do everything that she ordered, marvelling in a dazed sort of way at her energy and forethought that was driving both their lives into a channel that would broaden and open onto a new and strange landscape. He never questioned her judgement and it was only on that quayside, anchoring himself anxiously to the spanking new trunk which was the only familiar thing in sight, that he began to wonder what their plans really were.

The enormity of it all suddenly overwhelmed him, as he realized that his round-eyed Elise, the only daughter of doting parents, was giving up her whole life to him. He swallowed air in a great, nervous gulp with the sudden knowledge that neither of them would return to Germany; she was losing her life to him, making a total commitment, and now Frederic knew that he must do the same.

The tender rush of love eclipsed all his feelings of loneliness and bewilderment and he stood up tall, eyes bright and arms straight down by his side with triumphant, clenched fists. And then, miraculously, there was Elise, with eyes as bright as his and dancing feet and laughing face, little hands clutching at his arm. He held her with a love and a need that he had never felt before and they both collapsed, still bright-eyed, onto the trunk, to talk over their plans, with the cold Dover wind blowing around them and the milling rush of the busy port cocooning them. They had begun their new dialogue that day and the conversation had never flagged. Not until Elise had died. And here, in this trunk, were the letters that Frederic wrote to her, not being able to bear the loneliness of his unshared thoughts.

Petra woke suddenly and easily, without that transition from dream images to waking reality that often put a strange mood or slant in her mind to colour the first few hours of the day and make the ordinary business of life seem unreal.

She thought of the packing, which she should have done the day before and which must be done now. Putting this off, she looked critically at Philip, still fast asleep beside her. He seemed weak and chinless while he slept. His hair, dark and slightly greasy, hung unattractively over one eye – he always left it too long in between washes and cuts – and his eyes with their tightly screwed-up lids seemed small and shrunken without his glasses. He breathed heavily, making odd popping noises with his mouth, which was pursed into a tight round red 'O'.

Petra became cross with herself for spying on him and judging him while he was defenceless in sleep, but at the same time she felt like prodding him into awareness. Instead she got out of bed and went downstairs to make a cup of tea. It was very early, but the sky was cloudless, a soft soulless blue, and the sun already up. Dan, dressed in shorts and a T-shirt, was sitting on the kitchen floor, pulling on a pair of rubber-soled shoes. Petra marvelled at her son's independence; Dan never needed direction on anything but he just plodded on sturdily and surely, taking his own unshakeable course.

'Why are you up so early – is William awake, too?' she asked him.

'No he's not.' Dan's solid round-eyed face was serious as always. 'I'm going to pick a piece of meadowsweet for Mrs Beckett.' Petra watched through the window as he marched steadily down the length of the garden and climbed the two stone steps built into the low wall that separated their piece of land from the meadow beyond. She wanted to go with him and hold his hand and run in the wet grass and exclaim at the early morning tracery of spider's webs picked out by a fine mesh of glittering dew. But she turned from the window and filled the kettle, then poured a glass of milk for Dan, thinking of the times that she and Caroline had crept out early in summer mornings to look for mushrooms in the damp fields.

At breakfast Petra lost her temper with Fiona, who was teasing Dan. Fiona, slim and neat, long dark hair wound tidily in fat plaits, slender brown legs rounded off neatly with white socks and clean shiny brown sandals, long lashes hiding the expression in her large brown eyes, seemed at times to be a changeling, a fairy child, nothing to do with her. Yet Petra remembered how she had loved the tiny baby Fiona with a sentiment that was out of touch with all practicality.

'Flesh of my flesh,' she would whisper to herself, the phrase moving her, as she gazed at the perfect, beautiful baby with violet eyes.

But now Fiona was a secretive child; at ten she had her own friends, a cluster of neat little girls who whispered and giggled together, her clubs, the secret societies of childhood, and she treated her parents as if they were kindly idiots and her brothers with unmerciful contempt. Petra often wanted to scream: 'I'm your mother – I understand – I remember!' but instead she found herself saying, through clenched teeth: 'You don't run this house, do you understand, Fiona?' when faced with the look of dumb contempt or blank amazement that Fiona turned on her from time to time.

It was this look that the child affected now when Petra asked her to stop teasing Dan about taking flowers to his teacher. Petra could see that M was shaken by her outburst, although both Fiona and Dan remained completely unmoved. In fact, thought Petra, guilty at her own depth of feelings against her daughter, she need not have remonstrated with the child in the first place, as Dan obviously did not notice a little thing like being teased. William, however, was visibly unhappy and kept asking Petra how long she would be away.

'Two nights,' she told him. 'Two nights and three days.'

'Can't I come – why can't I come, Mummy?'

'Because you must go to school and Daddy is staying at home to look after you.'

'But I want to go to Granny's too. I want to see Grandpa.'

'You wouldn't like it, William. Granny and I will be in the car a long time. We're going all the way to London, to Aunty Caroline's.'

It was strange, thought Petra, as they drove away from the house in M's smart little car, that she had not been on her own with her mother for years and years; probably the last time was when M had driven her and her great pile of luggage up to the Midlands for her first term at university.

Chapter Three

Petra looked gloomily out of the car window at yet another set of small, even, brick houses and she wondered how people could bear to put such awful colours on their doors and windows. Lime-green and watery mauve competing with each other. She didn't want to go to university. She started working out, yet again, the cost of the train fare home each weekend, and hoped, desperately, that she would not have to share a room with anyone.

Caroline had seemed amused at the prospect of Petra having to live in one of the university buildings.

'Never mind,' she had said. 'You can just use it as a base while you look out for a flat of your own. There are bound to be lots of people wanting to share.'

'No – we've got to live in for the first year – and anyway, I couldn't afford a flat.'

'Of course you could. Dad would cough up if you went about it the right way. I'm sure you don't really have to live in. Does that mean you've got to be in at ten every night and no visitors? Just like boarding school?' Caroline was being rather condescending, Petra thought, and she hated her for it. It was all right for Caro; she had no trouble making friends and seemed to like being at the centre of a great crowd of people, changing her plans to suit the moment and not needing a safe place to touch for luck.

M was also thinking about her daughters and their independence. She accelerated as they left the small Midland

26

town behind them, and her round blue eyes made sudden darts from the road, to try to get the measure of the countryside which was flashing past.

'Lovely views, dear. I'm quite surprised. Dad said to tell you that if you find you really can't manage on your allowance, to let us know. But it should be enough. You're lucky to be in that hall of residence, you won't have to worry about food. I'm surprised that Caroline's managing as well as she is, although those who she's sharing her flat with are very sensible girls and Caro seems so much older than seventeen, somehow. She's always been so independent.'

Petra said nothing. She had watched, jealously, still in her school uniform, while her younger sister had scraped her way onto a nursing course. It was hard to see her sister leaving school while she was committed to another year of study and even harder when, suddenly (it had seemed sudden at the time but Petra accepted that was the way things happened to Caroline), the way was opened to a career which so suited Caro it seemed like a cliché. At that point the thought of Caroline in nurse's uniform seemed like a joke, obviously something that was never meant to become reality.

Daddy (Petra could never think or speak of her father by any other name, although M and Caro never called him anything but 'Dad' now) – Daddy's attitude to the whole business had been so strange that she still could not sort out in her mind Caroline's position as far as he was concerned. Caroline, leaving school at sixteen, waiting for her nursing course to start, quickly and easily made a new set of friends in the coffee shops and Wimpy bars in town. She went to parties and to the cinema and even to pubs. Different boyfriends drove up to their house to take her ten-pin bowling or dancing or swimming or sometimes even to the theatre. Petra sat up in her bedroom, revising, saying she could not go out because of exams.

Then, suddenly, Caroline was famous. Infamous, M had said. Well, not famous exactly, but everyone in their village and in the town knew that the girl with a wide white-toothed, perfect smile and a jagged necklace that looked like rows of

27

shark's teeth, posing blandly and unselfconsciously naked on the inside pages of a newspaper that Petra's parents never took, was Caroline Appleton.

It appeared on a Wednesday and, that morning, Daddy had gone to his office as usual, to find his secretary and one of the typists making excited little smothered giggles over a newspaper draped over the top of the new electric typewriter. They had hastily tucked it out of sight when he had come in but Daddy, being Daddy, could not bear not to know what was going on. He opened the paper, glanced automatically at the naked girl on the facing page, and it was only the shocked quality of the silence from the two women standing next to him that made him look more closely.

He later told M that he simply had not recognized his daughter. Petra, poring closely over the picture later on, understood this. The girl in the paper seemed larger than Caroline, her smile wider, her eyes bigger, but she supposed that was just a trick of the camera.

When Daddy had realized that the naked girl with slicked-back hair and sparkling raindrops on her healthy young body was his younger daughter, he had snatched up the paper, marched straight through into his own office and locked the door. No more was heard of him that day. His staff, worried, rang M, but she told them to leave him alone. She was right, of course. Daddy came home that night and roared at Caroline, who remained completely cool and unselfconscious about the whole business. Who, he wanted to know, had taken the photograph – and where? Why had she not told her family?

Caroline had laughed then, rather rudely, Petra thought. She told Daddy and M that the photograph was one of a series (here M shuddered visibly) taken in a proper studio by a freelance photographer whom she had met whilst he was holidaying nearby. It was all perfectly respectable (Daddy snorted) and she had, that morning, received a cheque for fifty pounds. At that point Daddy stopped roaring and snorting, lost his cross-bullfrog look and began to calm down. It was not the money that pleased him so much as the fact that Caroline had had the wit to earn it, showing sound com-

28

mercial common sense, and would now need some professional advice about using it wisely.

He puffed up a bit again when Caroline talked about another set of pictures, but Petra could see that he was feeling rather proud of his daughter now and the brightness of his eyes and the solid placing of his thickset thighs in their good strong tweed reflected this pride rather than the anger he had felt before. Caroline, sprawling back in the nicest chair in the room, one leg folded underneath her and the other swinging slowly, the little red straps of her sandal caught daintily across her toes, over the velvet-covered arm of the chair, took Daddy's slow admiration for granted, just as she had accepted his outburst of temper.

Petra clutched her sherry glass and sat well back into the corner of the long settee. She and Caroline were each given a minute quantity of sherry at half past six in the evening and this was to prove that M and Daddy were bringing up their daughters in a civilized way. Normally they talked about solid sensible things like the weather and the garden and holiday plans during this time.

Caroline would look bored or rebellious, waiting for the obligatory half-hour to be over, so that she could get ready to go out, or telephone her friends, or play records in her room. Petra, on the other hand, enjoyed the evening contact with her parents, feeling that here she was accepted, while her prospects of getting a degree or a job as a researcher or a teacher or a civil servant were discussed and Daddy could hold forth and tell her the best course to take. She had not minded tonight when Daddy lost his temper; she just hid under the outburst. But now she could see that he was feeling expansive and wanting to assert himself as head of his clever family.

He was talking to Caroline as if she were a grown-up, Petra realized. Asking questions and listening to her answers. Instead of being scornful and negative when Caroline told him that she had received a tentative offer of a place at a London modelling school, he admitted the possibilities, poured Caro some more sherry and puffed out his cheeks knowingly as he talked to her. Petra's throat tightened and she became panicky but unable to move, glancing first at Daddy, big and pink and confident, fingering the pointed hem of his waistcoat. She looked at Caroline, slowly swinging her long leg, a little, secret, knowing smile on her face as she looked sideways at her father. M was still there, a pleased grin on her face, as she sat straight, upright in the big winged armchair with the floral cover, rubbing her pointed finger slowly up and down over the dewy sides of her sherry glass, nodding as Daddy spoke and broadening her grin as she looked at Caroline. There they all were: big, proud smiling Daddy, responsible for all the good things that were happening to his family; secret, smiling, concession-making Caroline; and M, happy now that everything was going to be all right.

Petra found that she could not smile and she could not bear it. Red-faced and ashamed, she stood up hastily and bumped her way out of the room, dropping her glass awkwardly onto the top of the polished table that stood by the door. No one called after her.

Now Petra sat, watching M's little hands, capable on the steering wheel. Big solid stone-built houses slid past them, fields flashed by in gold and green blurs, curving bumpily up hillsides bounded by walls made from chunks of rock and slabs of slate piled in eternally locking patterns; the small red car throbbed steadily on, up the wide streets that parted villages granite-built and dark, with no gardens or trees to soften the hard stone.

'Poor Caroline, oh poor Caroline.' The squeeze of pain tweaked Petra's mind as she focused on the purpose of this journey, and she swallowed hard.

'Do you remember how cross Daddy was when he saw those photos of Caroline?' she asked M, who blinked rapidly a couple of times and shook her head.

'Oh no dear. He wasn't really cross. He was very proud of Caroline. Poor Caro.' M echoed the pain in Petra's mind. 'He was proud of you both – still is of course. He was very upset when you left university, though. You see, dear, Dad felt that he should have gone to university himself and he would have done, but the war came and we were all called up and so he had to do his training the hard way. He always wanted one of you girls to go, though, and he was so proud when you were accepted.'

'Christ!' thought Petra, violently. 'All he said was: "Pity it's only a red brick one." I bet she doesn't remember that, either.'

University had been the beginning of a time of great change for Petra. The first few days and weeks, she had cocooned herself against any sort of contact which she felt she could not cope with. Her room – she was not sharing, she found out with a flood of relief – became a refuge, a sanctuary like 'home' in a child's game of tag. Make a dash for home, leave the way clear and then nothing can get you. She did everything she was meant to do, went to lectures and tutorials, vowed that she was going to apply herself rigorously to her books and studies. But this deliberate policy of cutting herself off from the mainstream of college life could not last. At mealtimes in the big bright modern refectory, she often sat next to people who attended the same course as herself and she found that she was talking, answering their questions, making an odd comment now and again with a certain sense of surprise and a feeling of daring. No one seemed to find her odd in any way and she enjoyed listening and being listened to. But her room was always there and she would hurry back, head down, books tucked under one arm.

Gradually she grew bolder and started to explore a little, walking round the campus and in the streets of the town, looking at the other students, trying to find a key to the proper way to behave by seeing what they wore, what they said, the food they ate and how they ate it, the things they did in their free time. . . . M had always led her daughters to believe that there were only two ways of doing things in life – the right way and the wrong way. Caroline had always got away with doing things the wrong way, simply because she was Caroline, and a separate rule existed for her. Or so Petra had always thought.

Now she saw that no one was going to stare at her if she ate

31

at odd times, wore clothes that she automatically criticized mentally in M's precise voice but secretly longed for, or even if she smoked a cigarette in the streets. Her own wardrobe, chosen with care, ostensibly by herself, but with a lot of guidance from M who had always insisted on accompanying her on shopping trips, consisted mainly of smartish casual type clothes, all bought to last and look 'good'. Low-heeled leather walking shoes, tan-coloured tights, skirts with matching tops and discreet navy blue and cream wool dresses. Now she longed for blue jeans and rollneck sweaters, coloured stockings and pink lipstick and untidy hair.

So Petra spent the money she had earmarked for her train fares home. She bought tight denims and bright sweaters, coloured shoes and T-shirts. She had lost a lot of weight in the few weeks since she had been in college (mainly through the awful selfconsciousness she had felt at eating with strangers) and for the first time in her life she became conscious of her body. She danced in front of the mirror and went out and bought a black sweater and put on pale pink lipstick and lots of eyeshadow.

With each dip into the eyeshadow and each stroke of the lipstick, M's face, smiling politely and saying: 'Very nice dear, but, if you don't mind me saying so, you've put on everything just a little too thickly,' receded, tunnelling back firmly to its place in the small, leather-framed photograph which stood, well back, on the bookshelf on the wall of her narrow room.

Petra liked her room. It was tiny and cramped, nothing like her spacious, well decorated bedroom at home, but here M and Daddy had had no say in the furnishing. It was a perfect oblong, with a door which opened inwards from the long corridor at the narrow end. A cupboard occupied the space to the right of the door as you looked into the room, and this was just behind the head of the neat divan which fitted along the right-hand wall. There was just room for a fitted desk at the foot of the bed, and on the narrow wall at the end of the room was a window which looked out across the brick-paved courtyard filled with rapidly growing young trees and racks of frames for the students to keep their bicycles. The leaves of one of these trees, a sycamore or a maple of some sort, Petra thought, almost brushed against her third floor window; she would lie in bed imagining that she heard the leaves rustling at night and she watched the sunlight as it filtered in through the tender branches in the morning. Directly opposite the desk was a small washbasin, against which Petra banged her chair every time she sat down to do some work. Next to this, parallel with her divan, with its brightly striped blue and green cotton cover, was a long set of shelves, spaced to take books, clothes, shoes, records. The walls were lined with dark-brown cork tiles, chipped or picked away here and there, and Petra set about pinning up pictures and photographs, even scraps of bright material, on these.

One evening, at this time when she regarded her room as a special haven, she had smoothed out the newspaper picture of Caroline and pinned it up, just to see what it looked like on the wall, as she had imagined it pinned up in factories and offices all over the country.

She stood there looking at it, and she suddenly felt a degree of meanness for gazing at Caroline, frozen for ever in that silly, innocent, provocative pose. She felt guilty for the resentment and jealousy which she knew she would never lose. The guilt became worse as Petra remembered times that she had been sent up to bed without tea for some minor misdemeanour and Caro had brought her up smuggled-out biscuits and apples; there was the time that Smoke, their little grey cat, had been hit by a car and had limped back home, where Caroline cradled him in her lap for hours, until the vet came. It was Caroline who had held the wet and shivering cat whilst the vet administered the final injection. Petra, because of her loneliness, remembered this and snapped the picture off the wall, tearing it slightly before she smoothed it out, folded it up and put it in the middle of a large volume of poetry which she was studying for her course.

For all Petra's gradual thawing, slow unclenching, the aloofness, born entirely of her own insecurity, stayed with her well into the first term. She worked hard and steadily but, despite her new clothes and altered appearance, still confined herself to encounters and experiences which she knew she could cope with. At first she refused invitations out of any sort; when a group of others from the same lecture or lunch table made plans to go swimming, or to the cinema, Petra backed away. Not because she did not want to go, but because she remembered her inability to join in with Caroline's huge crowd of friends with their special catchphrases and jokes which she never understood. She associated a group outing with wisecracking and witticisms, with words and behaviour outside the sphere of her experience, and she was afraid that she would be tried and exposed as the boring, pedestrian person she knew herself to be.

So perhaps it was not so strange that Petra had her admirers. Her terror of being found wanting, concealed by a polite aloofness and a pretence of always being occupied, of always having something else to do, was seen by the others around her as self-confidence; they saw her as a person with a special sort of self-containment, a sufficiency, an independent person, the kind to look to for support.

Petra had no inkling of this general view; she was just happy to be coping with the mechanics of life, 'managing', M would have said. Managing her washing, feeding herself at the right times, using her room to discover her likes and dislikes which, up until now, had always been coloured by the opinions of others. She did not know that she was slowly growing into the person which her altered appearance with slimmer figure, easier clothes and longer hair made her.

One afternoon there was a knock at her door and she opened it to find a girl she knew only as 'Susan' standing diffidently outside.

'Er . . . mind if I speak to you for a few minutes?' Susan, a lank person, started insinuating herself round the doorway. Thin and angular, she seemed to have no round edges. Even her thickish spectacles were squared off and her long, mid-brown hair hung below her shoulders in flat, dull strips. Her voice was drab and toneless and her yellowish skin looked as though it never changed colour. She wore dull browns and greys; nylon blouses and Crimplene skirts.

34

Petra enjoyed playing hostess, asking Susan into her room. This was the first time anyone had actually knocked at her door, and she liked the sensation of ownership which the invitation to enter confirmed. Susan, however, hardly glanced round, and if she liked the way Petra's belongings and pictures were arranged, she said nothing. She sat down, solidly, on the bed and turned to Petra, who was pulling out her chair by the desk at the window.

'Did you know that the whole of the Students' Union is run by men?' This was not at all what Petra had expected, so she just shook her head and looked at Susan, whose prominent eyes were gleaming zealously behind her spectacles.

'It's nearly all men, anyway. There's only one woman on it and she's only there as secretary because they expect her to do all the paperwork. No wonder all the activities here are male-oriented. Hadn't you noticed?' Petra shook her head, slowly. She had not realized that there were any officially organized activities.

'I mean,' said Susan, warming to her subject, sitting bolt upright on the divan and gazing earnestly at Petra, clutching one hand in the other so that the bony knuckles showed white, 'some of the societies are one hundred per cent male as far as membership goes; the hang-gliding club for instance has no women at all in it and neither does the model aircraft society. I think we are just being pressured out.'

'But I don't want to go hang-gliding.' Petra felt resentful that this girl should assume that she felt strongly about the alleged lack of things for women to do.

'No, that's just the point. I've noticed that you always seem to have plenty to do. But some of us feel that there should be more organized for the girls here and that's why I've come to see you. I thought you might be the sort of person who would have some ideas and help to get things going. Even stand for election for the Union's Entertainments Committee – that sort of thing.' Petra noticed with distaste that her visitor's teeth were bad.

But she was at once flattered and absolutely terrified. No one had approached her before with the assumption that she was capable of doing anything that required initiative and energy. Although she knew that she would not be able to put herself on view for anything like an election, here she was, confronted by this earnest girl who seemed to think that she could provide some of the answers. She could not bring herself to destroy this image that had been falsely created in Susan's mind, so the girl kept on visiting Petra's room and Petra often made her way down to the next floor to see Susan and to listen while she held forth earnestly about women's rights and the exploitation of their sex by men, and Petra, for the first time in her life, had a cause. But, although they talked a lot about what ought to be done, it was with little conviction on Petra's part, and they never actually did anything.

Susan, with her flat, nasal voice and her bad teeth, would inch up to Petra as they hurried along the long passageways of the college to and from lectures, her eyes gleaming large as she turned her head and her glasses caught the light. She insinuated herself into the seat next to Petra at mealtimes and borrowed notes and books after each class.

The attention was, at first, flattering, but Petra grew bored and annoyed with the girl who became a droning, constantly whining voice at ear-level. If someone spoke to Petra during a meal or a coffee break, Susan would interrupt, claim Petra's attention, cutting her off from the contact that she was just beginning to accept and enjoy. She was too new at making and having friends to deal honestly with Susan's whining possessiveness and too frightened of offending, of hurting the girl's feelings, to say anything. So she took the coward's way out; avoiding the area near Susan's room, arriving late at lectures and tutorials so that she could slip in at the back, taking devious routes round the university buildings. She stopped going to the refectory for all her meals.

Petra's first term passed and she took the train home at Christmas.

'How well you look, dear,' said M, who immediately noticed the change, the new brightness in her elder daughter;

but she said nothing more. Daddy wanted to know what sort of work she was doing and whether she had joined the right sort of societies. She was noncommittal on both counts. Daddy seemed a lot smaller now she had been away from him for twelve weeks.

Caroline did not. A term's absence had blurred the clear vision of Petra's mental image of her younger sister. She had looked at the newspaper picture of Caroline and seen her naked, vulnerable, helpless. She was shocked when the sharp, clear reality of Caroline swung into the house to spend Christmas Day with her family. Petra had forgotten the startling contrast between Caroline's cream-white skin with its delicate scattering of minute freckles across her tiny perfect nose and the glossy thick darkness of her heavy hair. She had forgotten the perfect evenness of Caroline's thick eyebrows, their slight heaviness accentuating the peculiar quality of the green-blue light in her eyes. Petra's spirits dropped, and she felt something approaching despair as she remembered, too late, that when Caroline was in the room, everyone else was eclipsed by the atmosphere which diffused from her in such a way that it was almost a physical emanation, like a glowing light, or a heavy scent. It was as if Caroline's self-absorption was so strong, so complete and unselfconscious, that her whole physical presence and personality was rolled into an aura, a covering blanket which protected and surrounded her, and completed her presentation to the world.

Petra had dressed carefully for that meeting. She had bought a straight, clinging dress of a jewel-like greenish silky material which caught and reflected the light. High-heeled shoes and sheer tights, nail varnish, lipstick. She felt attractive, well dressed and ready to meet her sister.

Caroline looked like a lily; tall and white-spathed. Her face was unblemished and un-made-up. Her eyes were enormous against her pale skin and her hair hung simply and straight onto her shoulders in one shining fall. Simple white cotton trousers, gathered at her ankles, flat little white straps on her feet and a plain, fluffy white jumper made Petra feel hot and overdressed.

37

'My God, I feel dreadful.' Caroline kissed M and Daddy briefly, waved a hand at Petra and strode gracefully into the drawing room. Just before she collapsed into the big armchair by the window, the chair that had just been re-covered with brown velvet, she said vaguely: 'Oh, this is Henry. I said of course you wouldn't mind him coming, there's always plenty to eat.'

Petra and M looked at each other and thought instantly of the family present-giving ceremony which always took place just before lunch. Henry was going to be dreadfully in the way, thought M, as she smiled at him with her teeth showing, and shook his hand. Petra glanced at Daddy, but he strode over to the drinks cupboard and dealt with the situation by offering refreshments in a very loud voice. Petra knew that if she had been the one to bring an uninvited guest home to share the family Christmas lunch, M would have nudged her out into the kitchen and hissed reproaches at her. But no one would dream of doing this to Caroline.

Petra, feeling daring, asked for and was given a gin and tonic. She watched Daddy shudder as Henry asked for a rum and Coke and Caroline looked amused and said she would have a mineral water, please, because she was working tomorrow and must not have bags under her eyes.

'Working tomorrow! On Boxing Day!' cried M, looking shocked. 'Are you sure you're looking after yourself, Caroline?'

'Caroline not looking after herself – that's a good one,' said Henry, who had swallowed half his fizzy-looking drink in one gulp.

'What's your line of business . . . er, Henry?' asked Daddy, standing in front of the Christmas tree that Petra and M had decorated the night before. His legs were straddled and he shifted his weight gently from right foot to left foot and back again, as if he were trying to hypnotize his audience with the gentle, repetitive movement.

'I'm a photographer – or rather, I'm learning to be a photographer.' Henry gazed back equably at Daddy.

Petra knew that her father was put out at being confronted

in this self-possessed manner by a trainee photographer, but Caroline, holding her glass in the curl of her long fingers, laughed and reproached Henry.

'Don't be boring!' Henry beamed at her.

'Henry's over here from America. He's setting up a job for Dimrill and Mudie.' Everyone looked blank and Caroline raised an eyebrow. 'I'm working for them tomorrow, in London. They do big advertising features for glossy magazines.'

M started to ask Caroline what magazines in particular and what she would be wearing, and even Daddy looked impressed. Petra sucked her lemon and spilt gin on her dress. She looked up to find the peculiar-looking Henry gazing at her.

'I say, did Caroline say that your name is Petra? I thought so, what a wonderful name.' He had a dome-shaped head, bald almost to the crown, with a fringe of soft, slightly curly baby-like brown hair, bordering the shining curve. He wore round spectacles which looked like the very cheapest, National Health sort but Petra was, by now, worldly enough to realize that they were very expensive ones. His face wore an earnest expression, but his eyes, which were blue and round, seemed shrewd and pleasant. Henry's cheeks were very smooth and pinkish brown, full like his mouth, which pouted slightly below a little moustache fringing his lips in the same way that his hair framed the dome of his head.

'Don't tell me I'm being rude, I know I am.' Henry settled himself comfortably down beside Petra. 'But you would look just wonderful if you had your hair cut in a softer way – layered, like this.' He leant forward and picked up strands of Petra's fine fair hair, which he wound in his thin fingers and twisted this way and that, squinting at her to get the effect. Petra stiffened, but then she laughed and relaxed. The gin made her feel slightly dizzy.

'I'll get you another drink,' she offered. 'Another one of those?'

'God, no – that was awful,' Henry hissed, making her laugh again. 'I only asked for it because Caroline said I wouldn't dare. Get me a dry sherry would you?

39

They opened their presents and Henry managed cleverly not to be in the way; in fact he helped things along by exclaiming loudly and admiringly as each piece of paper was peeled away, and this generated a feeling of good will, becoming more genuine, so that they all became caught up in a traditional happy family atmosphere, smiling and joking with each other. They ate their lunch in the same spirit and then all, except for Caroline, went out for a brisk walk afterwards.

Petra was by Henry's side down the steep hill, slippery in places with an early evening frost, through the dark church-yard with the glimmerings of the Christmas offerings of bright flowers put on the graves that morning, and up the little lane that completed the circle back to their house.

She stood outside with M and Daddy, waving goodbye, as Caroline and Henry drove away in Caroline's little car, and she went to her room early that night, to think about Henry. Petra knew that she was in love. She went over every detail of the day in her mind and lingered mentally and indulgently on every word Henry had spoken to her. She did not want to touch Henry, to hold him, but she needed to think minutely of the things he said, how he had made them all laugh, his appearance (his hands had very long pale and tapering fingers, she remembered, with an involuntary shudder of pleasure).

He had worn black trousers, cut high and tight across the stomach, like those of a Spanish dancer, with a full-sleeved loose white cotton shirt with an open, casually frilled neck. He had carefully fastened his fancy dress black velvet cape around his neck with a brooch decorated with a yellow-brown stone, when they had made ready to go out for their walk. She brooded on his appearance and his eccentric dress and then pondered on all that she had gleaned about him. He lived in New York, sharing his apartment there with a guy called Peter, who was in Real Estate, whatever that was; she knew that his job took him all over the world with his cameras and a list of contacts to set up location shots for firms who used the most beautiful girls to advertise their products. Petra thought gloomily about the glamorous girls, but then she thought, Henry talked to me most of the day and seemed to ignore

Caroline. Perhaps, she mused, lying face downwards on the pink shiny bedspread, pressing her hot face into its slippery coldness, perhaps he is so used to beautiful women, he just does not notice them.

Caroline paid another of her flying visits one evening at the beginning of January. Petra, sorting out clothes and books to take back to college, came flying downstairs when she heard the car, hoping that Henry would be with her sister. By now he had become enlarged in her mind to a perfect, gentle figure and she compared all men she saw when watching television or walking in the town with her mental image of him. But Caroline was alone and wanted to see Daddy.

'Business, dear,' hissed M importantly. 'She's making some money now, you know, and your father looks after it for her.'

Daddy and Caroline came out of the little room which opened off the hallway and which Daddy called his study. It had been a cloakroom but Daddy had had the washbasin and lavatory taken out and had enlarged the window, so that he could look out on the rather scruffy little shrubbery at the side of the house. Petra knew that he never did any work there, but it was his room and no one entered it without an invitation.

Caroline, it seemed, had been signed up by one of the biggest and best-known modelling agencies in London. She had come to ask Daddy to sign the contract for her, as she would not be eighteen for another month. Petra felt ten years younger than her sister as she listened to them talking about fees and contracts and tax allowances. M beamed with pleasure and poured out drinks and patted everyone on the shoulder with little dry feathery taps of her hand; she asked Petra to pass round small bowls which she had filled with savoury biscuits, crisps and nuts.

Caroline said that she would have to move to London now; commuting from her flat in the suburbs was out of the question, as many of the jobs she would be offered were at odd hours. M started to speak, alarmed at the thought of Caroline on her own in London, but Daddy held up a big hand.

41

'I've given this some thought. Caroline can't commute any more, she's quite right. Most of her work is in London now, so she'll have to buy a flat.'

'But I can't possibly afford a flat in London.' Caroline sounded amused. 'Have you any idea of the prices?'

'Of course I have. Now I've not spoken about this to you girls before, because the question has never arisen. Your grandfather,' Daddy paused and looked across at M, who bowed her head to acknowledge that he spoke of her father, 'your grandfather left each of you a sum of money, in trust, until you reach the age of twenty-five or marry, whichever comes first. Now' – again he held up his hand to forestall Caroline's questions – 'there isn't enough to buy the lease of a flat outright, but you should be able to put down a very good deposit on one and I will guarantee your mortgage repayments until you can do it in your own name. Your present earnings and the sum mentioned in this contract should mean that you have no problems on that score.'

'But you can't live on your own, Caroline.' M sounded very worried. 'Not in London. You're far too young. Isn't she, Tom? Why can't she just share a flat as she's doing now?'

Tom Appleton looked impatiently at her. 'She would do well to buy. It's a buyer's market at the moment and she's earning enough to get on the property ladder. It's a wonderful investment for the future and she's very lucky, very clever, to be able to start out like this.'

M still looked unhappy, but she conceded Tom must know best and she brightened up as she thought of helping Caro choose her curtains and furniture and of stocking up the kitchen for her.

Petra had to speak.

'Daddy, does that mean that I've got some money, too? From Grandpa, I mean?'

Her father still looked impatient. 'Yes, yes, of course you have. I said he'd left money in trust to each of you.'

'How much is there?' asked Caroline in a matter-of-fact voice. She didn't seem at all excited, whereas Petra, who had been dying to ask the same question, was leaning forward in her chair, thinking about spending her share.

'Oh, I haven't looked at the figures lately,' said Daddy. 'It's all invested of course. I think it would work out at around £15,000 apiece.'

'What!' exploded Petra. 'Can I buy a car? Caroline's got one but I can't even drive.'

'Caroline paid for her own lessons and bought her car,' replied Daddy. 'And I told you, the money is looked after by trustees. We would be able to get Caroline's money released as she has very good grounds for needing it and buying property is just a reinvestment – and a very sound one right now. I'm afraid the trustees wouldn't let you have any just for a car which you don't really need. No, Petra, you'll have to wait until you're twenty-five – unless of course we marry you off first!' Daddy winked at M and burst into hearty laughter.

'I think I'll get Henry to help me look for something,' said Caroline, slowly. 'He's very good at that sort of thing and of course he knows London well. He'll be over next week. He's on holiday with his boyfriend in New Orleans at the moment.'

Petra couldn't work out the meaning of Caroline's words. 'With his boyfriend?' she laughed awkwardly, and Caroline grinned at her.

'Oh yes. Didn't you realize? Old Henry's as queer as a nine bob note!'

Chapter Four

'Well, here we are!' M pulled briskly at the wheel and the little red car turned into the gravelled driveway of the house that Petra often referred to as 'home'. The rose beds, spilling over with full-blown colour by the side of the neatly edged drive and the precise clumps of scarlet sage and dusty blue ageratum made her think, hopelessly, about the overgrown state of her own, much smaller, garden, back in Somerset. She stepped out on to the neat crunchy gravel and saw that Daddy's car, a nice, solid, dark green Austin, was sitting in its place in the big double garage.

'Daddy's home,' she said in surprise.

'He must have left the office early because he knew that we'd be home by tea-time,' said M. 'I'll put the car away later. You go in and find him, dear – he's been looking forward to seeing you.'

Petra disappeared into the house through the back door and M, gathering up her handbag, reached into the little boot for their overnight cases. She stood stock-still for a moment, her fussy small bird-like movements stilled, as she worried about Petra. When the girls were younger, she remembered, Petra had been so normal, so healthy. She had been a little shy as a child, a little inclined to hang back, and she had gone through that awful teenage phase of surliness and clumsiness and uncertainty – but then so did most children. Caroline, of course, had sailed through all that with careless charm and ease, but then Caroline's problems had started later.

44

Petra was a grown-up now, a married woman – M screwed up her eyes a little, head on one side, as she tried hard to remember how long ago Petra and Philip had been married – twelve or thirteen years. Yet she seemed no further forward now, no more definite about her life, than she had done on the day she became Philip's wife, although she had three children and there was that pleasant old house to look after. Petra seemed forever wrapped in thought, totally preoccupied, and she wandered around doing very little that was useful, as far as M could see. But what was upsetting M and what she was trying very hard not to think about was the feeling she had that Petra was quietly despairing about something.

M sighed. She did not suppose it was Petra's marriage, it was just the girl's attitude towards it. M had never felt that Philip was the right man for her elder daughter; he was too easygoing, lazy even, too happy to let Petra direct him in everything, and that was no good for someone like Petra who was often unsure of herself and pushed too hard, nearly always in the wrong direction, just for the sake of reassurance.

The weight of the two small cases roused M and she gave a shrug and her automatic bright smile. Oh well, no use worrying, she thought, things generally work out in the end.

'Petra! How nice!' boomed Daddy, looking fresh and dressed with care in an expensive, casual, middle-aged sort of way. His hair, now very thin on top and a salt and pepper colour, bushed out into little curls behind his ears and his high-coloured face seemed soft and newly shaved and smelt of cologne as Petra kissed him on the cheek. He wore blue, canvas-topped sneakers with spotless white trim around the eyelets and his pale blue trousers of well cut linen had not a crease out of place. A cream and navy shirt, open a little way at the neck, showed off his brick-coloured suntan (he and M had gone to Africa earlier in the year for their holiday); Petra had the absurd feeling that he had just stepped off someone's yacht.

'How well you look!' Daddy sounded as if he meant it, and indeed it was true. Since the birth of her children, Petra's appearance, which had at times threatened to alter in all sorts of directions, had become stable. Her hair, once mousy and unruly, had, by some strange process, grown fair and smooth and her skin, at one time liable to betray her by breaking out into fiery blushes, was now close-grained and brown. Her face had lost the plumpness which once hid the fine straight lines of her cheekbones and nose. Petra, her father thought, would never be a striking figure, would never make heads turn as Caroline had done, but there was no doubt that he had produced two fine-looking daughters.

Petra herself, once so concerned and so despairing about her appearance, especially when she stood next to her sister, knew that what she was now, outwardly, was the person whom others would see for the rest of her life. Her skin, her eyes and mouth and hair would change slowly as she grew older, but the structure that showed through now was the Petra who would be there for the next thirty or forty years. She had some time ago stopped worrying about what other people thought of her physical appearance, but inside she still carried around the leaden lump, the nagging worry of her own inadequacy. Although she had reached a goal, a base point physically, the restless uncertainty about the things she should do would not leave her. She knew that there was some achievement she must make, a space somewhere that only she could fill. Although she laughed and called herself lazy when she neglected the house and failed to tend the overgrown garden and did not start the reading programme she planned five years ago, it was a laugh with bitterness in it for the things she should be doing instead, if only she knew what they were. She despaired, waiting for the little creation of which she should be a part.

Daddy was right, she knew. She did look well even if it signified nothing at all. She scrutinized him closely as he turned to tidy a pile of magazines on the polished yew table by the french window and she realized that her first impression of a big hale and hearty man had only been a surface one. He stooped as he turned; the bullfrog had deflated into a dry tortoise, with a loosely fleshed neck sagging into his shoulders. The gay boating clothes were a pathetic cloak for ageing and a defence against the terrible sadness that he and M must be feeling. Petra noticed his hands trembling slightly as they sorted through the heap of *Illustrated London News* and colour supplements on the table and she saw, with a wrench of sadness, the spreading brown blotches of age marking his knuckles, and the creases where the suppleness had left his skin.

Tom Appleton cleared his throat. 'It's very good of you to go up there with M tomorrow,' he said in a formal voice. 'Very good indeed – she's very grateful, but I'm sure she's told you that herself. Painful business for her – well, for all of us, of course, but especially difficult for her. You know what I mean.'

Petra hated this difficult humility of Daddy's far more than all of his shouting at her when she was a child. 'Aren't you coming up with us? To help with the heavy things . . . I thought M said . . .'

'Well, no, much better not. I think it's better that you go with her, just the two of you, alone. I'd just be in the way. Besides, I'm very busy at the office just now – recession and all that – everyone seems to need an accountant when they're going bankrupt.' He smiled bleakly at his little joke, which rolled out so glibly and easily that Petra was sure he must make it several times each day.

'M seems to be taking everything very well,' she ventured.

'Has she spoken to you about it?' Daddy asked, quickly and eagerly, not looking at her.

'Well, no. Not this time. Of course she did when – when we heard about it, you know, when it happened. I did try to say something on the journey here, but I'm not sure if she heard. She just changed the subject, and I didn't like to make things worse for her if she felt she couldn't talk about it.'

'Yes. Your mother,' said Daddy slowly, 'she finds it very hard at times to face reality. She bottles it all up inside and then pretends that it just hasn't happened. That's no good, Petra – you can't go through the whole of your life wielding an enormous mental umbrella.'

Petra was surprised and a little embarrassed to hear her

father talk like this. He had never spoken to her before about M and, although she accepted what he had said, she found it hard to believe that he understood her mother so well – they had always seemed two very separate people to Petra. She had not known before that her father had any kind of sensibility.

That evening they ate one of M's delicious meals; cool tasty summer soup, chilled and creamy, made from cucumber and lettuce and herbs, roast lamb with fresh summer vegetables and a raspberry shortbread with thick cream. Petra praised everything and M looked pleased.

As they sat round the polished table, eating and drinking and talking about people in the town and the shops that had changed hands, Petra looked at the formal, pretty, William Morris wallpaper and the shaded lamps on the wall, the gleaming dresser with its shining complement of silver and at the watercolour landscapes and she thought, we are, after all, a family. It's just me now. Philip and the children and Caroline seemed to be part of a life that was disjointed, nothing to do with the present. M and Daddy paid court to her, treating her as an honoured guest, a beloved daughter – the beloved daughter – and she found herself laughing and making witty jokes, coming to life; they all came to life, she thought later as she undressed in the room that had once been hers, but now bore traces of more recent occupation by Caroline. We came to life thought Petra, a little drunk, just as we did that Christmas when Henry came to lunch and made us forget ourselves.

She opened her old wardrobe door to hang up her trousers and the jacket she planned to wear tomorrow, and she gasped as she saw the neat rows of clothes hanging there, each dress or skirt, each fur jacket protected by a little collar of thick polythene. Petra, who had rarely been able to afford good clothes (the legacy which came to her on marriage had paid for the deposit on their house, a new car and one mad shopping spree), was overcome with sheer envy. She pulled out a short soft fur jacket, a smoky brown wrap, and stroked it before trying it on. It smelt of expensive scent but looked quite new and she snuggled it round her shoulders and wondered how often Caroline had worn it.

48

'I must ring Philip,' she thought suddenly, guiltily remembering that she had promised to let him know she had arrived safely. Exasperated, she took the jacket off and hung it carefully back in the wardrobe, feeling like Cinderella when the clock chimed midnight and the spell was broken. And broken it was – at once she hated all the clothes, meaningless in their neat rows, most of them unworn, she thought, and she shut the light oak door, hearing the catch click with a sense of satisfaction. She did not want to see them again.

Wrapping her dressing gown around her, Petra crept downstairs to the telephone on the hall table. It was dark – past midnight by now – and she knew that Philip would be grumpy at being woken. Why on earth had not he rung her, she thought crossly, and supposed that it just had not occurred to him. But when she got through to Coombe, Philip answered the phone quickly and was pleased to hear from her.

'Sorry I didn't ring you,' he said, 'but I took the children out for a walk this evening and they wanted to pick wild strawberries along the old railway lines. And when we got back I had to look up a flower for Dan, so by the time Fiona and I made supper, it was rather late.'

'What was Dan's flower?'

'Well, as far as I can tell,' replied Philip, who scarcely knew a dandelion from a buttercup, 'it's borage. Dan says the old bee man gave it to him – he must have picked it from his garden, though, because I didn't see any growing wild when we walked that way this evening.'

As Petra put the receiver down and prepared to slip back upstairs, she heard a muffled noise from the back of the house. She gripped the edge of the hall table and concentrated until she heard it again; a kind of tight muffled screech, the sort of noise one would make through clenched teeth, a suppressed sound of pain. She crept round the foot of the stairs to the dark side of the hall and stood motionless in the deep shadow outside the kitchen. There it was again, an inhuman, dragging moaning which suggested something in great pain. She was sure that it came from inside the house, from the kitchen. Petra felt her own breathing coming harshly and quickly and her

49

heart thudded, while her knees felt weak. Prickles of sweat broke out on her face and the palms of her hands as she tried to make out the dark blob that was the kitchen door handle. It really was very black. When she had been using the telephone, she had been able to see a little from the moonlight that came in from the hallway window, but on the other side of the hall the bulk of the stairs blotted out this light and there was only shadow and deeper shadow. She knew that she could not go back upstairs and wake M and Daddy, much as she wanted to turn around and run away from the noise, which now seemed louder and was accompanied by a rhythmic rattling and banging.

Her reasoning petrified, completely numbed by fear, she shot out a hand, fumbled with the dark shape of the door knob and said, in a high, nervous squeak: 'Who's there?'

'Mmmmmmmm aarrrrrh!' The keening noise changed pitch and assembled itself into some kind of coherence, and the rustling and banging stopped for a minute.

Petra scraped her hand down the wall by the door, frantically feeling for the light switch, and she finally succeeded in flicking it on. In the flicker of the fluorescent strip lighting she had a ghostly vision of a hunched-up dwarf of a figure, dressed from head to toe in an all-enveloping green robe, clutching at its face whilst shuffling its foot, which appeared to have some club-like deformity, to and fro. Petra shrieked in horror and then started in amazement as the light came fully on and the dwarf resolved itself into M, in full-length green velour dressing gown, frantically scraping at the inside of her mouth with a finger and shaking her right foot, which was stuck inside a round, red biscuit tin. Petra's heart eased its agonized thumping and she again felt weak as she leaned back against the door frame and started to shake with hysterical laughter.

'Oh dear, M . . . you do look so funny . . . I was so frightened . . .' she wailed between bursts of giggles.

M glared at Petra. She had stopped moaning and poking her finger in her mouth and her face was red with pain and indignation. She swallowed, controlling her impatience. 'Do

50

stop it, Petra – it's not at all funny. Not funny at all. I was in absolute agony.'

'But why? What were you doing? I was so frightened,' repeated Petra, gasping for breath as she tried to stop the bubbles of laughter bursting from her. She reached across and tore off a piece of kitchen paper and blew her nose and wiped her eyes. M had shuffled over to the sink and was pouring herself a glass of water.

'Why were you in agony – was it you making that awful noise?' she asked.

'Yes, it was. For some reason I couldn't sleep tonight – I suppose it's because of tomorrow,' admitted M, who by now had succeeded in freeing her foot from the tin and was picking out the squashed ginger nuts and chocolate digestives. 'So I thought I'd come downstairs and have a biscuit – something to eat often does the trick if you can't sleep, I'm told.'

Petra immediately felt contrite, remembering what Daddy had said that afternoon. It was unlike M not to be able to drop straight off to sleep.

'I didn't bother with the light. I know where everything in this kitchen is, and I got the biscuit tin out of the larder and put it there on the table. I opened it and ate one – a ginger nut it was, and I thought I'd just have one more, because I didn't feel at all sleepy. Your father's fast asleep, and really it's rather depressing lying there, wide awake, when he's so well away. Well, the next biscuit I picked out must have had silver paper on it and I just didn't realize. I took a bite and suddenly I was in absolute agony – on my fillings, you see. It felt like an electric shock.' M poked her teeth ruefully. 'It was so painful. I didn't want to make a noise and wake everyone, but I was trying to scrape the bits of paper from my teeth, when I knocked the wretched tin off the table, and what with hopping around a bit, my foot got jammed in it. Oh dear!' Her face crumpled up and she looked as if she were about to burst into tears. Petra was horrified. She rushed over to M and put her arm clumsily around the green velour shoulders and kissed the papery cheek.

'Don't, dear. Please. You'll make me cry.' M turned away and Petra was hurt.

51

'You should cry, then,' she said awkwardly. 'It might do you good.'

M turned round briskly, shoulders straight and all traces of weakness gone from her face. She busied herself with clearing up the remains of the biscuit crumbs and the scraps of silver paper from the tiled floor. 'Nonsense, dear. Time for bed. Busy day tomorrow – today rather.'

Petra sighed and bent down to pick up a round, silver shape which was underneath the table. The neat crescent of a bite marred the roundness of the smooth outline. 'Like a moon in reverse,' thought Petra wearily as she trailed up the stairs.

Frederic spent the evening in the garden, methodically clipping the long grass round the three hives which faced the east and stood just behind a bed of flowering shrubs and bushes.

The air was still warm and soft and, although it was nearly eight o'clock, the sun felt pleasant on his skin, dressed as he was in a thin, short-sleeved shirt and a pair of old shorts. The coffee-coloured shorts, which were longish and which flapped around his skinny thighs as he worked, were made of a good, strong cotton twill which had resisted years of wear on summer hiking holidays all around the country. Elise and he would shut up their flat for three or four weeks at a time, carefully making arrangements for the old man who lived across the corridor to come in and water the pots and tubs of herbs on the balcony, that Elise called her garden and which always seemed to flourish for her.

'One day,' Frederic would tell Elise, 'we'll go and look for a place with a garden and then you can grow all the herbs you want.' But Elise would laugh at him, because they were both perfectly happy where they were, and the tubs of mint and parsley, clumps of sweet-smelling oregano and thyme, the chamomile and feathery fennel and the pungent basil were just as she wanted them. There had never been any 'if only' for Frederic and Elise as they grew older together – neither thought life might have been any better had they lived another way.

Frederic became a senior houseman in a large hospital and had no ambition to go any further in what seemed to him to be the complicated structure of hospital life. It suited him. He was quietly, totally involved in his work whilst he was on duty, excellent at his job and efficient rather than committed. Elise had given up her classical studies when she left Germany and had never tried to resume them in England. When the war was over and they had married and gone through the lengthy business of becoming British subjects, she had trained as a physiotherapist, and one of the reasons she gave for this choice was that she could feel close to Frederic in his work, also part of the healing process. She never said that she felt she should work at something that benefited the community in some tangible way, grateful as she was to the country that had, by its acceptance of two young refugees, helped her to convert her blueprint for life with Frederic into easy reality.

Elise was aware of her power. She knew that she was the stronger partner, the decision-maker, but it never occurred to her that she had an extraordinary ability to create an atmosphere of peace and comfort. This was why her impossible escape from loving parents and her marriage to a penniless Jewish refugee succeeded totally; this was why, later, her services as a physiotherapist were so much in demand. It was Elise and her still calm centre which provided Frederic with a mantle of complete security, so that he never questioned his happiness or the love which seemed to him to be as natural as the rhythm of daybreak and nightfall. When Elise died, Frederic suffered the loss of her physical presence deeply, but, more than that, he was completely puzzled and alarmed at the surge of a whole flood of emotions whose existence he had forgotten, been secured against during her lifetime. There was fear, depression, loneliness and a frightening bewilderment about the world, which had never before seemed to him to be a hostile place.

Frederic finished clipping and tidying around the hives, noting that the bees' activity was ceasing now, as the sun dropped, and he carefully raked up the long pieces of grass. He then went indoors and returned with his supper, which he took across to the mossy, herb-strewn bank which ran at right-angles to the line of hives and, as he ate his bread and cheese, he thought about the picnics that Elise had prepared with an immense, childlike pleasure for each day's hike on their holidays.

In the early days they had explored Scotland, Wales and Norfolk. They both loved Suffolk with its great green spaces and the juxtaposition of endless sea and countryside. But, as they grew older, they turned again and again to the West Country, to Cornwall and Devon and Somerset, travelling by train and on foot, with all their luggage in the rucksacks. They wore walking boots and shorts and Elise always managed to produce a bar of thick, very dark chocolate from somewhere when they stopped to rest or admire a view or just to sit and talk. She laughed at the solemn way Frederic was always scrupulously fair over the division of the bar.

Frederic would not have worried about where they slept on these holidays – he would have been happy to camp out or to sleep in a corner of someone's barn. To him, the activity, the sheer mechanics of walking along a loosely planned route with Elise, was as much as he wanted. But Elise insisted that they stay in good hotels and Frederic never questioned her choice. Neither of them thought that a pair of middle-aged hikers, wearing long, unfashionable shorts, thick socks and heavy boots, with no car, no luggage apart from a couple of battered rucksacks, would be looked at askance by young hotel reception clerks used to the better type of commercial traveller or to well-dressed couples booking in for long weekends. And, oddly enough, they were never turned away. They generally timed their trips at the slack end of the season when business of any sort was not to be sneered at, and both were so serious and businesslike, so gravely unconscious that there was anything odd about the way they holidayed, and so certain of a welcome, that no hotelier could contemplate refusing them.

Each morning, after breakfast, which they always took in the dining room, Elise would slip away for half an hour, an hour, whilst Frederic studied the map and planned their route for the day, or wandered around the hotel, looking at the pictures and ornaments; or he would sit in one of the reception rooms, or the garden, making notes about anything that had impressed him the previous day. They would leave when Elise returned, her rucksack full of newly baked bread, local cheese, fruit and salad for their picnic. Once, in a little village store, she had found a stock of pumpernickel and she had bought some of the hard dark bread for old times' sake, but they had laughed together as they both made wry faces over it.

Frederic sat on the bank in his garden at Coombe, chewing at, but not tasting, his bread and cheese, and the memory of those holidays was very precious.

He could not, at this moment, select one event, one holiday, one route that they had taken, one picnic they had enjoyed on a cliff top or in a wood or a grassy clearing; but the essence was there, like a scent, whose release evokes waves of feeling rather than specific memory. Throughout the collage of half-remembered pleasures fixed firmly in his mind, was Elise, her brown curls untouched by grey and her bright round poodle eyes making laughing love to him.

They had first seen the wooden bungalow when they had visited Coombe during a walking holiday in the Black Down Hills, about ten years before, Frederic remembered. It was a hot, late July day, the sun making a hazy shimmer as they walked past fields of ripe barley, and they had decided to make for a small market town for the night.

The little village was asleep as they tramped through it in the middle of the afternoon, the warm yellowish stone of the walls of the houses throwing back the heat into the narrow street, where the only sign of life was an old black and white farm dog lying in a dusty patch in the road. He gave a low, half-hearted growl as they walked past him and then thumped his feathery tail in mitigation, raising clouds of dust. Elise laughed at the dog and said she was thirsty. The beer that they had drunk with their cold sausage and fruit at lunchtime, a couple of villages back, seemed a very distant memory. They walked on, down a narrow, tree-shaded hill, which snaked out of the village. As the curve of the road flattened out they saw the playground of the school, beyond the bend. Then, right in the elbow of the curve, was a wooden house, set back from the road, with a largish paddock between the little bungalow and the hedge. Four white goats were tethered and lazily grazing in the paddock and there was a chalked sign which read 'Goat's milk, Cheese and Honey for sale'.

'Just the thing,' said Elise, who had stopped to read the sign. 'I hope it's nice and cold.'

Frederic laughed at her. 'You've never had goat's milk – how do you know you will like it?'

'I don't care what it tastes like,' said Elise. 'I'm so thirsty, I feel I could drink anything!'

They bought the milk from a small, slow, round man with watery blue eyes and pointed teeth. He seemed puzzled that they had no jug or can with them, but when they explained that they simply wanted to quench their thirst, he fetched two long tumblers, which he carefully polished with a spotless cloth, before pouring out the milk for them. Frederic drank his out of politeness, disliking the strong, musty taste, but Elise appeared to savour her milk and stood there, drinking slowly, her bright eyes darting round the homely room with its wooden walls, rag rugs on the floor and oil lamps suspended from the planked ceiling beams.

They learnt that the little man lived on a war pension and on the sale of milk and cheese from his goats and jars of honey from his bees. When Frederic expressed an interest in the bees, he lent him a curious hat and veil and led him out to the big garden at the back of the bungalow, where he lifted the cover from one of the hives and explained the structure of the colony and showed Frederic how to handle the frames, each one covered blackly with a crawling furry mass of workers.

Elise sat on the topmost of the three wooden steps which led out of the back of the house and looked happily at her husband, absorbed and serious as he peered into the hive, his face stern and sharp and intelligent. She relaxed completely as she looked around her, the taste of the milk, which she had in fact enjoyed, still in her mouth. At right-angles to the hives there ran a long bank, which appeared to be the borderline

56

between the garden and a field which rose steeply into the hillside. She noted with pleasure the drifts of thyme and marjoram, the latter fully in flower, and the big clump of borage in the corner. Nothing here had the air of being well tended, but on the other hand there were no rank, straggling weeds, just a happy mixture of grass and herbs, shrubs and wild flowers.

When they left, the old man, whose name was Frank, smiled his sharp-toothed grin and refused to accept payment for the milk, although he did let them buy some tangy white cheese and a jar of thick honey.

Whenever they were in Somerset after that, they visited Coombe to see Frank and to buy some honey and some cheese. They always drank a glass of his milk and, when they had drained the last drop, the old man, who stood smiling and nodding at them as if they were good children, led Frederic out into the garden. There they inspected the bees, whilst Elise sat on the wooden steps and enjoyed a slow look over the wild garden.

And then, one April, they took a week's holiday at Easter, a short break in the part of the world that they were growing to love more than any other, and as was now their custom they called in at Coombe, walking from the railway station at the next village, to see the old man. There was no reply to the knock at the front door and Frederic went round to the back of the house, to see if Frank was in the garden. Elise suddenly realized that there were no goats grazing in the paddock and, just as she registered this fact, Frederic came loping round the side of the house, looking puzzled.

'The hives have been neglected,' he told her. 'One colony appears to have died out, and the entrances haven't been opened up properly after the winter, even though the weather has been beautiful.' He turned to go back to the bees and Elise followed him, noticing the daffodils springing up in grassy patches and the bluebells, just beginning to show hazy blue at their tips. But, while she admired the spring colours, she noted that the garden was untidy and overgrown. In the past it had looked natural and wild, but not neglected. Now there were straggling weeds winning the battle with the flowers and it had the forlorn look of a place which had once been tended and was now slowly being strangled through lack of care. Frederic was more concerned about the bees.

'They must have a bigger entrance,' he declared and, using a strong twig, he eased out the wooden block which cut down the size of the opening to each hive. Elise knew that he had read a good many manuals on bees and beekeeping since they had met Frank and she never questioned Frederic's practical ability to know the right thing to do. So she watched, fascinated, as he gently eased the lid from one of the hives, prised off the inner cover and started to examine the frames in the brood chamber, tutting over the wild comb that the bees were building at the top.

Then she remembered that, really, they had no right to be here, looking at the old man's bees, and she reminded Frederic that they should search for Frank, try to find out what had happened to him.

'Frank is dead,' Frederic told her. 'No goats, bees untended. If he were alive this would not be happening. There should be more frames on top of this brood chamber – they are already bringing in a lot of nectar. I wonder where he keeps all his equipment.' Elise had also felt instinctively that the old man with the pointed teeth and the lazy, blue-eyed smile must have died during the winter, and that saddened her. But, at the same time, she was amused by Frederic's serious preoccupation with the bees and by his impressive theoretical knowledge. He was so utterly absorbed in the hives and their occupants that he did not even flinch when a bee, irritated by the intrusion, stung him on the back of his hand. Elise was, though, as practical as ever. 'We must make some enquiries, Frederic,' she reminded him. 'After all, the house may belong to someone else by now – the bees too. Frank may not be dead – just ill in hospital. Or even – ' and she stiffened as a horrible thought struck her – 'even ill, or dead, alone in the house.'

'No,' Frederic replied, calmly. 'I looked in all the windows – you can see into every room. The doors are all open inside. There's no one there. But you're right. We must find out about him. We'll go to the pub and ask there. It's only just after one.'

Nine months later the deeds of the bungalow and the bees belonged to Frederic and Elise, and they decided to move into the prosaically but accurately named 'Hillside' at Easter, just a year after they had discovered that the old man had died. After a lot of discussion, the decision to buy a house of their own had come easily. It seemed the logical next step, because they both wanted it to happen. Frederic was nearing retirement age and Elise had gone past it, without really noticing. It was a big step only because they had never owned anything large before, not even a car. But, thought Frederic, sitting on his herb-drenched bank, his bread and cheese half eaten on his plate, surely it had been the right move, although the events on the very day of the journey had completely overshadowed any pleasure of ownership.

He gazed mournfully at the piece of yellow cheese and broke off a piece of bread to eat with it. As he chewed, his thoughts turned to the little boy who had sat on this bank with him earlier today and who had been intensely interested in the tall patch of bright blue flowers with rough hairy stems and big coarse leaves. The bees loved them, Frederic knew, and he often watched them visiting each black-centred flower in turn, probing into the nectary and then making their steady way onto the next one. What, the little boy had wanted to know, was the name of that plant?

'Oh, dear,' Frederic had told him, as he bathed the child's cut knee with a piece of damp cotton wool. 'I don't know. It is a herb, like those others, and it dies away each year but it drops its big seeds which make more plants in the same place, sometimes in other places, but I don't know its name. Elise will know.'

'Where is she, can we ask her?' The boy had not flinched as Frederic smoothed in some antiseptic cream, although he had cried earlier when he fell in the lane on his way home from school, and it was this sobbing that had brought Frederic out of his garden to pick the child up. Frederic looked gravely at Dan and then sat down beside him on the fragrant bank, smoothing the long grasses over gently with his hand.

'No, we cannot ask her. I am afraid that she is not here. Do you like flowers?' he asked.

Dan nodded. 'I know the names of fifty-four wild flowers and several in the garden,' he said. 'May I take just a bit of that one home with me, so that Daddy can help me look it up? Mummy's better at looking up flowers, but she's away with Granny, until Sunday. Daddy's taking us to watch the village cricket match tomorrow,' he added, doubtfully.

'And do you like cricket, too?' asked Frederic, his eyes solemnly upon the little fair-haired boy who sat firmly on Elise's bank.

'Well, I don't know really. Daddy said I might.' Dan wriggled. 'We've seen you before. Mummy helped you knock your bees off that tree in front of your house when we were going past one day. When they swarmed. They stung her, on her knee, but she didn't say anything until we got home.'

'I remember. So, you have a brave family – all getting hurt on your knees and not making too much fuss!'

Frederic, living alone for the past five years, was unused to any lengthy conversation and he found that he was enjoying Dan's company. He led the child towards the row of hives, just as the old man used to lead him, and he showed the boy the one which now housed the swarm, explaining the life cycle of the hive, and Dan understood something of the instinct that drives each bee to work herself to death, so that the community survives. Frederic, who had brooded long and often on this phenomenon, forgot he was talking to a child.

'You see,' he said, leading Dan back to the bank where they both sat down again, 'each bee has no thought for herself. She is programmed, it is imprinted in her that she must work only for her hive and for her queen who is in the hive. Do you know,' he said, smoothing and patting the seed-laden heads of the tall grasses that tickled Dan's bare knees. 'I have seen a bee working on those pink flowers over there. She could not fly any longer and was clearly about to die. She could hardly move her wings, yet her only instinct was to stagger over to the next flower head to gather the nectar. She only thought of what she had to do, not of what was happening to her. Yet we are so different. Humans think only of themselves, but our actions affect those around us, those to whom we are close. One human being can so influence the life of another, that a whole personality can be changed or twisted in some way, although the person who has this power may be quite unaware of it. It can be like an invisible force, driving us to achieve the impossible, or it may be the most wonderful strength we shall ever know. But each of us bears this responsibility for another, or for many others, and that is the most awesome thing. The bees look to the immortality of the colony, but we must see to our individuals before we can start to care for humanity as a whole.'

'Please,' said Dan, who was beginning to feel hungry, 'I think I should go now. They will wonder why I'm not back from school yet. Daddy's getting tea, you see. Can I take a little piece of that with me?' He pointed at the tall, hairy borage and Frederic's face relaxed.

'Of course you can. Come and tell me what it is when your father finds out. We must try to find a piece that isn't covered with bees, don't you think?'

When Dan had trotted off home, clutching his small bunch of flowers, Frederic stayed on the sunny bank, thinking about what he had just said, more to himself than to the boy. When Elise had been alive, he had had no difficulty in accepting the fact that she had taken over his life – she was his life. There was no reason not to let her lead him onto paths he wanted to take and he had always felt complete and whole and satisfied. Now, after her death, he knew that he had been one of the happiest men alive and, having lost the source of that happiness, he was now the most sad. Just how she had bent his will to hers, twined his life to the stem of hers, he did not know, but that was what she had done. He remembered children's fables about inventors, creators who discovered a source of power to breath life into some inanimate object, a doll, a toy of some sort. Elise had given him that breath and her fund of life was so rich and her will so strong, that there had been enough for the two of them.

How was it that one person could be as strong as Elise was, and become part of another, Frederic wondered. He had nothing that had not been hers, also. His skill as a doctor, perhaps, but he had been trained to heal and diagnose and prescribe and he knew that was not something that came from deep within him, as all his communion with Elise had. Elise had loved him, cared for him, supported him in all things; but had she known that, when she was gone, he would be left broken, half a person, like this? In his darkest moments, Frederic wondered what sort of a man he really was and he knew that he could never find out, because without that part of her within him, he was nothing. But, he speculated, during those years with Elise, those thirty-eight years, had not he been someone then, or had he just been a shadow, an extension, an overflow for all her thoughts and feelings? Could he have existed for all that time without her?

Chapter Five

'Look!' said Henry, speaking through his teeth and hissing slightly as he always did when he started to grow annoyed, 'I'm trying to get in touch with Petra Appleton. I'm afraid I can't remember her married name. Her sister, Caroline Appleton, gave me this number some time ago. Is she there, please? What? Yes.' He spoke clearly, enunciating every word slowly. 'Yes, of course I realize Caroline is not there. May I speak to Petra, please?'

Henry, speaking from a crowded hotel in tourist-bound Cornwall, was feeling distinctly frayed. He had arrived in England the week before from his base in New York, with a brief to set up a location for some shots with dramatic sea and cliff backgrounds, that could be linked up by the advertising whizz-kids with folklore and legend to promote a new scent. He had dismissed the wilder parts of Scotland as inaccessible, and that left the West Country with its lingering traces of giants and mermaids and tales of King Arthur. But Henry only remembered the bare beauty of the dramatic rocky scenes of his childhood holidays, forgetting that the whole county of Cornwall was alive with its annual complement of summer visitors. Disgruntled after a week of trying to take test pictures of Zennor, Tintagel and Boscastle without an inch of solemn landscape that was not peppered with figures crawling up and down cliffs, he remembered that Caroline's sister lived in Somerset and thought that perhaps she might know if there were any suitable legend-ridden cliffs and headlands in nearby

Wales. Henry, always careful and methodical if there was a face to be remembered, an address or telephone number to be listed, had taken Petra's number some months before from Caroline, when he thought he might have to go to Somerset to do some work in the caves at Cheddar. But the assignment was cancelled and the number, unrung, had stayed in Henry's bulging book with all his other contacts.

Henry had often thought of Petra during the fifteen years since that Christmas when he had been very unhappy and she, by being grave and courteous, had helped him not to think about the bitter argument he had had over the telephone with Peter. Caroline propped him up in any misfortune simply by taking control for a while and ignoring the problem. He often did the same for her and they looked upon each other as straight guys; not the sort of friends who fell, sobbing, on each other's necks or who sat up together for half the night, spilling out tales of woe. But Petra, serious and reserved and obviously unsure of herself, had been someone to coax to life and who had responded so magically to his attention that the bitter words and the hurt that he and Peter had inflicted on each other had been eased. She marked that particular time for him as much as the scent of a flower or the song of a bird will evoke any memory that is also a feeling.

She had cropped up the following Christmas, too, by the most peculiar set of coincidences, and the last time he had seen her was on her wedding day, when he had been Caroline's guest. Now, when the surface of his unhappiness was only just being coated with the bland necessity to go on living and working, he thought of Petra again because, although she did not know it, she was linked to him with a frail and tenuous chain by the circumstance in which Peter had died.

Now he supposed that this guy on the other end of the line was Petra's husband, and he wondered what was wrong with the fellow. He thought Philip seemed a bit stupid. Henry's world did not embrace the type of marriage where husbands and wives felt they had a right to know who was telephoning their partners, and he could not think why this guy did not go and get Petra; in fact he did not seem to know whether Petra

64

lived there or not. Oh hell! thought Henry, trying to remember if he had any other contacts in that part of the world, and he was just about to ring off when Philip seemed to get himself together and explained that Petra would be away until Sunday evening, but if Henry was up this way then, well, he might as well call in. Henry, amused by the grudging invitation and bored to death with the traffic-jammed lanes of Cornwall, accepted.

'Sod it!' said Philip violently as he put the receiver down. He was cross, not because that softly spoken idiot with the twangy accent that sounded like a bit of wet elastic had rung up to speak to Petra, but because he felt that he had made a fool of himself. He looked at his watch. Christ – it was nearly ten o'clock. He had stayed up long after the children had gone to bed the night before, and Petra had telephoned quite a time after the late film on the television. This call from whatsisname, Henry, had woken him up – no wonder he felt stupid. He rolled himself slowly out of bed and reached for his spectacles to bring the world into focus, while he wondered why the children had not woken him before this. Had that Henry idiot said when he was going to turn up? Well, he was not going to miss the cricket match this afternoon on his account. Philip dressed and went downstairs, trying to remember if Petra had ever mentioned one of Caroline's old boyfriends called Henry. It did not occur to him that Henry might have been one of Petra's old flames.

Petra woke up early on Saturday morning, comfortable in the bed that had last been slept in, she supposed, by Caroline. Despite the fact that she knew that today's task should not be a pleasant one, she looked forward to the day ahead. She had no decisions to take, no food to choose and prepare, no children to entertain or help with homework, no housework or gardening. All she had to do was to support M, and Petra knew very well that her mother would draw her own peculiar defence system very firmly around her, before they had to face the emptiness of Caroline's home in London.

Petra lay in bed thinking that she had not liked the sight of Caroline's clothes, part of her working wardrobe, she conjectured, hanging up so neatly and clinically in her old cupboard. But that, she told herself, was not because of what they represented, but rather because they all seemed to be part of some dry investment, a calculated plan, and she felt sure that many of them had never even been worn. They were like exhibits in a glass case in a museum – part of a late twentieth-century model's working outfit – thought Petra, wondering if she was romancing because she was simply jealous and if, in her heart, she did not really covet the silk shirts and the suits and jackets and dresses. She tried to picture Caroline wearing the little fur jacket which she had tried on the night before, but she could not see her sister; Petra pulled up the sheets and realized that she could no longer visualize Caroline's face, could form no mental picture. She closed her eyes and tried hard to concentrate, but nothing came, nothing but a fuzzy reproduction of the newspaper picture of the neat little pin-up who was not really like Caroline at all.

That tattered bit of paper, screwed up and creased, had in the end been indirectly responsible for what Petra later thought of as freedom from the self-imposed restrictions on her personality and behaviour. It was because of that newspaper photograph that she had thrown off her self-centred pose at university and had become one of the crowd. It was because of that picture, she thought, with the wryness lent by the perspective of years of security, that she had over-reacted to the power of her newly found self and had wilfully wasted time, been thrown out of university and lost any chance of a degree.

But that came later; at the end of those first Christmas holidays she had returned, her course still firmly fixed in her mind, everything steady and in order and her reading and study marked out neatly. As before she kept to her room, joining forces with Susan when it was unavoidable and she began to take a new and deepening interest in the works of the English metaphysical poets. As the days lengthened towards the end of term she could see the swelling buds on the young

66

tree whose bare branches had been scraping against her window pane during the stormy winter nights and she would feel excited and restless for no particular reason. She would stride up and down, up and down in her room that was like a slice of passageway, five paces up and five paces back, muttering snatches from Cowley and Marvell and Donne. Donne especially suited her mood.

She yearned for the thin young lecturer who read them poetry on Thursday afternoons and Tuesday mornings and all her heart went into the essays she wrote for him. He wore a nasty checked sports jacket with leather patches at the elbows and his wife, whom Petra had seen once and had hated, was tall and very thin with dreadful teeth. Petra invented excuses to ask Mr Dagger – Geoffrey Dagger, she had discovered – involved questions about the works they were studying. But he, weary after another day on poets whose works he did not feel too much for (he was, after all a Wordsworth man, having written several papers on the Lakeland poets), was short with students who held him up when he wanted to get home to Margery, who had just told him that she was expecting their first child.

So Petra read and paced and yearned, and tried to dodge the whining Susan. She often wished now that she was one of the noisy friendly crowd who joked and threw books at each other and paired off and were easy enough to borrow a few quid from when the grant ran out. But a terror of deviating from the path she had set for herself, the image she had made and fixed for her own safety, held her back.

'Twice or thrice had I loved thee, Before I knew thy face or name . . .' muttered Petra as she paced, feeling the rush of longing for something, she knew not what, as she quoted the incantation, which was so beautiful that it should have the power of revealing new worlds; but all that happened was a tap on the door and a familiar drone.

'You in, Pet?' No one had ever reduced her name to that pathetic syllable before and she loathed it. Dragged out of her glazed excitement, she put down her book and opened the door to Susan, who was cradling a pile of notebooks under her skinny arm.

'My God, these books are so heavy,' whined Susan, tossing her head to flip back a lank strand of hair and flopping down, uninvited, on Petra's divan. 'Look, Pet – can I have a sight of your big blue book of ballads? I don't know where mine is and I need to look something up.'

Petra heaved the thick book across without a word, feeling mean because she resented Susan's intrusion, and knowing that she was being ungracious. But Susan did not seem to notice and she opened the book, making Petra wince as she licked her thumb and forefinger to squeeze the pages over. The book, resting on Susan's bony knees, tilted slightly and, as she turned more pages over, the creased and folded newspaper cutting fell out into her lap.

'What's all this?' she said, picking it up and unfolding it. 'Guilty secrets, eh?'

'Leave it alone!' Petra snatched at the bit of paper, but she was too late. Susan had unfolded it and was gazing at the blurred picture, reading the caption aloud: 'Who cares if it's raining? Not Miss Wednesday, lovely seventeen-year-old Caroline Appleton, who says that there's nothing like a shower to make her feel as fresh as a daisy!'

'Is that your sister?' Susan pointed self-righteously at Caroline's crumpled bare body. Petra nodded. 'You poor thing.' Susan looked genuinely concerned. 'You must be so ashamed of her.' Susan's gooseberry eyes, large and solemn behind her thick glasses, goggled as she gazed at Petra, who began to feel light-headed. She giggled at Susan's po-eyed indignant face.

'Of course I'm not – why should I be!' she spluttered. 'You should see your face. I'm not ashamed of Caroline. In fact I'm very proud of her – she's on her way to becoming a top model and she works very hard and earns a fortune.'

'But Pet, you can't be proud of a girl like that – she makes us all look stupid.'

Petra's mirth turned to cold fury. She snatched the piece of paper from Susan's waxy hand, ripping it in half as she did so. 'What do you know about it? All you ever do is whine about things. And my name is not Pet – it's Petra!' she roared.

Susan, pink-cheeked and pop-eyed but otherwise unruffled, pursed up her lips and gazed back. 'I'm sorry, Petra, but I always believe in saying what I think. I'm sorry if I offended you.' She started to gather up her books. 'Can I borrow this one?' she said as she scooped up the thick blue book of ballads.

'No, you bloody well can't. I think you're bloody rude,' shouted Petra, who rarely swore and never told anyone what she thought of them. She squeezed past the offended Susan, who was making little shrugging movements with her shoulders, and opened the door for the lanky girl, slamming it hard after she left.

That evening Petra stood in a long, jostling queue outside the Great Hall, where a rock band was to play. She chatted easily with the other students in the queue and, when the doors opened, she pushed forward with the rest of them into the great darkened room which had been stripped bare of all furniture and furnishings. There were no seats but she saw that everyone was pushing towards the stage to sit down on the floor, as near the front as possible. She squeezed in and, in her blue jeans and Indian cotton shirt, felt just the same as everyone else. A strange sweetish smell drifted round the hall and there was a blue haze caught in the beam of the two high spotlights.

The stage was crammed with enormous pieces of electrical equipment which were stacked in great square heaps, with untidy masses of wire poking out of the backs of huge speakers and trailing across the side of the stage. The little area with the drums and the piano and the three microphones was tiny, dwarfed by the black boxes. Nothing happened for ages; stage hands trailed up and down, plugging in odd leads and twiddling dials which made weird electronic howls of static wash over the muddle of heads on the floor. They all made thumbs-up signs at a long-haired man who sat on a platform in the middle of the audience, playing with the knobs and dials of what looked like a giant radio set. Somebody passed Petra a cigarette and, although she rarely smoked, she greedily inhaled a stream of hot smoke which tasted like the smell that drifted round the hall.

Immediately she felt dizzy and light-headed, and she only giggled when the young man squashed up next to her nudged her and said, 'Hurry up with the joint, man, we all got to have a drag.' More and more people were cramming themselves into the hall and Petra, who found that she was with a crowd that seemed to have some sort of connection with the band, was shoved and jolted as each newcomer pushed as far forward as possible.

And then, suddenly, everyone started clapping and cheering and the band was on stage. There was a drummer, a very tall thin man with a glittering array of saxophones strapped around him, and two guitarists. Petra forgot herself in the lights, the loud music which washed over and pounded through her head and stomach. She leaned against the fair-haired man next to her, taking a deep drag on each hand-rolled cigarette as it was passed round and swaying and clapping in time to the music. The insistent pounding throbbed out from the enormous black speakers, setting up waves of sound which, as they rolled louder and louder, pulled the audience to its feet so that, towards the end of the set, the great high-roofed hall held a jammed mass of swaying bodies. Up on the stage, bathed in ever-changing coloured pools of light, the band played on and a strange Old Testament figure, garbed in flowing white robes, leapt up in front of one of the massive speakers and was dancing his hands in a series of complicated twining movements in time to the pulse of the drums. Petra found herself laughing out loud in sheer pleasure at the power of the noise and lights, which had forced all consciousness of self out of her, and as she did so she felt the blond boy put his arms round her shoulders and squeeze himself close to her.

When she looked back at her university days from the safe haven of her marriage, Petra shuddered as she thought of the way she had behaved during that year. Some of the students managed to combine evenings of concert-going, dancing, drinking and drug-taking with a serious application to their studies. Not Petra. Once she had discovered the freedom that could be taken simply by wearing the sort of clothes that would be sure to upset M if she ever saw them, by going to rock concerts that the old Petra would have sneered at, by drinking and smoking and sleeping around, she found that this easily created new image of herself could not cope with a proper day's work as well. She studied in a desultory fashion, wrote the scantiest papers that she could get away with, and gave up her day-dreaming and Donne altogether. She had several love affairs, cramming all the adolescent rebellion which had been suppressed and overshadowed by her aware-ness of Caroline's successes into a few months.

Then she met Adrian. She had started her second year with warnings from her tutors that both her work and her attendance record must improve, or she would not be able to finish the course. By this time she was becoming convinced that it would be beyond her to sit down and take her examinations in any case. The conscientious Petra, channel-ling everything into her study, dividing her work up into neat little sections to be completed and ticked off – done, done, done – had lost hold of the security of her notebooks and reference volumes and now, looking back at the unfinished and unstudied patches, she knew that she had neither the will nor the inclination to cover the ground that she had wilfully set fire to.

Adrian was thin and monkish-looking. He had wispy, slightly long, grey hair in which unexpected patches of black still showed. He also had a soft, grey-black moustache and a beard which was trimmed to a fastidious point. He was very round-shouldered, so that he appeared to be stooping slightly all the time, and when he spoke, tilting his head to one side, he smiled with his thin lips drawn back over a set of strong white teeth. He was at least thirty years older than Petra, who met him in the bar of the Lamb and Blackbird. She had gone with a group of friends, who had left her there, defiantly drinking a pint, when they decided it was time to go back to do some work. Adrian bought her another pint of bitter and told her he was a publisher. Petra was impressed by this title and by the twenty pound note with which he paid for her drink. He was married, she discovered, with a young second wife and two small children.

Petra, downing her third pint of beer, was full of plans for her own future, and she told him that she was going to pack in her course and look for a job. Adrian pretended to look astonished and told her that he was, right now, looking for a new personal assistant and had she anywhere to live? Petra, rather frightened now that someone seemed to be offering her the means to leave university, said, no, she had not and she would have to think . . . when Adrian said that he had just signed the lease for a new set of offices and that there was a little furnished flat above, which could be hers if she took the job.

Petra left her studies on a wave of bravado and, once installed in the two miserable damp rooms that passed as a flat over the shabby premises that were to be Adrian's 'offices', she felt as small and as lost as she had when she first went up to university. Her friends had not seemed too impressed – they clearly thought she was mad and she could not screw up the courage to let M and Daddy know what had happened, although she supposed that the university authorities might.

She soon discovered that Adrian's publishing business meant that he produced the monthly *What's On* information and advertising sheet that was pinned up everywhere in the town, and that his personal assistant was the one who had to go out collecting the advertisements for it.

Petra was totally inexperienced and completely unfitted for persuading worldly businessmen and women that their pubs, clubs, bars and cinemas would see an upsurge in customers if they advertised with her. She hated trailing around the streets, map in hand and her feet hurting because her shoes were rubbing, and then having to knock at the back door of a club which really did not come alive until the evening. The owner, or manager, still bleary-eyed from the night before, did not really want to see her, and she would wait awkwardly in the corner of a dim, badly lit room which at night would be bright with coloured lights and women's dresses and alive with loud talk and laughter and music, but now smelt of stale smoke and sour drink.

The bad-tempered cleaners would bang around her with their mops and buckets and she would apologize for getting in their way. Petra would flush and she knew that she was being sniggered at. She normally managed to sell her space simply because people advertised in the brochure through force of habit, but it never occurred to Petra that it would have been a lot easier to ask Adrian to have the telephone in the office connected, so that she could simply do the whole thing over the phone in a brisk, businesslike way. Petra had never earned any money before and she was now working on a commission basis, which meant that she was paid a small percentage for securing the repeat advertisements and a larger figure came her way for new orders and for an increase in the size of existing displays.

After three dreary weeks in the dismal flat, she reckoned that she had only earned a few pounds and she had not seen Adrian to broach the subject of her money. He had told her that he was going away for a few days with his wife, whom Petra had not met, but who was called Sarah. Petra, who was utterly captivated by what she saw as Adrian's buccaneering air, his obvious detachment and independence from his family, loathed the unknown Sarah with an unreasoning venom.

The Sarah that Petra visualized was fat and dumpy and dowdy and she made Adrian's life at home a misery. He was always out and about in the town without her and Petra reckoned that he must be doing his best to escape the constant nagging. She pictured a plump, greying shrew, who tried to force Adrian to conform and shave off his dashing beard and work at a desk in a suit and tie from nine to five. Petra knew that, if Adrian would only let her help him, she could do so much more than Sarah to encourage him to sit down to write the novel about which he often talked and which he said was bursting inside his head. Where Adrian's money came from was a mystery to Petra, who had heard him talk of other business interests, but only in vague, half-hearted terms, and

73

she knew from her own involvement in the December issue of *What's On* that the publication's advertising revenue would not even begin to pay for the upkeep of his new, white sports car.

Petra was beginning to worry about her own finances. She was living off the remnants of her grant until Adrian paid her and she had a sneaking suspicion that the authorities were going to make her pay some if not all of it back. A woman from the university's welfare department had tracked her down and had made her feel defiant, childish and very foolish as she looked with obvious pity at the badly furnished office and had listened, without belief, to Petra's tale about her career in publishing.

'Where are you living?' she had said.

'Oh – there's a very nice flat which goes with the job,' Petra, red-faced, had told her, knowing that the woman had seen her eyes straying to the door in the corner of the office by the scratched counter, which led to the dark wooden stairs, giving away her miserable rooms. She saw her situation from the welfare officer's vantage point, and she wanted to cry.

But there had been days when Adrian had been around and had taken her out to lunch, to good restaurants where he seemed to be known. He had captivated her, telling her how easy it would be for her, a smart, clever, good-looking young woman, to sell his advertising space. Then she had formed pictures of herself sitting coolly on a swivel chair in a comfortable, well carpeted office, charming agreeable businessmen into buying large display ads.

But she had to admit to herself afterwards that the reality did not square with this image. The question that they all asked – 'You tell me what I'll get out of it, and then I'll advertise with you' – always floored her. She did not know the answer.

Adrian's return and his cheque – drawn on a joint account with Sarah, she noticed with distaste – cheered her. She came back to the office one dark evening, dreading the traipse upstairs to the dreary rooms which despite all her efforts with posters and cushions had never felt like home, as her college room had done, and found him waiting by the desk, tapping his pointed fingers on the telephone.

'Hallo, little Petra – it's on.'

'What is?' she asked grumpily, cross because he did not greet her in a special way after he had not seen her for so long.

'The telephone. What's the matter? Business bad today? You don't look too happy.' Adrian seemed to be brimming over with good health and vitality, with glowing cheeks, pink with health and sparkling eyes. Petra thought that his weekend away must have done him good and she was upset that she had not been part of it.

'Oh, I don't know. It's all so – so humiliating!' Petra, trying desperately to control the lump in her throat, found herself snivelling and then crying. She wanted to wipe her nose, which was dripping and, failing to find a tissue, started to charge blindly up the stairs, knocking Adrian's arm aside as she did so. He followed her and at the top of the stairs a strange little dance ensued, as she tried to open first one door then the other, but Adrian blocked her way each time she turned and the little landing was so small that there was barely room for both of them to stand without touching.

Petra, her head down, sniffed and was aware of the smell of the suede jacket that Adrian wore. She looked out of the corner of her eye to see his pointed gaze spearing the side of her face. He looked like a witch with his stooped shoulders, his little beard accentuating the sharpness of his chin and his long, thin nose and intense eyes. He clutched at her wrist, wrapping his long fingers round it and, slowly stooping towards her, he kissed her.

This was in the middle of November which, that year, was warm and bright. Petra went to bed, woke up, ate and worked in a cloud of happiness for just one week. Her affair with Adrian knocked her into a higher gear, brightened up her attack on life by a good few notches. Once more she became the pretty, bright girl who had walked confidently out of university. She raced around the city, knowing that she could not fail to sell a lot of advertising space. Every day she met Adrian for lunch and on a couple of occasions he stayed overnight with her. At this time Petra often felt as she walked, or rather bounded, along the streets that, if she willed it, she could, with one tremendous burst of concentration, lift her body from the ground and float above the earth. For the first time in her life, she reflected, something that she really wanted had happened, had become reality. That reality was spoiled, just a little, the second time that Adrian stayed the night with her. She had, that morning, received a puzzled letter from M, who was obviously doing her best to disguise a good deal of anxiety.

'We have had a letter about your grant, dear,' M wrote. 'There has obviously been some mistake because they say that as you are no longer a student, part of it must be repaid. I can't imagine what has happened, but could you find out your end? Ring me and let me know.'

There was a PS in typical M style: 'You father doesn't know about all this fuss, as the post arrived after he had left for the office and I don't want to worry him. So telephone me as soon as you can, please.' The letter had been forwarded, Petra supposed, by the welfare officer. She put it to one side as she did not want to think of that part of her life, although she supposed that, sooner or later, she was going to have to let them know at home what was going on, especially as the Christmas holidays were looming. But today she was to meet Adrian for lunch and they were going to the printer's, where he always introduced her as his Personal Assistant, and then she supposed that he would take her out for another meal, or a drink, before they came back to the flat.

They arrived back very late and rather drunk, laughing and staggering together into bed. Petra, giggling, asked Adrian how he had managed to fool his wife. She felt him stiffen beside her and he told her that Sarah and the children had gone away to London for a few days to stay with relatives. Petra should have been warned by the coolness in his voice, but she was too young and sure of herself to know when to back away from forbidden areas and too sure of her newly found power over Adrian to care.

'Then we should have spent the night at your place,' she

teased him. 'Much better than this seedy old flat.' Adrian was quite still for a minute. Then he got out of bed and went over to the door, where he fumbled for the light switch. Petra thought he looked rather silly, naked in the full glare of the bare bulb with his skinny white chest and humped back. Only his face was still imposing and she was suddenly stricken by the shadow thrown on the wall by his profile.

'Adrian!' she shrieked. 'You look just like the devil!'

He turned to look and the stark image disappeared. They both started to laugh. But Petra's euphoric mood gradually dissolved and, soon after that night, she began to be irritated by Adrian, by his fussiness, his constant worry about catching colds, his passion for tidiness. He complained if the flat looked messy and he nagged her if there was any washing up lying in the sink, or dirty clothes piled up. Petra grew to hate the way that he spent what seemed like hours deciding whether he should wear a coat and a scarf, or just a jacket, or if he needed a jumper and gloves as well. She did not like the fact that he could not keep up with her if she felt like running and she began to despise him for his grey hairs and hunched back, and started to avoid his embraces.

Petra also knew that she must reply to M, and she was beginning to realize that her hasty, unconsidered exit from university was the biggest mistake she had ever made. She could not spend the rest of her life, or even the next few months, selling advertising and she doubted if her course tutor would consider having her back. By the beginning of December she told Adrian – who by her reckoning owed her fifty pounds – that she was not going out touting for advertising for his rotten news sheet any more. He was infuriatingly calm.

'Now, Petra, I don't understand. You agreed to work for me on a percentage basis and I pay a pretty good commission.'

'And you owe me fifty pounds,' Petra told him, wincing inwardly as she heard herself whine and feeling grudging and mean and in the wrong, as he bent over her with a patient look on his face.

'Well, you only had to ask. I can't remember everything. I'll give you a cheque now.' He pulled out the chequebook – still the joint account, Petra noticed – and started to scribble, filling in the wrong date. She was about to point this out, but he carried on: 'I didn't force you to work for me – you were quite keen at the time, I remember, and I've even given you a flat, completely rent-free.'

'It's a horrible flat. It's not a real flat at all and I never see anyone I know apart from you and I hate it here.' Petra gave herself up to her petulance. Adrian looked pained.

'You've never asked for it to be decorated. What does it need – brightening up a bit? – painting perhaps, new curtains, light shades? You just tell me, and I'll get it done.' His easy compliance completely took the wind out of Petra's sails. She wanted an excuse to stop working for him, but she did not know how to go about it. She did not have the courage to tell him that she was not the girl he had taken her for when they first met in the Lamb and Blackbird.

'Come here, little Petra.' Adrian held out his arms and he looked like a stiff old ballet dancer, posing in front of a cracked mirror. With one foot pointed outwards and a silly smile on his foxy face, he gazed at her. She shook her head and put her hands behind her back, like a child, and he changed his tactics, becoming brisk.

'Very well, then. I was going to ask you if you'd like to come to a party, tonight. Sarah is having a few friends in for the evening and I know that she would like to meet you. Will you come? You've just said that you never see anyone.'

'But I haven't got anything to wear,' was what Petra thought. She said: 'Does she know about me, then?'

'Of course. I've always had a personal assistant in the past to help me with this side of the business and I've always worked from home before. It was only when she – I – bought this office, that I decided to run the *What's On* guide from here.' His voice dropped a tone and he looked slyly at Petra. 'She doesn't know about us, though.'

Petra blushed and looked away. 'I don't know where you live.'

'I'll pick you up – at about eight? You can't get to Ashford

78

by bus, so perhaps you'd better bring an overnight case, because I probably shan't feel like driving at the end of the evening.'

Petra was still intensely curious about Adrian's home life, even though she had no intention of letting him touch her, ever again.

'Let's put the hood down,' she said when he arrived, exactly on time, to pick her up.

'In this weather? We'll freeze!' He was genuinely horrified and Petra shrugged. To her surprise, he climbed out of the car and, without another word, unclipped the leather hood and folded it neatly back. Petra had decided to arrive at Sarah's party on her own terms. She was wearing a pair of very tight dark pink trousers and a thin blouse of near-transparent cotton. Her jeans were tucked into high-heeled boots and she hoped fervently that the sports car did not break down, because she could not walk very far in them. A dress, with long sleeves, would have been the thing she imagined, but that was not the image she wanted.

Adrian stopped the car in a layby outside a brightly lit shopping arcade. 'Just going to get another couple of bottles of gin,' he told her. 'I'm sure we've got dozens, but Sarah's worried in case people want to drink spirits.'

As he went into the off-licence, two young men sidled up to the car and Petra, without the protection of the roof, felt apprehensive and looked straight ahead.

'Nice motor!' announced the taller of the two. 'Take you for a drive, darling?'

'She's nice, too, isn't she?' said the other lad. 'Rather have her than the motor. You from the university, then?' Petra swallowed and looked up. They both had pleasant, open faces and she realized that they were only chatting her up. She relaxed.

'Yes. Yes, I am.'

'This your boyfriend's car, then?' asked the tall one, settling himself on the side of the bonnet and talking to Petra over the top of the windscreen.

'Yes – and he's coming now,' Petra told him, looking in the direction of the off-licence.

'Oh yeah – that old git?' The tall boy sniggered as Adrian, well wrapped up against the December wind, came closer. He got off the bonnet, but stayed leaning against the side of the car.

Adrian, saying nothing, opened the door and slid into the driver's seat. The young man still made no move, so Adrian said, pompously: 'Would you get off my car, please!'

The boy slowly uncurled himself and looked down at Petra. 'OK, Grandad – keep your hair on. 'Bye, sweetheart!'

He and his friend turned and sped away. As Adrian started the motor, Petra heard one of them shout 'Sugar Daddy!' She clenched her fists and stared straight ahead. Adrian did not say another word until they pulled into the gravelled driveway of a long low building, which seemed to be about a mile away from any other house, through a small village some way out of the city.

Petra followed Adrian through a thick wooden door in the side of the house and they walked along a passageway with uneven walls and two or three doors opening off to the left. The house was obviously extremely old, very large, and the floor was thickly and expensively carpeted, while shaded lamps made pools of light on the bumpy whitewashed walls.

'I don't expect Sarah is down yet,' said Adrian.

'Putting the children to bed,' thought Petra, who asked for a cloakroom, so that she could comb out the tangles that the cold wind had whipped into her hair.

The downstairs lavatory was large and warm with lots of lights, big soft towels and large mirrors. Petra, who had chucked away her bra along with her university course, bit her lips as she saw just how transparent her blouse was – the poor lighting in her flat had been rather deceptive. She combed her hair, wincing as the teeth pulled at tangles, and she put some more eye-shadow on. Outside the cloakroom she bumped into a youngish woman, plump and pleasant-faced, neatly and discreetly made up and smart enough, with tidy permed hair, an expansive tan dress and matching shoes and bag.

80

'How boring,' thought Petra unkindly, as she immediately assumed that this was Sarah.

'Hallo! You must be Mr Bell's *What's On* lady? I'm Janet Taylor, Mrs Bell's secretary and personal assistant. I'm pleased to meet you,' said the brisk young woman, politely averting her eyes from the front of Petra's blouse. 'I was just on my way to the drawing room – a lot of the guests have arrived by now. Would you like me to show you the way?'

'This house is very old,' she threw out the information over her shoulder to Petra, who walked a little behind along the narrow corridor. 'Over six hundred years, in places, but I do think Mrs Bell has made a lovely job of restoring it and doing it up. Don't you think it's wonderful?'

Petra did, but she was not going to say so. She asked carefully: 'Does Mrs Bell spend a lot of time here – she must do, if she's restored the house?'

'Well, it all depends on the business,' said Miss Taylor, cautiously. 'She's abroad a lot, of course, tasting and buying. Such a shame that Mr Bell doesn't have any interest in it, but then, he's got his own little concerns,' and she gave a laugh which sounded rather nasty to Petra, whose boots were hurting and who was beginning to wish that she had never come to compete with this superwoman. Sarah was not upstairs putting the children to bed, that was certain. She probably had an army of nannies to do the job for her.

There were rather a lot of people in the drawing room. Petra, who had visualized a party of eight or ten, was relieved to see that she could lose herself in this crowd of forty or more. The room itself was enormous ('Three old rooms knocked into one, isn't it wonderful?' whispered Miss Taylor) and they entered by a door set in the wall of what must originally have been the middle room. Large log fires blazed at either end, and as Petra gazed from the doorway she felt the same curious panic she had experienced as a child when teams were being chosen for games at school, and she knew that her name was going to be the last called. People were grouped around each of the identical fires and she could not decide which way to go – to the right or to the left. All the men seemed to be fairly formally dressed but many of the women were, like herself, wearing trousers. She turned to Miss Taylor.

'I didn't realize that there would be so many people – I'm afraid I don't know any of them.'

'Don't worry,' began her companion and, at that moment, a door by the side of the fireplace on Petra's right opened and in walked a very tall, blonde woman, with Adrian at her heels. Everyone at the other fireplace immediately surged up the room and Petra and Miss Taylor were caught up in the general rush towards the magnificent blue-eyed giantess whom Petra recognized with a sinking heart to be another version of her sister Caroline.

'I'm so sorry, I'm late. At my own party, too. I was putting the children to bed.' Petra ground her teeth as she gazed up at Adrian's wife, who must have been nearly six feet tall, with a great mane of red-blonde hair pinned back from her smooth face. Adrian was a hunch-backed old man beside her. Everyone seemed to know her and want to speak with her and they all started jostling for her attention, so Petra found herself shoved to the edge of the crowd and that was where Adrian found her.

'You didn't tell me your wife was a businesswoman!' she said to him, meaning: 'You didn't say she was young and beautiful and clever.'

'Didn't I?' he said, gloomily. 'She's very good at it. Got the family palate – not my family. Hers.'

'What does she do?'

'She's a wine merchant. Family business, you know, and she's taking it over from her father and uncles. No son, you see, but then there doesn't have to be. Funny, isn't it? Have a drink.' He led Petra over to a table which ran very nearly the length of the wall opposite the door by which she had entered, and poured her a glass of wine. There were no spirits, she noticed, and wondered why Adrian had been buying emergency bottles of gin at the off-licence. More and more people seemed to be coming in.

'Who are all these people?' asked Petra, beginning to feel sorry for Adrian, whom she had never seen at a loss before and who was clearly here by accident, as she felt that she was.

'Oh – business contacts, press – trade press, that is. She's bought out a lot of good stuff, here' – he pointed at the table, a good half of which was covered with bottles of red and white wines. Petra sipped at hers, enjoying the fruity, slightly peppery taste and the feel of the thin glass in her hand.

'I can tell you that's a claret from the shape of the bottle,' said Adrian, gloomily. 'But, without my glasses on to see the label, I couldn't begin to tell you where it comes from. I'm no use to the business, you see.'

'But can't you help run it, organize things and so on?' Petra patted his arm. 'You run the *What's On* guide, after all.'

'I've been doing that for years. It runs itself if the truth were known. No, they wouldn't let me near their precious warehouses. 'Scuse me.' He lurched away and Petra realized that he was rather drunk and must have bought that gin for himself. She reached over and poured herself another glass of wine and wandered off, down the room to the far fireplace which was now deserted and looked inviting. The first glass of wine, drunk quickly on an empty stomach, had made her feel rather light-headed, and as she settled herself on a seat which flanked the blazing fire at a comfortable angle, she squinted at the crowds milling round the wine at the other end of the room and felt that she was peering through the wrong end of a telescope. Sarah's bright head stood out in stark contrast to the dark suits and jackets of the men clustered around her, and Petra smiled as she thought of the fat, nagging wife she had enjoyed hating for Adrian's sake.

She rather liked the look of Sarah, perhaps in some perverse way because the tall blonde reminded her of her sister and she found herself discounting Adrian who, only a few weeks before, had seemed to be a person of depth, a romantic, a glorious man. He was a miserable failure and a mistake. She knew that she could not stay here tonight and she also knew that she would not go back to the cold echoes of the flat. Her mind raced; doors were slamming, one after the other, in her face. No study, no work, nowhere to live. But she sat and enjoyed the warmth of the fire and the red wine and the unreality of the people at the other end of the room.

'Petra! It is, isn't it? May I sit with you?'

She gaped at Henry, courteous and grave and wearing a ridiculous suit of Lincoln Green with a big, flatly frilled lace collar. She started to giggle. 'Where's your bow and arrow?'

He grinned and sat down and handed her another glass of wine. 'Have you eaten?' She shook her head. 'Stay here and don't let anyone cut me out.'

Henry disappeared into the throng and came back in minutes with a loaded plate. Petra could not stop eating once she had started, and Henry looked on admiringly as she demolished pâté and duck and little bits of smoked salmon and tiny bread rolls and odd bits of pastry. At last he remarked: 'How nice to see a girl with an appetite. I'd forgotten what one looked like.'

'I didn't know I was so hungry. Oh, Henry, thank goodness you're here. Where are you staying?'

'Well, my hostess seems to want me to stay overnight, but I have to be in London very early tomorrow.'

'London!' The name offered refuge to Petra, whose one desire now that she had fortified herself with food and drink, and with contempt for Adrian (and for herself for getting involved with him), was to get away, as far as possible, from the mess she had made. Henry gazed at her, and his sharp eyes behind their spectacles slipped past her to look into the depths of the fire.

'I'm not going to ask you what you are doing here, when I thought you were safe at university. But I'm telling you not to get mixed up with this lot.' He nodded towards the centre of the room, where a crowd of black jackets and a blazing blonde head showed Sarah's progress. 'She's rich and spoiled. Very clever, mind you, and a shrewd woman when it comes to any sort of business. He's a loser; the one mistake she's ever made. Adrian was all right as a fairly successful small-time con man, but he's right out of his depth now.'

Petra hung her head, trying to think how she could have been so stupid. A vision of her narrow room at college, with the pictures on the walls, the crammed shelves and the young tree tapping on the window, filled her mind and it blotted out the threatening figure of Daddy, always in the background ready to roar at her for abandoning the university education that he had never had. The heat from the fire was beginning to redden her cheek, making her feel uncomfortably hot.

'Can I come to London, with you, Henry? I've got a bag in Adrian's car.'

Caroline's house was cold and dark when they arrived in London at four in the morning. Henry always stayed there when he was working in England and he told Petra that Caroline was away on a job in North Africa.

'Sleep first,' he told her as he efficiently sorted out blankets and sheets and switched on the heating and bustled in and out of the kitchen with hot water bottles and a cup of tea. 'Sleep first and we'll get you sorted out in the morning.'

Petra drifted off to sleep, trying to make a complete picture in her mind of Caroline's house, which she had never seen before and which seemed to be situated in a small mews, with cobbles outside. She suddenly realized that she had taken Henry's appearance at that awful party very much for granted.

'What on earth was he doing there,' she wondered sleepily, 'and how did he come to know Sarah?'

Chapter Six

'Coffee or tea, dear?' called out M in a bright, early morning voice as Petra yawned her way down the stairs. There was no sign of Daddy; Petra did not blame him as she knew that M's chatter, brittle and cheerful to the point of insincerity, would ring very false today. Petra did not really want any breakfast, but she accepted a cup of tea and drank the orange juice already poured out and waiting neatly by her place at the dining room table. She and M buttered toast and spread it with chunks of expensive-looking marmalade. M hummed slightly to herself in between mouthfuls.

'What on earth are we going to do with everything?' Petra asked, abruptly.

M stopped humming and looked pained, but she knew what Petra was talking about. 'I rather thought we'd worry about that when we got there, dear,' she warned.

'But what about all the things here – in my room?'

'Oh yes, well . . . I thought that you might like them all. I'd like that and so would Daddy.' M looked hopefully at Petra, who simply shrugged and shook her head.

'Well, never mind dear. We'll sort all that out later, don't let's worry about it now. I know what I meant to ask you – what would the children like for Christmas, do you think? I know it's a long way off yet, but I like to start early and get it all done in good time. Clothes for Fiona this year, would you say, and perhaps William . . .'

'M! It's still summer!' Petra was truly shocked. 'You can't think about Christmas yet. Not today.'

M shrugged slightly and looked sideways and Petra felt guilty. 'Oh hell!' she thought. She said: 'How's your tooth this morning? I really thought you were a burglar last night.'

M giggled. 'Oh, it's fine, dear. That was silly of me. I was thinking about it all when I got back to bed and I'm going to buy digestives next time and put them in a separate tin, in case.' She paused, fiddling with the handle of her tea cup, and then asked: 'Petra, dear – how long have you and Philip been married? I couldn't think last night when I went to bed and I think that's why I found it hard to sleep in the first place. I did remember that it was the year that Caroline had the contract for that big cosmetics firm . . .'

'Eleven years,' muttered Petra, but M, lost in her train of thought, took no notice.

'That's right – it *was* that year – what did they call her on the posters? "Miss Starglow, the Face of the Seventies." She always used Starglow cosmetics after that.'

'They probably gave her a lifetime's free supply,' said Petra, and then she stared at her mother in horror and embarrassment when she realized how hurtful her words must be. But M was not listening.

'Now I remember – it was twelve years ago – oh yes, Petra, and do you recall all that fuss on your wedding morning when we couldn't find her anywhere and it was time for you girls to get changed and she'd got into a panic about being a bridesmaid because she didn't want to outshine the bride? That funny man she liked so much found her in the end so it was all right. Do you remember?'

Petra clenched her fists under the snowy mantle of the tablecloth and thought, how like M to put such a romantic gloss on a thoroughly unpleasant scene. Caroline had simply not liked the colour or the cut of her bridesmaid's dress, which had had to be made without a proper fitting, as she had always been too busy to try it on in the weeks before the wedding. She had sworn at Petra and walked deliberately out of the house.

87

Petra had not seen her sister during her short stay in London after Henry's rescue and her flight from the Midlands. She had woken up warm and comfortable, and it was pleasant to see a bright, well furnished room, pretty curtains filtering the daylight and soft coloured lampshades giving a rosy glow to the world. She felt a warm carpet tickle her toes as she levered herself out of bed and she shuddered as she thought of Adrian and of the clammy feel of the lino on the floor of the chilly flat with its sooty view, threadbare mats and stringy curtains at the dirty windows.

This room must be Caroline's bedroom and she looked around with interest, for never since the days when the two of them had shared a room had she seen how her sister lived, how her tastes had developed. She was disappointed to find no clue here; the furnishings, all pretty but practical and beautifully matched, could have been chosen by M, and Petra, after a close look round, surmised that they had been. There were a couple of pictures on the creamy coloured walls which Petra recognized as prints that they had had in their bedroom at home but, apart from the little porcelain figurine which Caroline's godfather had given her on the day she had been confirmed, there were no ornaments.

The dressing table sported, rather incongruously, a couple of angled built-in spotlights, and Petra realized that they were there so that Caroline could achieve a flawless make-up. There was also a tortoiseshell-handled brush, comb and mirror set which was clearly never used, a box of tissues resting in a frilly case (M's touch again), half used, and two quarter-full scent bottles. Petra squirted some of the scent on the inside of her wrist and sniffed at it. It conjured up visions of expensive jewellery and thick fur coats and she gave herself another spray. She then moved over to the wardrobe, which contained several pairs of trousers, a plain dress or two and a few jackets or skirts. All severe-looking and plain and certainly nothing that was the height of fashion.

The chest of drawers which matched the dressing table had

three lace mats on top, but that was all. Petra opened the top drawer, which contained neat stacks of letters, bulging folders and a few small cases containing sticks of professional make-up with clinical names – 'Base Number One', 'Tan Tint Strength Four', 'Highlight Three'. Petra swept those back and opened one of the folders. There was Caroline, Caroline's face, full and profile; left side, right side, tilted, smiling, frowning. Caroline lying, jumping, stretched out, standing, bending, sitting. She was sulky, sexy, pouting, healthy and wholesome. Each large glossy coloured photograph was carefully mounted and notes beside each one gave the date and the photographer's name. The printed script could have been in Caroline's hand, but Petra was not sure. She didn't know if these pictures – and there were five folders full – were mere records of jobs that Caroline had undertaken or if they were some sort of portfolio, built up so that Caroline could hawk herself wholesale to prospective employers. Petra shuddered at this thought and shut the drawer. She had not seen her sister for almost six months, when they had met at home during the summer, and these photographs, with their professional detachment, made her feel further than ever away from Caroline.

The other drawers held underwear and sweaters, all neatly folded and sorted into piles according to their colour. Petra was just shutting the bottom drawer when she saw something black and angular jutting from a pile of pink sweaters. She slipped her hand into the softness of the wool and pulled out a framed photograph which she recognized instantly. She and Caroline were sitting on the ponies they had had as young children. There was Caro, straight-backed and unsmiling, neat ginger hacking jacket and long slim legs in faultlessly shaped pale jodhpurs, firm around her bay pony, the Hon. Miss Someone fresh from *Horse and Hound*. While Petra, red-faced and untidy in a home-knitted red sweater and dirty trousers, crouched uncomfortably on her small shaggy pony, was far more Thelwell.

That photograph had been enlarged and sent to the aunts and uncles for a Christmas present, and Petra remembered the resentment she had felt when they wrote back and said thank you and what a fine little horsewoman Caroline was becoming. She stood the photo up on one of the little lace mats and looked hard at it, trying to think about the things that she and Caroline had talked about in those days, what Caroline's interests had been, what games they had played together. But nothing came and Petra was suddenly desolate, her childhood, that part of her life which she had shared with Caroline, turning into the other side of a dream. She wanted to carry on her search for traces of her sister, but at the same time she thought of Henry. He had said that he must be in London early, so she supposed that by now he was out, working. She washed quickly at the handbasin in the corner of the room and dressed in her pink trousers and blouse. There was a jumper in her overnight case but, after a moment's hesitation, she opened the bottom drawer, pulled out the cashmere sweater which had protected the photograph, and put it on.

There was no sign of Henry, but Petra saw, with a small sense of shock as she looked at the electric wall clock in the kitchen, that it was past midday. She put the kettle to boil on the gas cooker to make herself some tea and, as she fiddled with the unfamiliar controls, she saw a note on the blue work-top next to the draining board: 'Bread etc in the cupboard. Will be back this evening – don't ring your parents – we'll talk p.m. If you want to go out, lock up with the keys which are in the drawer by right of sink.' A neat arrow pointed downwards, presumably to the drawer, and the note, written in a tiny hand, the letters black and angular, was signed 'H'.

Petra had no intention of ringing home, but she wondered why Henry should worry about it. As she found the bread and butter – Henry must have done some early morning shopping, as the bread was fresh – she started to think about him and his relationship with her sister. Petra knew very little about homosexuals, but Henry, with his decisive manner and unquestionable capability, did not seem to conform to her stereotyped picture of a gossipy lisping introvert. Nor, though, did he conform to any of the standards to which she was accustomed. His dress was obviously eccentric and his appearance, with big baby face and balding head, little round spectacles and neat moustache, was unusual, while his job was glamorous in the extreme. Perhaps he and Caroline were lovers of a kind . . . but even as the thought came into her mind, Petra dismissed it. Caroline could not have been joking about Henry and his boyfriend or lover, or whatever the title was, in America. But if Henry had someone, what about Caroline? During the brief period at home when she had left school, there had been hosts of boys and young men wanting to take her out. But she always went as part of a crowd, never having anyone special.

Petra wandered around Caroline's house, a piece of toast in one hand and a mug of tea in the other; what had started off as an exploration out of pleasant curiosity was becoming an intense search for a clue to the part of her sister she had forgotten. She was surprised to find that Caroline lived in a small house and not, as she had supposed, in a flat. There was a large hallway downstairs and a good-sized sitting room which looked out onto a cobbled yard. The stairs, from the hallway, led directly into the open-plan dining room and then there was the tiny kitchen and two bedrooms and a bathroom which all opened off a small landing through from the dining area.

The two living rooms, the bedroom and the kitchen all bore traces of M's influence and no clue at all to Caroline's own tastes. But the bathroom was different. M would never have chosen that glowing juicy wallpaper which dripped with luscious fruits and shady leaves, she would have tutted at the wall of mirrors and the battery of spotlights, and although she would have admired the shaggy luxury of the thick emerald-green carpet, she would have told Caroline that it was not at all practical. The wall of mirrors ran above a long work-top, underneath which were cupboards and pigeonholes, like those in a luxury kitchen, and there were two deep-blue handbasins, each shaped like an enormous cockleshell, set into the wall. Bottles of bath oils and salts, body lotions and creams filled the recessed shelves at the sides of the enormous blue bath, and when Petra opened a door on the far side of the room, she discovered an airing cupboard filled with thick soft towels of all sizes. She had only switched on one light when she entered the room and the interior of the cupboard was in partial shadow. As she started to shut the door, she noticed that it had a huge poster pinned to the inside, so she reached over and snapped on a spotlight which was angled towards the cupboard's interior. She pressed the button of the light and looked at the inside of the door and she gasped as the strong beam made an enormous face, Caroline's face, gazing serenely out, jump sharply into focus.

Henry came back early in the evening, just as Petra, with the airing cupboard door firmly shut, was climbing out of the bath. As she heard his footsteps on the stairs she wrapped a thick warm towel round her body, feeling guilty for the warm scented air that wafted through the house.

'I had a bath. I hope you don't mind,' she said, politely.

He started to laugh, 'You are a strange girl! This house belongs to your sister, not to me. Look, you go and get some clothes on and I'll pour us a drink and take you out to dinner.'

Over the meal Henry listened while Petra poured out her sad little story and he looked sympathetic although the mere telling of it made her feel naïve and very stupid.

'Do you want to go back to college?' he asked, and Petra shook her head.

'I don't see the point,' she said. 'Even if I worked very hard now I'd only get a poor degree – and then what? I don't want to teach or work in an office; in fact I can't think of anything at all I'd be good at. No, that's wrong. There's something that I really want to get involved with, but I can't think what it is.' That sounds stupid, she thought and hung her head, gazing at the thin white china on the polished table, feeling sorry for herself.

'You sound just like your sister,' said Henry.

'Caroline! But Caroline doesn't have to worry about a thing. She's always done exactly as she wanted and she's always had her own way.'

Henry started to say something, but changed his mind and sat there looking thoughtfully at Petra, with a little smile on his face. After a considerable pause he muttered: 'Ah, well!

things aren't always as they seem, you know, Petra.' That was all he would say and Petra, becoming aware once more of her own predicament, did not have the energy to ask him to explain.

'I'm going to talk to your parents,' he told her over coffee. 'I think I understand the difficulties you're putting yourself through and I'm going to try to get them to see it, too.'

'But why should you? I mean,' Petra hoped that she was sounding as grateful as she felt but was afraid that her words seemed rude, 'what I'm trying to say is I've only got myself to blame. I got myself into this mess – why should you sort it out? And there's all my stuff still at that flat, all my clothes and books. Oh dear.' Her voice started to take on a wailing note as she thought of all the arranging to be done, explanations to be made.

'I'll get that idiot Bell to sort all that out for you and to send it on.' Henry was becoming angry, but not with Petra. 'This isn't the first time he's buggered someone about.'

Petra became curious. 'How did you come to know them, Henry?'

'Oh, Sarah occasionally shows in the same circles, you know?' He was deliberately vague and again she felt that she could not press him.

Petra never knew what Henry told Daddy and M, but, apart from one or two hastily suppressed outbursts of anger from her father, they did not scold her or question her decision to leave university. She doubted that they knew the true story and she certainly was not going to tell them herself about what she now saw as the sordid little episode with Adrian. Her luggage arrived, too – all neatly packed up and addressed correctly to her at her parents' home; inside the large suitcase there was an envelope with a cheque in it for the £50 which Adrian had owed her and which she hastily banked.

But all this was after her stay in London, when she and Henry turned the three days into a little festival, a short holiday. For Petra those three days of sightseeing, shopping, housekeeping, laughing at Henry's awful jokes and eating three huge meals a day seemed to mark the start of her adult

93

life. She was no longer 'in love' with Henry and she doubted whether she ever had been. She took pleasure in his company, and this was because of the overwhelming sense of relief with which she realized that he expected nothing more of her than her natural self. She felt no pressure to do or to say clever things, there was no need to prove herself, because they got on perfectly well without the automatic monitor that she often subconsciously employed. Henry, always full of energy, would put on one of his impossible capes or floppy velvet jackets, wind a scarf round his neck and drag her off to see London. He took her to look at odd little statues in small parks, out-of-the-way galleries that specialized in a few Asian paintings or Eskimo crafts, to the docks and the markets. She found herself gazing at paintings by artists whose names were unknown to her, at buildings in crooked streets, at aged trees. She said one morning that she would like to go to the Victoria and Albert museum and he grinned and took her there in a taxi and followed her in amusement as she wandered around, unable to settle on one object or one group of objects to study.

'You see – there's far too much. You can't take it in, yet, Petra. One thing at a time. Make one thing important and the rest will follow.'

She gave up trying to absorb the complicated and ancient pattern on a very beautiful and very large blue and gold carpet.

'Is that how you do it, Henry? One thing at a time?' He nodded. 'What is your one important thing?'

'That, dear little Petra, would be telling too much!' His round blue eyes were kindly but she knew that he was not really being flippant as he steered her towards the main entrance. 'You must know,' he said, once they were safely outside on the steps, 'that all the truly happy people in this world – and I wouldn't say that there were that many of them – are the ones who make other people more important than things, objects. Care about people and your ideas are right – care about ideas and you can lose touch with people.'

They walked along in silence until Petra spoke. 'I've never had anyone important in my life.'

'What about Caroline – your sister?'

'Caroline! Oh, I thought you meant, well, you know, a special lover or someone like that.'

Henry laughed. 'Oh, don't take any notice of me when I get serious, I promise I won't do it again. No, I didn't mean, well, you know, a lover or someone like that,' he mocked kindly and Petra grinned.

'I really can't feel close to Caroline. In fact, I've spent the past few days trying to think what she's really like. It should be easy to do that living in her house, but there's nothing there. I can't get any clues. Does she ever talk to you about herself?'

'Sometimes.' A little frown sketched itself on Henry's face. 'But Petra, you must know that there's only one person in this world who means anything at all to Caroline – and that's Caroline herself.'

Petra was distressed. 'But what about her friends? What about you? Does she have a boyfriend? There must be someone!'

'Oh, Caroline is very well aware of what she calls her frozen centre. She enjoys my company because I amuse her, provide somewhere for her to stay if she comes to my part of the world and keep her company when I'm in England. I'm no threat to her, sexually – you understand me? And I know rather a lot of people who often turn out to be useful to her in her career.'

Henry put his arm round Petra's shoulders and pointed at the fairy tale outline of Harrods, twinkling under its skin of Christmas lights. 'Let's get you sorted out first, Petra. Caroline knows very well what life is all about and she's chosen her own path, although I doubt very much if she'll ever be happy. She is single-minded in the extreme. You care for her a little, but you'll get nothing in return.'

Petra shivered, and in place of the twinkle and sparkle of the elaborate Christmas decorations, glittering frostily as they spun and swung in the thin wind, she had a vision of Caroline, beautiful and alone, floating sadly in vast empty galaxies. Henry squeezed her shoulders and laughed at her.

'Come on – let's go and find some lunch. All this morbid talk is making me hungry!'

Petra arrived home alone on the train, carrying just her overnight grip and wearing a new pair of boots and a thick coat which Henry had insisted on buying for her. M was at the station, and looked so pleased to see her that Petra felt wretchedly guilty.

It took some time for Petra to realize that both M and Daddy were under the impression that she had undergone some sort of a breakdown. M, in particular, treated her like an invalid and she began to suspect that Henry had posed as a doctor or a psychiatrist when he had spoken to them on the telephone. They also thought that she had come home directly from the Midlands, changing trains in London. Henry had warned her when he saw her off at Waterloo not to say that she had been staying at Caroline's house.

'Don't complicate matters. Let them think you're coming straight home. I'll square it with Caroline and I don't think they'll ask too many questions. I'll see you!'

But Henry never wrote and Petra, who knew that he was due to return to the States, to Peter, did not have his address. Over the months that followed, those first few days of adulthood in London became unreal, encapsulated in a thin haze like the early mist from cold rivers, as if she had dreamed away the days.

Caroline, still in Africa, did not come home that Christmas, and Petra and M and Daddy treated each other with extreme courtesy, considerate as one is to someone handicapped, anxiously polite. But once Boxing Day was over and the New Year approached, Daddy made it quite clear that he considered it was time Petra thought of her future.

Petra's removal, by her own actions, from university, diminished her, lowered the self-esteem which had flowered for such a short time. In those miserable weeks of slushy January she thought maybe I should have braved my tutor, confessed to M and Daddy, faced the others and humbly asked for my place back. Sometimes, when Daddy was at his office and M out, doing the shopping or at the hairdresser's or having tea with a friend, Petra would sit on the bottom stair, eyeing the telephone, planning to ring up the university authorities and plead to be allowed back. But the mechanics of the thing – who to ask for, what to say, how she would reply – defeated her, and in her own mind she became a small thing, relying on others to make decisions for her, too irresponsible to cope for herself.

She neglected her appearance, eating too much, not washing her hair, unable to plan what to wear and failing to notice when her clothes needed cleaning or washing. She started reading only what she knew would not disturb her – romances in women's magazines, old-fashioned detective stories, her old books from childhood. Often when both M and Daddy were out of the house, she would sit and weep, rubbing her hands over her wet face and through her hair. A postcard from Caroline, sent some weeks before from Morocco, arrived for M and Daddy; Petra, hating the casual message – 'Hard work and v. hot, love Caro' – scrawled in green ink across the back of the brightly coloured card, took it up to her bedroom before they saw it and cut it up into small pieces with her nail scissors. Caroline must be back in England now and she wondered if M had written about her. She guessed not, but she knew that Henry must have let Caroline know about their occupation of her house.

'I might go up to London for a few days to stay with Caroline,' she announced one evening as they were eating dinner. The words slipped out, more as just something to say rather than anything she had thought about, or even wanted.

Daddy raised his eyebrows and looked at her. M clenched her knife and fork very tightly and sat still. Petra knew, by the quality of the silence, that Daddy was about to be extremely cross, but she kept her head down, looking at her plate, where she cut up cabbage and mixed it with the bread sauce and the gravy. She concentrated hard on the appearance of the food, the smell of the white slices of chicken, the tiny yellow fat globules glistening on the gravy which smeared the clear blue and white of the plate.

'Petra,' said Daddy, too quietly. She had to look up. 'Petra, who is going to finance this jaunt to London?'

'Please, Tom, not now.' M had put her knife and fork down and was darting little flickering glances, full of concern, between her husband and her daughter.

'Why not now? For the last six weeks, Petra has sat in this house, burying her head in the sand, lounging around, looking as though butter wouldn't melt in her mouth . . .' Daddy, too, put down his knife and fork and he turned his head abruptly as he glared in turn, first at Petra and then at M.

'It's about time . . .' he started, but his words broke off as a strange, bubbling noise broke across the harshness of his voice and Petra, her shoulders heaving, started first to giggle and then to laugh, in great heaving sobs. She gasped, covering her face with her napkin, and tore in painful mouthfuls of air as her lungs felt near to bursting point; but still the waves of hysterical sobbing laughter rippled through the shocked silence.

M looked desperately at her husband. 'Tom! Do something. Please! That man from the university told us that Petra isn't well. She's hysterical.' At this Daddy threw his napkin onto the floor and tried to reach across to slap Petra's face. He only succeeded in cuffing her ear, as the blue napkin in her hand hid most of her features. But that was effective enough. Petra, still gasping and sobbing, tears now streaming down her blazing cheeks, pushed back her chair, which toppled and fell to the ground with a loud thud, and stumbled up the stairs to her bedroom, where she barricaded the door with the heavy armchair which normally sat underneath the window.

She climbed into the armchair and sat on top of a heap of dirty clothes that had piled up during the last few weeks, listening for what was going on downstairs. Like a child, she became filled with self-absorbed pity. She thought, what if I were terminally ill, or destitute, or even dead, and she pictured the shocked and repentant reaction of her parents. She could not focus her thoughts away from herself and her own predicament and on to M and Daddy's bewilderment.

Once or twice, she stiffened as she heard careful footsteps on the stairs and at one point there was whispering outside her door, M's voice sibilant and urgent and Daddy's breaking out of a cracked whisper, as he became agitated. Then M tapped, very gently, on the door.

'Are you all right, dear? Can I come in?'

'Go away!' Petra said gruffly and a new flow of tears spurted from her eyes and ran down her stained face.

After that she must have gone to sleep in the armchair, for she woke up later, cold and stiff, her face still swollen, with pieces of lank hair sticking to her cheeks where the tears had dried. It was very dark and, as she woke with a start, her heart began to thump violently. From her position in the chair the dim square of light from the window was not where it should have been and she panicked. She thought at first that she was back in that damp cold Midlands flat, and her heart started pounding more and more vigorously until she became convinced that she was about to die. Drowning, like a swimmer struggling from the clutch of a strong current, she pulled herself out of the chair, realized slowly that she was in her parents' home and tried to concentrate, through the buzzing in her head, to work out where the light switch was. The effort of standing was too much and she fell to her knees and crawled until she bumped into the safe outline of her bed and felt her way round to switch on the lamp that stood on the miniature chest of drawers which served as a bedside table. The pink-tinted light blurred and darkened the secure perimeter of her room while black spots danced and fuzzed the air in front of her as the noises that filled her ears grew louder and louder. She half crawled, half swam onto her bed and lay there, gasping in absolute terror until the air cleared and the noise began to subside. With a great effort she kicked off her shoes and, still fully dressed, eased herself in between the sheets, where she slept until morning.

Petra waited until she heard Daddy's car drive away, then went down to the kitchen.

'All right now, dear?' M clearly was not going to say any more about last night – if she did not discuss the scene it would soon stop worrying her, and she could not bear the thought of any more strong displays of emotion. Petra nodded and poured herself some cereal, which she ate quickly, still standing up, before making for the door.

'Where are you going?' M asked, anxiously.

'Out for a while.' Petra was short, noncommittal.

'Just a minute, dear. This probably isn't the best time to give you this – from your father, you see. He was going to tell you all about it last night, at dinner, but, well, there wasn't really the time.' She handed Petra a note, written in Daddy's firm hand.

'Petra – John Kingswear tells me he is looking for a trainee librarian. I've given him your A.L. qualifications and they are more than good enough. I've made an appointment for you to see him at 11 o'clock this morning. Ring me if you are not well enough to keep it.'

Not – would you like the job, Petra thought mutinously, and why should I ring Daddy if I can't go. And then she realized that Daddy thought she was not capable of cancelling her own appointment. She wondered what he had told this John Kingswear about her – 'Just needs a firm hand and a bit of guidance – thinks she knows it all, they're all the same these days – very bright, but won't settle to anything.' So Daddy was going to sort everything out for her, get her a job, get her settled nicely.

She stomped up the stairs to make herself look presentable for the interview – she felt too tired to resist. Although she grumbled to M and honestly felt resentment at Daddy's interference, she sensed a new lightness, a tiny bit of happiness at the prospect of a deadlock being broken. And she knew that she wouldn't have come up with anything better by herself.

'He doesn't say who this John Kingswear is, or where I'm meant to be seeing him,' she complained shortly to M as she came downstairs again, and M fluttered anxiously crumpling up the note.

'At the library dear. In town. He's the librarian. If you like I'll drive you in and wait for you. You'll get wet if you catch the bus.' So M was in on it too thought Petra, hating herself for her easy compliance.

A few weeks later she had settled down easily into the library routine. The cataloguing system was simple and the day-to-day work, stamping the books, taking fines for those that were overdue, filling shelves and doing her stint in the junior library, was more than easy enough to cope with.

The other girls and the women with whom she was now working accepted her without comment and were generally kind and helpful, although some of the older ones seemed a little put out when she grasped the complexities of the catalogue files without any trouble. They were jealous too of small privileges, signs of status embodied in the best cloak-room locker or the new tea cups, and there was endless suppressed bad feeling over whose turn it was to wash up the tea and coffee things. Petra put up the line of least resistance, was careful to offend no one, and her days soon took on a calm uniformity.

She enjoyed her new status at home. She paid her mother a nominal sum towards her keep, although M protested each month when Petra handed over the money. But her stock had gone up with Daddy, not because of her cash – he too protested that she need not pay anything now – it was just that before, she was not earning her keep, which seemed not at all logical to Petra but, as she did not want to destroy the new atmosphere at home with arguments, she just smiled.

Daddy was polite to her and he would discuss matters concerning the library, or events in the town, with her in the evening, asking her opinion as if, now she was out in the world and in the midst of things, it somehow counted for something. M would sit with them, nodding and smiling, turning her head from one to the other, pleased that things had turned out for the best after all, just as she had known that they would.

But M was not able to nod and smile for very long. One day Petra was on duty in the library, routinely stamping books, giving out little pink plastic tokens in exchange for returned novels and periodically taking an armful of books from her haven in the island counter to refill the shelves and racks. One moment she was lifting up her black date stamp to mark a big bright picture book for a small child whose mother was gently chiding him, hurry up and give it to the lady, and then she had dropped it. She bent down to pick it up and gasped at the little black spots dancing in front of her eyes and at her heartbeat which altered to the crazy thumping it had produced on the night of the scene with Daddy.

Petra could not bear, on later occasions, to think of the fuss and confusion caused by her semi-faint. The little boy, upset at the breakdown in the order of things, screamed all the way out of the building, while the girls on duty with her left their growing queues of borrowers and returners to half carry, half drag her out of the middle of the circular counter and across the expanse of wooden floor to the staff rest room, where she lay on two chairs, awkward and miserable, until Daddy, summoned by his friend, the librarian, arrived to take her home.

At that point she was more concerned with the confusion she had caused in the library than with her own health, telling herself that she had simply straightened up too quickly after stooping. But M made such a fuss, talking about high blood pressure, that even Daddy became concerned and doctors were summoned, so that by the time she was tucked up, pale and clean, in her own bed, she became convinced that there really was something very wrong with her. In the days that followed Petra's fears enlarged themselves into an obsession about the frailty of her body. She would sit very still, absorbed with the mechanics of taking one breath and then another, and another, and would try to work out how many times she did this each day and how often her heart should beat and she would put her fingertips gingerly onto her wrist to feel her pulse, convinced that the steady beat was becoming irregular.

She sat there quietly, but she was in torment inside, quite sure that the whole delicate balance was about to break down – how could something so frail not break down? – and, as she worried, her heart would begin, as if in response, to thump madly, hard against her chest, slamming her body. She knew that if she moved, or even took a deep breath, something was going to burst with stringy bloody tendons and slippery muscles inside her, ripping and tearing. Her body was a thin shell, pink and transparent to the strong light, ready to be crushed.

M and Daddy brought the family doctor to her and he examined her thoroughly, listened to her faltering complaints, and tried vainly to convince her that there was nothing wrong. But Petra knew that her body was going to let her down. Her whole life was tainted by unquantifiable fears. She became afraid to go into a shop, any shop, to stand in a queue, to be trapped in conversation; her fears were not specific but she knew that she would be faint, giddy, perhaps vomit or fall unconscious. Working in the library became an enormous burden.

The office was not so bad. There was a safe chair in there and a way out which did not involve walking through the crowded public part. But when it was her turn to stand inside the island counter to collect and stamp books, she felt unmercifully exposed and her heart would sometimes start its crazy beating, making her gasp and stiffen. It was even worse when the pile of returned books had to be carried across the floor, out of the island, which now represented a haven, to be put back, one by one, on the shelves.

She became very thin, unable to enjoy the physical process of eating or drinking, caught hopelessly between the fear of collapsing and disgracing herself in public and the weightier terror of Daddy's scorn if she failed to pull herself together. When she thought about the future, and she tried not to, it was blank, with nothing to look forward to, nothing to act either as a marker or a goal, no point between now and the end of her life. Her twentieth birthday, just before Easter, came and went, unremarked for the most part, and later, when she looked back, always darkly, on that dreary frightening period of her life, Petra never could remember what presents M and Daddy had given her. What she could remember was the quality of the fear that haunted her at that time, but not its intensity, and she never knew the cause.

Throughout those months, the hard light that was Caroline and her career was there, always in the background but always

103

a threatening contrast to the dreariness of Petra's own life, pushed back into the foggy haze that cloaked events out in the world, away from home and the library and the well-worn track that connected the two. But – and this seemed, later, to be just and fair in the balance of things – it was Caroline who was, indirectly it is true, to dispel the haze and bring Petra's life back into focus.

'Caroline's coming home for Easter, dear.' M was making breakfast, toast for Petra and an egg for Daddy. 'Doesn't that jumper need a wash? – you can't wear that to work.'

'Oh, it doesn't matter, it'll do another day.' Petra found it far too much of an effort to plan different things to wear each day. The pale-blue sweater did look a bit greyish at the sleeves, but that was just too bad.

'Here's a postcard from her – rather an odd picture, I thought.'

Petra looked at the card, which was a colour photograph of a cigarette end which had been stubbed and twisted out in a plate of greasy bacon and egg. The mashed-up filter tip had a trickle of thick yellow egg yolk curling over it. Caroline's handwriting was curiously unformed – the letters angular and crooked as if, at some point, she had started to learn an italic hand, but had given up the attempt. 'Have a couple of weeks off, will join you for Easter, Caro,' it said, and Petra felt a flare of the old resentment at Caroline's assumption that there was no need to ask.

But as the time drew near for Caroline's visit, she found herself strangely excited. It was a year since she had seen her sister in the flesh, although there had been plenty of photographs in the house.

M kept a scrapbook, or rather what had started off as a scrapbook and was now filling several large folders. She bought every publication which featured pictures of Caroline. Petra never looked at these in her parents' presence but, when they were both out of the way, she would open the carved wooden chest in M and Daddy's bedroom and take the files to her own room.

Most of the pictures were in colour, cut from glossy

magazines. They were big and clear and smooth. Petra marvelled at Caroline's long sun-tanned legs, the camera picking out the fine grains of sand brushing down her slim calf and, on the next page, the sparkling drops of water glistening on her body as she walked out of a flat blue sea.

One photograph in particular disturbed Petra. She had always seen Caroline in relation to herself, an individual who, by virtue of those qualities which she possessed and which Petra did not, could affect her sister's life. Caroline was never associated in Petra's mind with any other person except perhaps Henry, and Petra knew that, in a way, Henry did not really count. There was a picture of Caroline and another model, a tall blonde girl, square-jawed and elegant, and the two girls, one dark and the other fair, had their arms twined round each other's waists as they strolled along, dressed in a designer's interpretation of flowing Eastern garments. There they were, brilliant, as they walked along a dusty road, past a dingy building, oblivious to a ragged crowd of native workmen in torn shorts, bony-legged, leaning on their spades to marvel at the two girls. There was no caption on the picture and Petra supposed that the colourful dresses and veils and scarves were the product of some fashion expert's imagination rather than the ethnic dress of an Eastern country. Caroline and the big blue-eyed blonde were posing as they had been asked to do but Petra was hurt and curiously stimulated by her sister's physical closeness to someone she did not know. She couldn't think of the last time she had touched Caroline, given her a hug of greeting, tapped her on the arm. Probably not since they were children.

When Caroline arrived in her little blue sports car, she was smaller than Petra remembered – much smaller than she appeared in all the photographs. She was dressed simply, in cord trousers, a shirt and sweater, flat boots and with little or no make-up. In the reality of her presence there was none of that total sophistication and self-absorbed detachment that

105

came across so strongly in the pictures that Petra had pored over.

'Is she all right, do you think, dear?' whispered M, as she and Petra stood at the foot of the stairs, gazing upwards in Caroline's wake.

'Why on earth shouldn't she be?' Petra was irritated at M's obvious concern.

'Well, she didn't say much, did she, and I think she looks tired. And her tan's fading – that always makes people look peaky.' M started to cheer up as she thought of ways of spoiling Caroline and making sure she had the good rest which she felt sure was prescribed.

They all ate breakfast together in the dining room the following morning and Petra saw how Caroline set herself apart. Daddy was being bluff and hearty, asking about the places she had been to for her photographic sessions, but her answers were short and distant and her eyes said, you can't possibly understand anything I'm talking about, my experience is way outside yours; she was polite enough and ate an enormous breakfast, which delighted M, who liked nothing better than watching her family put away bacon and eggs and slices of toast and honey.

The phone rang as Petra and M were clearing away and Petra was shaking the white tablecloth outside the back door. It was a reporter from the local newspaper. He had heard (from Daddy, wondered Petra?) that Caroline Appleton was at home for a few days, and could they come and do an interview with her and take a few photographs as it was not often they had a chance to feature a top model.

Caroline was polite but, again, distant. Petra tried to imagine her own feelings had she achieved something (what sort of something though?) and a newspaper wanted to write about her. She knew that she would be in a frenzy of excitement. She and M both tried their best to conceal their childish pleasure, because Caroline clearly thought the whole business a bore and had only said 'yes' because she had nothing better to do.

The photographer, a smallish man with greasy, slicked-back hair and eager eyes in a lop-sided face, was obviously nervous. He was hung about with an array of cameras and flashes and boxes containing lenses; although Caroline said nothing as he and the young reporter stood in the hallway, he fidgeted under her scrutiny and slight smile. Petra felt sorry for him as he trailed after Caroline and the tall dark-haired reporter when they went into the sitting room to do the interview. She imagined Caroline, cool and aloof, raising an eyebrow each time he tried to pose her, and the poor man, knowing that she was comparing his provincial equipment and techniques with those of the highly paid top fashion photographers with whom she worked as a matter of course.

'Should we offer them something, dear?' said M. 'Coffee, or a drink, or something. I should think perhaps that they'd like beer, wouldn't you, but I don't think there's any in the house.'

Petra tried not to sigh. 'It's only ten thirty,' she reminded M. 'I'm sure coffee will be fine. Put it on now and ask them when they've finished.' She could not bear to go into the room and see the humiliation that Caroline was inflicting on the photographer. But, when M and Petra took in the tray of coffee and biscuits, she was surprised to find the greasy-haired man, whose name was Ron, chatting happily about lighting and lenses to Caroline, who was giving him technical details of sets with which she had recently been involved. She spoke with an interest and an authority that was new to Petra, who contrasted this enthusiasm with the cold boredom at breakfast when Daddy had talked about mosques and sun-drenched beaches.

The reporter, sitting on the sofa with his notebook shut, had clearly finished the interview and accepted his cup of coffee and two chocolate digestives with the quiet satisfaction of someone who is happy with the job he has done. Petra perched herself on the far arm of the sofa whilst M twittered at Ron and Caroline until they were all drinking coffee and crunching biscuits. The reporter was tall and dark and sluggish-looking. He wore heavy, dark-rimmed spectacles and all his movements were slow and deliberate, calm, ponderous even, thought Petra, as she tried to talk to him. She received the impression that his calmness wasn't born of any sort of superiority but that he was a bit slow naturally, perhaps not thinking too much about other people. It seemed odd that someone who responded so little should choose to be a journalist.

She gave up the effort of small talk after a minute or two and sat, moodily drinking her coffee and thinking about Henry, who had been next to her on that settee sixteen months earlier and who had made her laugh. Suddenly she felt the familiar lump in her throat and her heart started to beat, fast and hard. She put her cup down, slowly and carefully, as she felt her cheeks flush and her whole body prickle with the heat of panic. Negotiating the stretch of carpet from the sofa to the door right across the room was not easy and, once outside, she pulled herself up the stairs, hanging onto the banisters, feeling that she was behaving rudely and idiotically. She lay down on her bed until the mad pounding ceased and the hot blood left her face. Oddly enough, this time she had been more concerned with the impression she had made on her clumsy exit from the room than with her own physical condition. This was an interesting discovery and it cheered Petra up a little as she heard footsteps scrunching on the gravel below and the banging of car doors as the newspapermen left.

Early that evening, just as she was thinking that she really ought to wash her hair, which was hanging dankly round her face, the telephone rang. Caroline's voice, clear and precise, called up the stairs: 'For you, Petra.'

The voice at the other end of the line was slow and deep. 'Petra? This is Philip – Philip Garlick. We met earlier today when I came to your house to interview your sister. Would you like to come to the cinema with me, this evening?'

Chapter Seven

'Your wife,' said Henry, sliding his empty Guinness mug onto the thinly hammered copper bar of the Horse and Jockey, and following through so that his elbow slumped behind the glass, supporting the weight of the right hand side of his body, 'your wife was, is still, I suppose, a very sensitive, aware sort of woman. Very aware,' he repeated carefully, turning to look at Philip, who found the magnification of Henry's stare from the centre of his hollowed eye socket disconcerting.

Those little round spectacles must be very thick-lensed, thought Philip, touching his own black-rimmed glasses, pushing them back from where they had slipped to the end of his nose. He drained the last few drops from his fifth pint of bitter, made a noise that sounded like a cross between a laugh and a hiccup and tried to remember how Henry knew Petra. 'Petra is unfulfilled,' he said ponderously and solemnly, and he too slammed his glass on the bar and watched it gloomily as it slid a few inches along the pinkish surface before coming to rest against the squat smugness of Henry's Guinness glass. 'Two more of those,' he said to Donald the barman, who was big and blond and too healthy-looking, like a member of the national rugger team. 'Guinness in that one and a pint of rubbish for me, Don.' God knows what I'm talking about, he thought as he tried to sort out the remark in his mind – he knew it must be true, but he couldn't work out any specific instances from the generalization.

'What do you mean, unfulfilled?' Henry straightened up a

little and fiddled with the bright emerald green strings at the neck of his navy blue two-piece towelling tracksuit.

Philip averted his eyes from Henry's costume, which seemed to him to be eccentric, irrelevant and unmasculine, and tried to concentrate on the nature of his wife's alleged discontent.

'It's hard to explain, really. I mean, we've got three children – well, you met them today. They're all right, but Petra doesn't really take that much notice of them. She loves them and all that, but they don't really seem to be part of her life, if you know what I mean. She doesn't take a lot of interest in the house or garden either, like some women seem to. She says it's all a waste of her time. But I don't know what she does do with her time. It's as if . . . oh, I don't know!' Philip pushed again at his glasses, which had gradually slipped almost to the tip of his nose as his face grew hot and sweaty in the warm crowded Saturday night atmosphere of the pub. He stared at Henry.

The two of them made an odd contrast, each leaning up against the ugly, uncomfortable copper bar, each with one leg hitched up casually on the rail that ran around the outside of the counter about a foot from the floor, and each bespectacled. But Henry, with his small thick gold-rimmed glasses, was almost bald, hollow-eyed and walrus-like. His shiny dome of a head reflected the colour of the bar and his faded blond moustache. While Philip heavily built and wearing dirty cord trousers, ill fitting and sagging at the back, had a head of thick dark hair, which flopped forward as he moved and hid the corners of his dark square glasses. Henry nodded encouragingly at Philip, who tried again.

'There's something locked away in her mind, something that is much more important to her than everyday things like running the house or seeing to the kids or doing the cooking or bothering about me, even. She doesn't know what it is, but she's waiting for it, saving everything she's got, I'd say.' Philip, trying to work out how many pints he had drunk, wondered if he really meant what he was saying. Henry said nothing, just carried on nodding in a Mandarin-like way, a

110

fleck of foam from his dark beer caught in his moustache. Philip laughed, uneasily.

'I'm just being fanciful, she's pretty normal really.'

'Don't say that!'

'What?'

'Don't say that. She's special – got to be. Especially now that Caroline's, well, you know. Now that Caroline's out of the way and she doesn't have to feel that she's second best.'

'How do you know anything about that?' Philip stared again at Henry, who smiled nicely as he looked back, showing small, even teeth under his moustache. 'How do you know so much about Petra? She's never said anything about you to me, or about Caroline for that matter. Caroline nearly ballsed up our wedding, you know. Silly bitch!'

'I know – I was there.'

'Of course you were, of course, that's where I've seen you before.' Philip gazed vaguely into his empty glass whilst Henry flapped his hand at Donald, indicating the two mugs. 'You were the chap who sorted things out, you talked Caroline round. I remember now.'

As their glasses were filled up again, they picked them up and made their way, a little unsteadily, over to a table in a corner where two old men who had been sitting playing cribbage had just wheezed their goodbyes and left.

'That's right.' Philip stabbed at the air with a stubby forefinger and his eyes were large and unfocused behind his lenses. A lock of slightly greasy black hair, just tinged with grey, flopped forward as he turned sideways to face Henry, who sat next to him on the bench. 'That's right, you were there,' he repeated. 'I do remember. Weren't you going out with Caroline at the time?'

'Oh, no.' Henry's expression became distant and guarded. He was neat, precise and dramatic in direct response to Philip's untidy clumsiness. 'Although I have done many things in my life, I have never "gone out", as you say, with Caroline. My relationship with her was rather more delicate, more that of a sister.' Philip did not protest at the use of the female image in Henry's description of his friendship with Caroline, nor did it

111

occur to him at the time to do so. Later, thinking about the conversation, he found it odd, but no more peculiar than many of Henry's small eccentricities.

Henry and Philip were becoming drunk together in the Horse and Jockey, a gloomy red-brick pub which looked out of place in such a pretty village. The brewery, at the time the pub was built, had not cared for local tradition, putting up all their houses in cheap materials, and they did so without being hampered by the planning officers and other officials who were later to become such a feature of modern life. The pub was just as dull inside, with a neat square bar and small dusty windows. The wallpaper was pink and the carpet a mottled red and the cheap chairs had overstuffed shiny leatherette seats. However it was, as the two old cribbage players would have said, within spitting distance of Philip's house, and so the two drinkers had left Fiona in charge of things for an hour or so. Petra would have been horrified, had she known.

It was Saturday night, but not the Saturday night of Philip's youth when the world, or your part of it, was there, the excitement enclosed like the kernel of a nut waiting to be cracked wide open in the right way. The right way was to dress up to the nines, after emerging from a scalding bath, hair slicked down, pink round the edges with the heat and the steam of effort and hot water. You had to have a good-looking girlfriend and you had to know where the evening's game was to be played. Pubs in those days were just for starters, thought Philip, regretfully, but with a comforting sense of security.

Henry's Saturday nights had been far less predictable, far more dangerous, but he would not have spoken of his past even if Philip had bothered to ask him, and Petra's husband was never to understand much about his guest.

Henry had arrived at Coombe that afternoon, to a small turmoil. Philip had organized a picnic sort of lunch, early, so that he could take the children, as promised, to the village cricket match, which was to be played at home against Compton Purlieu. The local ground, which doubled as a children's playing field, was situated between Petra and Philip's house and Frederic's wooden bungalow. Fiona had enjoyed herself that morning, bullying her brothers, playing the role of surrogate mother. William accepted this happily, but Dan, solid and unchanging, ignored her successfully. He remained aloof and upright when they arrived at the ground and Fiona immediately disappeared to find her little circle of friends who were all gathered, giggling and whispering, at the children's swings, slides and roundabout. Philip settled himself in a deckchair at the pavilion and young William, happily sucking his thumb, lay down on the grass beside him. Dan politely watched the teams as they strolled out of the pavilion and he showed interest in the first few overs, but he kept gazing longingly at the roof of the wooden bungalow which he could see on the curve of the hill. He would tell the old man that his blue flower was called borage and he would ask him for a stem of the pale pink flower with the ferny leaf that he had seen beside the bungalow, near the damp hedge. He sat down beside William, who was by now blissfully asleep, and thought longingly of the delicate musk mallow and of the old man who might let him peep inside his beehive, that magic contraption, like a conjuror's box, full of bits and pieces and more bees inside than seemed possible.

He knew the way to the bee man's house from here, out of the gate at the other side of the field, along the grassy footpath on the wide verge, and there it was, just on the corner. He walked that way every day to school. Surely Daddy would let him go, just for a short time. He looked up at Philip, prepared to ask him, and he saw that his father, slack-jawed, was fast asleep in the hot sun. Daddy was asleep, his lips loose and red, and so was William, but his lips were puckered around his small thumb. Fiona was on one of the swings, flying higher and higher, brown legs straight out in front of her and then back, showing off in front of her giggling friends, and not for the world would Dan have endured asking her permission to go.

He stood quite still for about ten seconds, his eyes tightly shut, his face screwed up with the effort of responsibility and decision, and then, without looking at his father or brother, he turned and plodded round the outfield to the gate, a small solid figure in navy blue shorts and T-shirt.

Frederic was also wearing shorts, but his shirt was a heavy khaki one, dirty and creased. He was out in his garden and he raised his head, looking at the small boy without recognition, as Dan marched purposefully round the side of the bungalow. As Dan approached the green bank, Frederic tucked the piece of paper on which he had been scribbling into the button-down pocket of his old shirt.

'I've found out that plant. It's borage, you know. Daddy looked it up and it says in the book that bees love it.' Frederic smiled. The small boy with the gashed knee and the passion for flowers.

'Oh yes. You are Daniel, aged six, and you've discovered borage for me. What else – the pink one, perhaps?'

'Yes, well . . .' Dan wriggled uneasily, not sure if the old man was teasing him. 'I was going to say could I have a bit of that one, please, because I think it's a mallow, you see. My teacher told me about them but there are different sorts, lots of different kinds, but I expect Daddy can find it, or Mummy will when she gets back tomorrow.'

'Your Mummy is away, then?'

'Yes. I told you last time, yesterday. She's gone to Aunty Caroline's house in London, with Granny. Aunty Caroline's dead, you see and we'll never see her again.' Dan was solemn and important and Frederic caught his breath. He had lately been much obsessed with thoughts of death, not that of Elise which constantly haunted him, but with his own death. But he never spoke the word aloud. Now to hear that word which described his separation from Elise aloud from the lips of a pink-faced child who stood, real and square, in his garden, gave Frederic a jolt. He felt agitated, as if there were some sort of action he should be taking.

Frederic had seen plenty of death. As a doctor in a large hospital, he had trained himself to see corpses as mere arrangements of non-functioning organs and limbs. As a man and a husband, faced with the dead body of his wife, he had become half a person; the spiritual needs within him only partly fed by his daily obsessive one-sided communion with Elise by means of the notes and letters in which he poured out his thoughts, jumbled up with the trivia of the day, his only safety-valve. The old trunk was stuffed full of these. But he knew that this was not enough, although in the past it had seemed some measure of compensation. Now he found himself, after all this time, talking aloud to her, and once or twice, on this bank, because after all this was the nearest he could get to her physically, he had thought that he caught a glimpse of his brown-eyed, sharp-nosed girl, whisking out of sight in a flash as he turned his head to see what the corner of his eye had caught.

This boy was the first person who had pushed Frederic's gate open to come to see him in five years (apart from the Minister who had called once and had understood Frederic to be a Roman Catholic, because of his foreign accent. Being Low Church himself, he had assumed that there was no need for any further visit). What an omen, thought Frederic, staring at the boy who was occupied with the clump of mallows. His pale blue eyes watered in his bony face. As I think of death, he mused, this child walks in and says the word. Frederic did not fear death – death was what had taken Elise, and he wanted to follow her as he had always done. But the method of travel was not so easy: although he knew plenty of ways to go to his dead wife, he had to admit to a certain fear of the processes.

When he had moved to Coombe and had contrived his half-life in the house that Elise had chosen for them, it was with the knowledge that he must carry out a sacred trust. He must live here as Elise and he would have done, tend the garden, just as she would have liked it, look after the bees and extract the honey, eat the foods they had always eaten together; he must enjoy the shape of the land, the rise of the hills and the long downs, he must observe the evenings and the pink dawns, the bird song and the wind and the rain, as they had done together. It was up to him, alone, to make the most of these things and, for her sake, he had done his best. But the burden was now heavy and lay in his chest like a large stone.

'Where do you live?' he asked Dan, almost fiercely, as he

thought, death is just a word to this rosy-cheeked child, who can speak so easily and simply of the great grey barrier that separates us. But Dan, thinking about Philip's possible anxiety at his absence, and with longing that eclipsed even that guilt, of the pink, fretty-leaved flower, did not notice the harsh black tones in Frederic's voice.

'Up the hill, a little way.' He pointed back towards his home. 'In the house with the yellow door, past the playing fields and the cows' field.'

Frederic nodded and, easier now, smiled at Dan. 'And you came to tell me of that flower, the blue one. What was it?'

'Borage.'

'Ah yes! Borage. And you also came to take some of my little pink cheesecakes.'

'Is that its name?' Dan was surprised and impressed.

'Oh, no. I do not know its name, but you go and pick a bit.' Dan did so and brought it back to Frederic, who showed him the little round fruiting bodies left by the spent flowers.

'You see, like little cheesecakes, wrapped up in this green case,' he said.

Dan was enthralled. 'That's where the seeds grow,' he said, and Frederic nodded and smiled. The boy took the flower and left, thinking of Frederic's hands with their twisted fingers and of the brown blotches on the thick-veined backs.

Frederic relapsed into the thought-conversation with Elise which the boy's visit had interrupted and, as he touched the bit of paper in his pocket which enclosed his love, he felt Elise brush behind him on the bank, but she disappeared into the thick tangle of elder trees before he could see her properly.

Henry just wanted to sit and doze in the sun which poured through the windows of his nice comfortable hired car, but he felt, having made the effort to come all this way, he ought to make contact with whatsisname, Petra's husband. By now he was regretting his phone call and would much rather have put up, anonymously, at one of the many comfortable stone-built solid hotels along the road. When he pulled up outside the

Garlicks' front door he was confronted with a white square of paper, held in place on the door by the brass ship-shaped knocker.

'Back early evening. Have taken children to cricket match just down the road. Join us in front of pavilion.'

The writing was elegant, black ink in a thick-nibbed italic hand, and this surprised Henry. He turned the paper over, but there was no name on it so he had to suppose that it was meant for him. There was no signature either, and he wondered why.

'Cricket, hey?' Henry did not stop to ponder why he was not the sort of person who took himself off to watch sport. He had given up this type of introspection years before, when he and Peter had both agreed that it was better to follow your own inclinations, be the person you wanted to be and not bother to develop minor character byways in the hope that something exciting might emerge. A dead-end or a cul-de-sac was what you generally found, they decided. Peter had opened Henry's wardrobe door in their New York apartment one day and had stared sadly at the odd, flamboyant collection of clothes: matador's capes, football jerseys, flying jackets, hats of all shapes and sizes, sportswear (Henry never played any sport, but he liked the clothes). Henry walked into the room and asked him, gently, what was wrong. Peter, in his neat slacks, Jermyn Street shirt, silk tie and cashmere sweater, his softly polished leather shoes, pointed at a wide-brimmed leather hat.

'How do you get away with all this crazy-looking gear? You're an odd-looking guy but it all fits and looks right. If I walked down the street with some of this junk on, people would fall around laughing.'

Henry, standing now on Philip's doorstep, gave a little shrug of his shoulders, gently pushing away Peter's image and the ghostly vision which had risen with it, like two photographs overprinted on the same negative, of Peter, fair-haired, tall and good-looking, and Caroline, pale, with a cloud of dark hair, loose around her shoulders, standing together, side by side, smiling at him.

117

He left the car parked in the warm sun outside the house, checking first that the boot with his cameras and suitcase inside was locked, and set off down the road to where he supposed the cricket match might be. He turned in at the gate of the playing field at the same time as a small boy who had approached from the other direction, carefully carrying a small bunch of pink flowers. Henry, who suddenly realized that he had no idea what Petra's husband looked like, thought perhaps the boy might know him. He fancied that he liked children, although he did not know very many, and certainly none as serious and honest as Dan. He said, politely, to the child: 'Excuse me,' and the boy stopped and blinked at him. They stood, sizing each other up, Henry skinny and bald, wearing his bright tracksuit and expensive running shoes, Dan in shorts, clutching his flowers.

'You don't happen to know someone called Mr Garlick, Philip Garlick, I suppose?' Henry asked.

'That's my Dad's name. I'm just going to find him but he doesn't know I'm gone. He was asleep, you see.' Now Henry could see that the boy was a little worried.

'Oh, I get you. You just slipped off, hey?'

'Well, sort of. I mean, yes. I had to go to the bee man's house about this flower and another one. Borage.'

'Borage – that's blue, right?' Dan nodded and looked at Henry with some respect and interest. Henry did not tell him that his sole acquaintance with the flower was when it floated on top of a glass of Pimm's. 'But what's the bee man got to do with all these flowers?'

'They grow in his garden, you see. He likes them, but he never knows their names. I like to find out the names. I know the names of more than sixty flowers now.' Dan looked pleased with himself. 'So I go and tell him when I find out. At least I've only been there once to tell him, but I'll go tomorrow if Daddy says I can.'

Philip's name reminded him that he could well be in trouble and he marched, Henry in tow, back towards the pavilion. It was there that they found an anxious family gathering. Philip had woken up fairly soon after Dan had trotted off on his mission; the opening batsman from Compton Purlieu had, in the opinion of the home team, clearly got his leg in front of the wicket and the hosts were gratified when the umpire duly signalled leg before. But the visitors obviously failed to agree and the noisy applause from Coombe supporters, countered by the howls of protest from the others, upset by the downfall of their local hero, had jerked Philip out of his peaceful doze. It slowly dawned on him that Dan was missing and he had summoned Fiona to look for him. She had searched (very unwillingly) the whole area of the playing field twice, but found no sign of her little brother.

It was just as Philip was growing cross with Fiona because he felt that he was to blame for going to sleep and not keeping a proper eye out, that the missing boy and Henry came in sight, still chatting to each other about the bee man and his garden. As they rounded the side of the pavilion, Philip started forward, scolding Dan, who stood patiently, twisting the flowers in his fingers. Henry, who was ignored, did not hear what was said. He drew his breath in sharply as he gazed at Fiona, standing beside her father, a sulky scowl on her pale face. The scowl and the set of the shoulders and the impatiently tapping feet were all pure Caroline.

Later, in the Horse and Jockey, William and Dan safely tucked up in bed and Fiona, bribed with television and crisps, in charge, Henry thought again, sharply and painfully, of Caroline. He was speculating romantically on the impossibility of the cribbage-playing ancients plying their skill on these plastic-topped tables when they should have been playing on ancient elm, deep grooved with time and wear, but they had seemed perfectly happy.

Henry, who was fastidious in such matters, sighed deeply and suddenly, for no real reason, was overtaken with a vision of Caroline, sulking in the bathroom of her house in London, refusing to go out because she said she felt ugly and could not face anyone at all. It would have been funny but for the depth of her despair. Caroline, so perfect, and yet increasingly so convinced that what she had to offer was not good enough, because she was competing with herself the whole time.

119

Henry told her you could not improve on what was already perfect but she would sit, slumped on the side of the bath or on the lavatory seat, refusing, by the set of her hunched shoulders and her floorwards gaze, to talk or to go with him to some reception or party. Henry understood the intensity of her silent self-hatred, but he could never acknowledge the need for it. He saw that when she was comparing herself to yesterday's Caroline or to the perfect photograph of herself on the inside of the airing cupboard door, she knew she had lost, therefore her existence was pointless. She could not justify herself and she could not speak about it.

Talking now to Philip, he gazed into his glass and saw the black and cream perfection of Caroline, sprawling loose-limbed and despairing, lovely in her pale green bathrobe, refusing to look up at him. He shuddered, remembering the concentration of self that emanated from her as she shut herself up in a solid state of introspection on these occasions. Once he had shouted at her, something about being a selfish bitch, and she had broken her silence and looked up with a bitter smile.

'There's nothing to say to you, Henry. You only really care for Peter but with me there's no one else. When I fall out with myself there's no one and nothing to understand. Now piss off.' Henry thought he did understand and he had said so to Peter, who was over with him that time for a short holiday. He looked at Philip, who was drinking his beer clumsily, spilling it down his chin, and he shut his eyes to shut out not the beer dribbles but the painful memory of that week and its sequel.

'She was bloody difficult you know. Bloody difficult.' Philip slumped his head against the hard plastic back of the bench as he rolled it in Henry's direction.

'Who was?' asked Henry, jolted out of his pain by the vehemence in Philip's voice.

'Caroline of course. Petra's sister. Bloody stuck up. Did you know her – course you did, I was forgetting. Did you know her well?' Philip peered intently at Henry, who was nonplussed.

'Well, you know . . .'

120

'Neither did I old man, neither did I, and I must say, I didn't want to!' Philip had assumed a negative answer from Henry's diffidence.

'She came to stay with us once, you know, here, just after Fiona was born. Petra was pleased, thought she'd be a help and all that, but she was just a bloody pain. Wouldn't get up in the morning and didn't like going to bed until very late. Wouldn't eat anything either, and had to go into town to buy a pair of rubber gloves before she would help with anything round the house. We took her to a party, too, and she wore some weird get-up and I remember there was this odd scene with Ailsa. Ailsa and Richard,' Philip explained, hiccuping as he did so. 'They were giving the party. He's an accountant and she's a witch.'

'I beg your pardon.' Henry, feeling a bit hazy himself, wondered if he had heard correctly through the hiccups. 'Did you say a witch?'

'Oh yes. We don't seem to see much of her these days but she never made any bones about it.'

'What does she look like, this witch?' Henry, used to all sorts of unusual encounters, was nevertheless impressed.

'Oh, quite ordinary. Long black hair, cut in a sort of fringe. Nothing special. She had a go at Caroline about something, though. It was an odd evening.'

Henry, who had spent many odd evenings in Caroline's company, did not reply at once. He shivered at the thought of an encounter between Caroline and the local witch; he did not want to know what had happened and he did not suppose that Philip, who seemed a nice enough fellow even if he was solid and unimaginative, would be able to tell him.

'What did she wear?' he asked, eventually.

'Who?' Philip looked as though he were about to go to sleep. The noises in the pub, the clatter of glasses, the drone of conversation punctured now and then by a shriek of laughter or a shout, the scraping of chairs on the floor, settled around them and Henry recovered his sense of time and place.

'Caroline, at the witch's party. You said that she looked weird.'

'Oh, I don't know.' Philip shuffled around uncomfortably on the hard seat, as he tried to think about Caroline's party clothes. 'Well, for a start she wore shorts, shiny pink shorts with some sort of purple tights. They had bits of glittery stuff in them and she wore black patent leather boots, with high heels and a blouse, only it wasn't a proper blouse, just made of fringes, a lot of fringes all stuck together. All the others had long things on or those Indian-type dresses and I thought Caroline looked very out of place. She didn't seem to mind though.' Philip was on the defensive. 'Probably all right for your London parties and things, but they're not used to that sort of stuff down here,' he said grudgingly. Henry smiled to himself. That was Caroline making a stupid point. In London she would wear very prim, simple clothes, but he did not feel like explaining that to Philip.

Petra and Philip had both felt a sense of foreboding, of not wanting to go through the next few hours, when they had turned into the long dark drive to the Gothic dower house built in a woodland clearing about fifteen miles away from Coombe. It was set well away from any other house and Richard and Ailsa had it on a ninety-nine-year lease from the trustees of the big estate to which it had originally belonged. Philip was uneasy, because he hated to be conspicuous and that was now inevitable with Caroline prancing around in this get-up. Petra, still tired after Fiona's birth, felt drab beside her sister. She was wearing a long, flowing Indian garment, which was fashionable at the time and which she had thought would hide the extra weight she still had to lose, but she was conscious of looking slightly eccentric and earth motherish rather than glamorous. She was also worried that the baby-sitter would not be able to cope if Fiona, only a few weeks old, woke up. She wished they had not come, but she wanted to show Caroline that married life in the country was not all nappies and long dreary walks, pushing a pram.

There was a dangling bell-pull fastened to the stonework on the side of the big front door. Lights gleamed softly through

122

the stained-glass panels at the top and they could hear music and laughter.

'Shall I?' Caroline pulled and immediately the door was opened by a tall thin man with a beaky nose and acne-scarred skin. He looked nervously at Caroline, but was reassured by the sight of Philip and Petra. This was Richard and, after the introductions, he handed each of them a small label.

'Pin these on,' he said. 'Ailsa's idea, to get people talking, you know. Characters in books – you've got to find others in the same book and get in groups.'

Petra and Philip, who both hated the idea, smiled politely, and he submitted to Gandalf, whilst she pinned Mrs Danvers onto her blue-flowered bosom.

'No thanks,' said Caroline shortly, waltzing off along the long hall, chequered with a black and white tiled floor. She made for an open door from which flowed light and music. Fifteen minutes later Petra had found a Maxim, Beatrice and Frank Crawley and they were wondering if they ought to search for a Rebecca (not Caroline, surely, thought Petra), Philip was gloomily drinking whisky with Bilbo Baggins, Frodo and Aragorn – and Caroline was nowhere to be seen.

Caroline had been furious at Richard's assumption that his guests would enjoy his party games. She decided, though, that this house looked interesting. Most of Petra's friends in Coombe seemed to live in tiny bungalows on bare new estates or in draughty, badly converted farm labourers' cottages.

After a brief appearance in a large comfortable room full of chattering guests ('I say, if you're Heathcliff, I think I should be joining you!') and lots of darkly polished furniture, gleaming in the flickering light of a log fire, she started a very thorough exploration. Shivering a little, for the house was full of long, chilly passages, warmed only by gently hissing fat radiators, she looked first into a little study, charmingly furnished in soft greens, with pink needlepoint cushions and a lot of small pieces of white china. There was a desk in here, its roll top open and a chair pushed back, as if the writer had just got up and left the room. Next came a big drawing room, very formal, with beautiful old moulded plasterwork ceilings and fireplace and great windows covered by heavy floor-length velvet curtains. She stood still for a long while in the double doorway, enjoying the luxury of the room, with its collection of porcelain and the silver curios scattered here and there. Bookshelves had been built into alcoves and there were a great many pictures on the walls, each with a discreet light over it. For Caroline, to whom visual awareness meant a great deal, the room was pure pleasure. That other room, the one with the guests and the fire, must be the dining room, she supposed.

The passageway widened outside the drawing room and study, which opened onto opposite sides of this small hallway. On the back wall was a half-opened door, and Caroline could hear the clatter of plates and cutlery and muffled yelps, as if there were animals in there. She slipped up the broad stairway, carpeted with dusky blue wool which was fastened down with shining brass rods. Petra had said that the woman who lived here was a witch, but Caroline had assumed at the time she was joking. She saw nothing now to make her change her mind.

At the top of the stairs was a small landing and a bareish room, lit only by dim red bulbs. A record-player, ready primed with a stack of long-playing discs, sat on a shelf in the corner and there were tables and chairs grouped around the walls. The boards were bare and Caroline guessed that any dancing at this party was to be done up here, later.

She left the red room and discovered five bedrooms, each well furnished but only one, a large room with a four-poster bed and a small dressing room opening off it, was obviously in use. This room also had a desk in it and Caroline opened the lid which came down to make the writing surface; when she peered inside she saw sheets and sheets of paper covered in fine scribbles. The bathroom was ill-lit and a bit draughty, plenty of room for more lights, cupboards and a bidet, and there was another, larger landing with an uncurtained, stained-glass window. The back stairs, wooden and with only a skimpy worn carpet, led back down to the ground floor from this landing and Caroline, growing bored, decided to descend this way. The narrow steps were steep and they twisted down into darkness.

At the bottom she found herself in what seemed to be a stone passageway, smelling bitterly of earth and damp. The floor was rough, probably cobbled, although Caroline could not see too well as the only light came in dimly from outside. It shone through the glass panels of a door which appeared to lead to some sort of a yard, but the door was either locked or very stiff; she could not get it to budge. But she really could not be bothered to go all the way upstairs again and, as her eyes grew accustomed to the dimness, she saw that there was another door directly opposite the foot of the stairs. She opened this. Immediately there was a terrific commotion, a flurry of yapping and barking. Caroline, blinking in the bright light which flooded the small scullery in which she found herself, stood quite still as the three dogs, yelping, surrounded and tried to corner her. Three rugs were squashed up together, close up against the wall, and the small room smelt strongly of animal. She wrinkled up her nose and swore aloud. She said 'Oh, shit!', not because she was frightened of the clamouring dogs but because they could easily nip and ladder her tights or scratch her boots, and they were all making such a row.

She was just about to slip back out of the door and bolt up the stairs, when the archway which led into the next room was blocked by the tall figure of a dark-haired woman, dressed in blue. Her black hair was long, a series of flat strips which hung almost to her waist, and it was cut into a severe square fringe in the front. She said nothing but just pointed at the dogs, a large golden retriever and two beagles, who wagged their tails and crept back to their warm, smelly rugs. Caroline looked squarely at her, and wondered if this was the witch.

'You'd better come and give me a hand with this food,' said Ailsa, turning back through the thick archway. Caroline, stepping over a recumbent beagle and its well-gnawed bone, followed her into a large, brightly lit kitchen, dominated just now by a square food-laden table in the middle of the red-tiled floor. There was plenty of space around the old-fashioned table and in the corner a black range, with polished coppery

125

fittings, grumbled away. Ailsa went over to this stove, pulled open the oven door and took out trays of pies and flans, all perfectly cooked.

'Would you get out the bread – it's over there and the baskets are next to it,' she said. Caroline saw an earthenware crock which was full of rolls and French sticks. She shared these out into the long baskets which lay on the floor and somehow made room for them on the thick-legged deal table, which already bore platters of cheese, bowls of fresh crab meat, salads, rounds of sausages and a great breadcrumbed ham, besides the savoury tarts which Ailsa was setting out on thick mats.

Ailsa, like her husband, had bad skin. It was thick and white with tiny pockmarks in the opaque doughy surface. Out of this chalky background her eyes, a bright turquoise blue exactly matching the dress she wore, glittered like gems underwater. In the bright light of the kitchen, Caroline saw that the black hair, not fine and silky like her own, was coarse and dull, absorbing the light rather than reflecting it. The thick fringe emphasized the deep frown marks which runnelled Ailsa's forehead. She was very thin but completely shapeless, and her hands, which were large for such a skinny woman, were red and ugly, with prominent knuckles. Up until now the pair of them had worked in silence to the hum from the range and an occasional whimper and scratching from the dogs in the scullery.

'What were you doing upstairs?' Ailsa asked Caroline, who was quite at ease, nibbling a lettuce leaf from one of the salad bowls.

'Oh, just looking,' said Caroline, unabashed. 'I like your bedroom – is all that work in the desk yours?'

Ailsa ignored the question. 'You're not like Petra, are you?' Ailsa's diamond-hard eyes were too bright. 'You are Petra's sister, aren't you?'

'Yes, I am. Her sister. No, I'm not like her.' Caroline considered a bowl full of tiny tomatoes, but she decided that if she bit into one, the juice might dribble down her chin and get caught in the fringes of her top, so she picked out a round of cucumber from the green salad.

'Are you the witch?' she asked, chewing on the tough skin and reaching for another piece. Ailsa said nothing, but went over to the archway which joined the scullery and the main part of the kitchen and fitted a wooden board across the entrance, barring the dogs.

'What sort of a witch are you?' asked Caroline, wandering around the kitchen and looking appreciatively at the collection of old tiles which formed a broad panel on the wall behind the black and gold range.

'Oh, I just push things around, a little this way, a little that.' Ailsa seemed amused. She had a lilting voice, musical, with a trace of some local accent, Welsh perhaps, or Cornish, in it. 'I frighten people and I encourage them. I frightened the Master of the Hunt so much that he will not bring his foxhounds anywhere near this place now. We have nearly one hundred acres here and they've always hunted it. But I barred the way to him with my words and he will never come back. I hate hunting.' She had been standing with the oven glove still in her hands, twisting it as she swayed to and fro, but she snapped upright and looked hard at Caroline.

'Why are you not wearing a badge? Didn't Richard give you one when you came in? I asked him to!'

'I didn't want one,' said Caroline, peeling back the stringy bits on the stick of celery she was chewing. 'What else can you do?'

'Oh, well now, I can put spells on the ground and on the cattle and I know the leaves and the plants to use to heal and help. I can see young mothers have their babies when they want them and I can see that when the babies are ready to arrive, the mother has an easy time. I am destined not to have children, you see. So are you.'

'How do you know that?' Caroline was becoming interested. She certainly intended never to have children, but it was novel to hear this crazy woman telling her what she already knew.

'It is my destiny not to have children. But for you, it is

127

choice. It is your choice. Not children, not love, not pleasure.'
Ailsa took a step closer to Caroline to peer intently at her.
Caroline, quite used to the close scrutiny of photographers,
stared back.

'You are someone I could neither influence nor help. I work
on the pleasures of people and on their fears and weakness, but
you are not afraid and rarely weak. You want to be totally in
control of your own life. I would say that no person other than
yourself has caused you unhappiness or pain, ever. No one has
given you joy. The cause and the control belongs to you alone.
It is a desperate way to be.'

'You're mad,' said Caroline calmly and indeed Ailsa, frozen
in the act of stepping forward, the oven gloves stretched taut
between her outflung hands, her brilliant eyes hardened to
narrow points of sharp light, could have been charged, on
appearance alone, with fanaticism.

They stood there, poised and finely drawn as two forces,
wavering and teetering between repulsion and attraction. A
painter would have noted the angles, the lines, the contrasts
and the geometry of their two bodies. Perhaps they stood,
each caught tautly in antagonism and a strange sympathy born
of strong emotion, for long moments.

After a time which neither would be able to determine
afterwards, the kitchen door was shoved open, and Philip and
Richard, leading a press of other guests, stood there, staring at
the two women caught in the finely balanced tableau. Again
no one moved and no one spoke, but the silence was
measurable. Philip thought of the scene in 'The Sleeping
Beauty', the instant before the Prince delivers the restorative
kiss, when the tick of the clock is lost and suspended, the food
lies untouched in preserved glory and a second is meaningless
in time. Unwittingly he stepped into the role of the Prince.

'There you are, Caroline.' He broke the spell. 'We've been
looking everywhere for you!'

Petra went home early that night. She left the party with
another couple from Coombe who had promised their
babysitter that they would be back at a respectable time. She
was worried about Fiona, her precious new baby, who was

128

likely to wake for her feed at any time now, and during the journey home, trying to make pleasant conversation from the rear of the car, she broke out in a cold sweat, thinking that her baby would be yelling for her, held by a stranger, wanting the warm comfort of her mother's breast.

So Caroline and Philip stayed on, Caroline dancing with a series of entranced strangers in the dim red cavern upstairs and Philip, haunted by his clumsy thawing of the frozen spell, staying close to the whisky decanter. Finally, flushed and breathing heavily, he went upstairs to look for Caroline, who appeared as pale and perfect as she had been when they arrived. Philip leaned against the door jamb of the stuffy room until he managed to catch Caroline's eye. She came over at once, giving a little wave of her hand to her partner, who stopped in mid-dance, gaping foolishly.

They went to look for Richard and Ailsa, to say goodbye and thank you, and found them seeing another couple off at the front door. Caroline ignored the witch who, stern-faced with blue ruffles at her throat, appeared in the light which filtered through the stained-glass panels like some noble boy or a crusader, a Joan of Arc. Richard said the usual polite things but, just as Caroline and Philip were walking to the car, Ailsa called out: 'Caroline! I am not mad, you know. Think about me!'

'What was all that about?' asked Philip as he started up the car.

'Oh, nothing. I think she's got some sort of a power complex. Tell me, Philip, does she really try to cast spells on people?' Caroline was laughing as she said this and Philip thought that she was joking.

'Yes, of course! You've got to watch what you say, or else you'll end up under a nice damp stone in the garden, croaking your heart out!'

'I didn't mean like that . . . oh, never mind!' Caroline snapped back and clearly did not want to speak any more. Philip, concentrating hard on the dark winding road that led through the thick woods that surrounded the dower house, did not press her.

He stopped the car outside his own house at Coombe thirty minutes later and gallantly went round to open Caroline's door. Neither had spoken again on the journey home. She bumped against him as she swung her leg out, because he was slow in stepping back. Some reflex action made him grab her shoulder and he pressed his mouth onto hers. He pulled back, swearing, as an unbearable pain shot up the inside of his right leg. Caroline, without a word, had viciously jabbed the thin spike of her heel at his instep.

'She was a stuck-up little bitch,' he told Henry, more virulently than he intended, as they stood up unsteadily to leave the Horse and Jockey. The landlord had called Time a while ago and they were the only people left in the bar.

'Well now, that's your opinion, but I have to say I never found her that way,' Henry said amiably as they rolled, a little uncertainly, across the road.

'Didn't she have a boyfriend, then, a lover, or whatever?'

'Well,' Henry hesitated, hit, as always, by the pain of the betrayal. 'Well, no one serious. That is there was no one serious for most of the time. I think there might have been someone, just before the accident.'

They were bathed in the light streaming from Philip's porchway now and Henry, not wanting to give any more away, turned his head so that Philip could not see his face. 'It's not too easy to lose someone you love, I guess,' he said at last and with obvious difficulty.

Philip, fumbling with the key, had a rare flash of perception. 'You sound as if you're speaking from experience,' he said as he swung the door inwards. They walked into the sitting room where Fiona, graceful in sleep, was sprawled on the settee. Philip bent to pick her up, to carry her upstairs to bed.

Henry felt that Philip's probe must be answered: 'Yes, I am,' he admitted simply.

Philip looked at him over Fiona's warm, soft body; her tightly plaited hair fell away from her neck, leaving vulnerable shadows and hollows. 'I am sorry,' he said, 'I should have realized,' and he was gone, off and up the stairs, bearing his beautiful daughter, before Henry could tell him that he was mistaken. Peter and Caroline. His Peter and Caroline, anxious to include him in their happiness, trying to draw him into their warm circle of recognition and sudden desire (Henry would not call it love, because he was convinced that Caroline, at least, was unable to love), but repelling him by their obvious guilt and pity. Peter and Caroline, sneaking away on holiday together, to India of all places. Henry sat down on the settee, warm and hollowed still from Fiona's body, and he leant his head on the arm, whilst great shudders shook his limp frame.

Chapter Eight

The heavy midsummer air of late afternoon wrapped itself, a thick cloak of timeless composition, warm and fragrant, round Frederic's beehives. The slow buzzing, charming and easy in its monotony, of the bees echoed perfectly the heavy embrace of the shimmering, heated air. Inside the newly colonized hive, the one with the swarm collected by Frederic with Petra's help a couple of weeks before, there was the chaos of action which resolved itself into well ordered definition.

The new queen, heavy with her thousands of stored, fertilized eggs, her destiny mapped out, went dexterously about her task of laying these eggs, depositing them unerringly in ready prepared cells, each one the same, each one to produce sister after sister, to replenish her always-diminishing stock of workers. Young bees, newly hatched, assigned to duties in the hive, rushed around on the brood combs, sealing cells, making wax, cleaning out the dry husk-like body parts of dead bees.

A cohort of workers stood busily just outside the hive entrance, their abdomens raised as if to sting, their wings an invisible blur as they fanned vigorously to cool the hive and its rapidly increasing stocks of honey. All the while other bees arrived, laden with little bags of pollen, orange, yellow, curiously blue from the great banks of fireweed at the back of the meadow, black from the dangerous hearts of silken-petalled poppies and pure white from the clean, tangy heather. They landed, stumbling a little, dazed by the nectar they had tasted, and marched forward into the hive, challenged at times by the guards, ever vigilant for strangers.

The queen went mechanically and skilfully about her duties in the pitch darkness, constantly touched and licked by her workers, anxious for the reassurance of her presence. One queen and thousand upon thousand identical sisters, all interdependent. Whilst the queen laid her eggs and ensured the future with the promise of an eternal supply of bees, the others worked ceaselessly.

Yet the queen, unable to forage for herself, unversed in the skills of pollen collecting, nectar extraction, honey processing, was in reality more dependent on others than the individual worker. But without her great maternal existence, larger than the rest and godlike in her capacity to create new life, the whole structured nature of the colony would have foundered and died. Frederic, on his bank, visualized the dark, secret places of the brood chamber, with this great saving presence moving slowly on the face of the comb, eternally making new life.

The boy had left the garden some time before and Frederic wondered idly if he would come trotting back tomorrow with the gift of the name of that pink flower. It was, he supposed, only the day before that the child had first visited him, but it might have been last week, last month. Lately all he had wanted to do was to sit here, on this herb-laden bank, close to Elise and to lose himself in the timelessness of the hot days and nights. He had not eaten since his bread and cheese of the day before but, as the queen bee went mechanically and competently about her duties, driven by blind instinct on the dark comb, Frederic knew with the same sort of instinct that he no longer needed food. He felt light-headed, spiritually wound up, excited. He was aware of every part of his taut, bony body. Every muscle, each nerve, the bones themselves, tingled to the call of his spirit.

He lay down, full-length, crushing the sweet wild marjoram under his body, until his senses were almost overcome by intense spiritual desires and the heady scent of the bruised herb. He knew that he could just melt, dissolve,

133

that these bones and muscles and nerves must just resolve themselves into pure spirit and, when that was done, he and Elise would be one again. An hour passed, two. Still the air was warm, although the quality of the life grew softer, less intense. Slowly, the activity around the hives decreased and still Frederic lay there, his face wet and hot with tears for himself and for Elise and for the frustration he felt when the will to join her was so strong but his body, too solid after all, had failed him.

Elise had, of course, organized their move to Coombe and she had been tireless in the pursuit of the logistics. She had informed the letting agents that they would be leaving their flat in three months' time and she had arranged the payment for their new home. Frederic had been mildly surprised when she told him just how much money they did have in the bank, although it never occurred to him to invest his cash to ensure a reasonable income for the rest of their lives. So Elise had seen to that, too, and she had arranged for them to visit Coombe before the actual date of the move to ensure that the old man's things had been taken away. They travelled, as usual, by train and she carried a large canvas bag which contained a carefully packed selection of young plants. When Frederic had laughed at her, she had wagged her finger at him in mock remonstration.

'You must not laugh because I am doing all this for you! These are all flowers for your bees, you see. Thyme, oregano and bergamot. I shall plant these today and by next year they will have spread – and the honey we shall have!' She had found an old trowel, stuck rustily in a weedy bed at the front of the bungalow, and she planted some of her small clumps there, planting extra borage seeds in case some of that year's flowers should fail. The rest she had taken to the little lawn at the back and had carved out pieces of turf from the bank to give the small hungry roots of her herbs a chance to take hold.

They had gone into the house and wandered through the empty rooms together and Elise had been like a small child, her round brown eyes wrinkling into cracks of excitement as she decided where they should have their beds – she had spent many evenings lately embroidering new coverlets – where they should eat and sit to read and write. Frederic, unused to this sort of domestic planning, had been dazed, but happily so, taking pleasure in her enjoyment.

She had fallen asleep in the train on the return journey and he had gathered her head onto his shoulder, clasping her small wrinkled hand in both of his. People walking past their carriage smiled to see the two elderly people, the woman sleeping so peacefully against her thin husband who was taking care of her with perfect seriousness.

But this was easy for Frederic, whose simple and honest heart had never been cluttered with any extraneous desires or complications. He was aware that he often puzzled other people and he suspected that his colleagues at the hospital thought that he was humourless and unimaginative. When he said as much to Elise in one of his rare moments of introspection, she had laughed at him and told him that it would not do to worry about what other people thought: 'One of the best things about you, Frederic, is that you are totally without selfconsciousness – if you start to worry about it, you'll change completely!' Frederic, neither needing nor looking for reassurance, had never thought again, whilst Elise was alive, that perhaps he was enclosed in some sort of emotional wrap, which rendered him impervious to blows of the spirit.

Now he lay on the bank in a semi-delirious state, a condition of spiritual fervour, his mind finely tuned almost to that point which inspires fanatics to speak in tongues, to cast out devils. Frederic would have said that he had no devils to cast out, but now he lay, sick at heart and feverish, willing his body, above that of his dead love, to slide down into the earth, to coalesce with the herbs and the grasses and the earth and the little stones and not to be Frederic any more. The burden of being one was too much, but to be Frederic with Elise, Elise and Frederic, that was the desire. As they were. As they always were.

It was Elise, naturally, who had arranged for the furniture van to call to pick up their sparse possessions and to take them down to Coombe. She and Frederic were to travel with the

135

men in the van. It was all arranged. They had spent the evening before the move packing china and cutlery, books (no pictures, they had none), stacks of Ordnance Survey maps, of which they had a massive collection, and the few remaining jars and bottles of food, into wooden tea chests. Elise had bought these, for a few shillings each, from a nearby warehouse which imported and stored tea and coffee.

They left the curtains for the new tenants of the flat and took up the two bright rugs which were all that adorned the parquet floor. All their small possessions fitted into three tea chests. That left only the comfortable two-seater sofa, two armchairs, a few lamps, dining table and chairs. The bookshelves were all built in, as were the cupboards. There was also the bedroom furniture – their two beds, a chair, and Frederic's trunk, which was now empty. It did not occur to either of them that it was strange that packing up should require so little space and effort. Elise asked Frederic to help her move the tubs and pots of herbs from the small balcony and, when they had positioned these outside their front door, in the hallway, by the lifts and the stairs, so that the removal men should have no problem with them, they sat together, as was usual in the evenings, to watch the sun going down. It was framed in their big window which looked out over the golf course on the edge of town to the blue-purple of the misty hills beyond.

Their supper of bread and cheese and hard-boiled eggs, which Elise had dressed in a herb-scattered sour cream sauce, lay on the table and they were going to eat it, as they generally did in the summer, when the sun had sunk. Neither of them was vegetarian through any sort of principle and they both ate meat when they were away on their walking holidays, but Elise, who bought and cooked their food, found it easier to ignore the great dark red heaps of meat displayed so heavily in butcher's windows and preferred to buy fish and fruit, eggs and cheese. She tried to buy food each day, keeping little in the small cupboard in the kitchen; just a tin or two of tuna fish or sardines, a few packets of pasta and rice and some dried peas and beans. Today she had bought perfect peaches for their supper and they lay, nestled together in a dish, glowing fuzzily reddish brown against the white and green of the cheese and the herb-strewn eggs.

As the great flat dull red disc of the sun dipped into the horizon, smearing the lower half of the sky with impossible colour, Elise expelled a long sigh. Frederic, who had noticed that her face was drawn, smiled at her.

'I can see how tired you are,' he said. 'You have had so much to plan.' But she did not smile back. Her thin, clever brown face, with its long smooth nose and chocolate-coloured round eyes, showed signs of strain and she seemed tense. Frederic waited for her to speak.

'Do you feel that we are right to make this move, Frederic? Can you settle down to looking after the bees and the house and the garden. Maybe we'll get some goats too.' She smiled suddenly. 'After all we've never had that sort of responsibility before – do you think we shall be able to manage it? You see suddenly I feel a little guilty about this because it's all my doing and you are so happy here. We are so happy here. Have I talked to you enough about it? It's a long way to go!'

Frederic took her seriously, as he always did. 'Yes, I think we shall be very happy. Of course we shall! I am going to enjoy the bees and perhaps you will too. You can grow many more of your plants in a proper garden and even teach me the names if you like! Will it be such a great responsibility do you think? We shall have plenty of time for walking – and no more railway timetables for you!' They both laughed. Elise, who planned their holiday trips and the initial rail journeys, found railway timetables totally incomprehensible. She had long voluble discussions with the man in the ticket office at the local station, who heaved a great sigh of discomfort every time he saw her march in, armed with notebook and pencil, to pin him down to exact connections, detailed times and probable delays.

She came away from these encounters triumphant and exhilarated but protesting that she was not going to do battle like that ever again, and Frederic would laugh at her and marvel gently at the neat interlocking of train times that she had managed to extract from the unwilling clerk.

137

Thinking of this on the evening before their move, they both laughed gently together and it seemed as if Elise's strange unease dispelled as the dull red power of the dying sun smudged and blotted the horizon. They ate their eggs and cheese with energy and optimism and cut into the two juicy peaches, talking of the future in their new home and of their past visits to that part of the Somerset countryside where their bungalow stood, recalling hills and woods and roads and streams, remembering, as they always did, only the sunny golden days, filtering out the cold and the rain which had no part in their life together.

The removal men were to arrive at half past eight, Elise said, as they went to bed. They had washed up the plates and knives and forks from their supper and carefully packed them away, wrapped in newspaper, in the last space in one of the tea chests. Two apples and two oranges were left out for their breakfast.

'Much better to have only fruit!' said Elise. 'Then we won't have to worry about packing away plates and things.'

Frederic agreed with her. They kissed each other goodnight with quiet satisfaction before Frederic pulled back his coverlet, embroidered in blue and green, and Elise climbed into her bed with its pink-flowered spread. Between them lay four feet of floor space, bare now of the stripy rug which usually lay there. This distance between the beds was determined by the width of Frederic's large, old-fashioned trunk, which also lay between them.

'Elise,' said Frederic suddenly, just as he was on the point of sleep. 'Elise, I know I will be happy at Coombe – as I would be happy anywhere with you. You know that. But, will you be happy? Was that the reason you were worrying this evening – can you make the move?'

But Elise did not reply and Frederic listened to her slow even breathing, marvelling, as he always did, at the ease with which she fell asleep. As he lay there he tried, for the first time in his life, to measure Elise's worth, her value. He tried to assess her, to see her through the eyes of someone else, a disinterested observer, who would gauge her desirability as a wife, her value as a companion, her use to him on his own trip through life, by a cold catalogue of her virtues and her faults. Frederic found he could not do this. He felt her good qualities, but he could not enumerate them. He grew warm under the vision, in his mind, of her smile and he felt safe when he thought of the neat parcel of arrangements that she had made. As he slipped into deep sleep, he was a small child, reassured and comforted by the knowledge that he had a mother who watched over him throughout the long night.

Frederic, embracing the warm earth and the grass on the bank in the soft evening light, shifted and stirred. Just up the road Henry was unpacking his overnight bag in the spare bedroom in Petra and Philip's house, noticing as he did so that there was no bulb in the bedside lamp. Philip was trying to persuade Fiona that of course she would enjoy keeping an eye on her brothers for just an hour or so, and Dan was carefully pressing his pink mallow between two thick white sheets of paper.

The air was still warm in Frederic's garden. The little lawn at the back, with its straggly flowers, bounded by the beehives and the bungalow and the bank, overhung by soft-scented lime trees, seemed enclosed, like a dim, green room. Or a private place, under soft seas from which the colour was slowly draining as the light was washed, imperceptibly, away. The greens and the blues merged into a shaded glaucous mystery and the reds darkened to empty holes. Only the whites stood out now, the small round roses and the phlox, sharp and shining, giving out their brilliance, whilst the rest of the dwindling light was slowly absorbed by leaf and flower and earth.

No one saw Frederic on his bank, his body moulded to the shape of the ground, welded to the earth, the grass and stones and the clumps of thyme and marjoram that grew there. As the light left the garden it seemed that he was surrounded by a thick golden haze, a beaded curtain of light, and, by the same trick, the herbs and grasses seemed to be growing over and around his unconscious body. Frederic, through the haze and the layers of sleep, felt the warmth of the golden light and, for an instant, he was sharply awake, an eidetic vision of Elise there, with him, for one moment. Then she was gone and he was back in bed again at their flat, the night before he moved to Coombe, dreaming just as before of Elise his wife, Elise his mother, Elise his wife-mother.

He had found it hard to shake off sleep that morning, which was annoying, as he knew that they must be up early to help the removal men, who were to be there before nine o'clock. Elise was still asleep and, as he looked across at her bed, he remembered his dream, the one he had had last night and very often before, when his mother, whom of course he could not remember (he had never thought of himself as having had a mother), had stood by his bed and had then taken the face and figure of Elise. It was strange that Elise was not awake; like that 'mother' it was always she who got up first and sorted out the business of the day. Then Frederic looked properly at Elise and he knew that she had died.

He stood there, helplessly, in his striped pyjamas, not knowing what to do. He wanted to be told how to behave, how he should act, but the only person who could tell him was gone. No need to call a doctor; he was a doctor. He walked back over to his own bed and stared hopelessly at it, feeling, illogically, that if he had not woken up when he did, if he could only go back to sleep now, if he had not dreamed about Elise last night, this would not have happened. He thrust his long feet into a pair of checked slippers and padded back to where Elise was lying, curled up, on her side. He started, with shaking hands, to examine the body of his wife and then he remembered everything that was to happen today. Elise had it organized, down to the last detail, and now everything had gone wrong.

He looked at his watch, which he had laid carefully across the curve of the domed top of his trunk the night before. It was already after eight o'clock, and the removal men would be here within minutes. Half-past, Elise had said. He thought of death certificates, of inquests, of undertakers and of funerals. He could not bear it and he could not cope with it. Not now. Things must go as Elise had planned, they must move to

140

Coombe. At the thought of their little country bungalow waiting for both of them, of the bees to be cared for, the garden to be planted, the windows to be curtained, Frederic groaned aloud and he flung himself down on the bed with Elise and banged his head hard and deliberately against the iron curves of the old-fashioned bedstead.

Hours, minutes, seconds later, he heard the creak and rumble of a vehicle pulling up outside the block. He ran to the sitting room and looked out of the window at the two men in blue overalls, climbing out of the cab. It was not an enormous van, a pantechnicon, but a medium-sized vehicle with an outward-folding back door and, he supposed, a platform, which slid out to form a ramp. He watched as the men began to unfasten the great sliding bolts, and their deliberate movements, their obvious sense of routine and ordinariness, made him remember that he must act. He could not delay now – he must do exactly as Elise had planned. He rushed back into the bedroom and flung open the lid of his trunk. Thank God it was empty. He worked in a frenzy, flinging back the bedclothes and lugging and dragging Elise, moaning as he did so, so that he could fold her neatly into the trunk. She was a small woman, but awkward in death, with stiffly flopping arms and legs. Dead flesh did not bother Frederic as flesh was, after all, his business. But he nearly faltered when the soft poodle curls stroked his wrist as he finally manoeuvred the body from the edge of the bed across to the trunk, and he sobbed dryly as he fastened down the lid. Then he scrabbled at her sheets and blankets, stuffing them into a large black plastic rubbish sack, which was one of several lying in the corner of the room. He supposed that Elise had bought these to put the bedclothes in anyway and he thought he ought to do the same with his.

At that moment there was a loud banging on the door and Frederic, now with the guilt of a murderer concealing his wife's body, checked the trunk fastenings – thank God it had those thick leather straps encircling it – and then shuffled out to the little hallway, just as the knocking started again.

'Doctor Mann?'

'Oh, yes . . . yes . . . of course . . .' Frederic opened the door wider. 'I'm afraid we, that is, I . . . I woke a little later . . .' He indicated his pyjamas. The men, good-humoured, laughed.

'Don't worry, sir. The lady, Mrs Mann, arranged that we should start in your sitting room. Here . . .' He thrust a sheet of paper into Frederic's hand and Frederic stared vacantly at it, his brain failing to register the words. He just stood there, nodding, his eyes blank and his thin hair tossed and dis-ordered. The men, who were young and competent and used to dealing with people confused by the enormity of moving all their possessions, dealt briskly with Frederic and sent him back to his bedroom to get dressed. They saw a tall, thin man with a long bony face and distressed watery blue eyes.

'Poor old bugger,' said one to the other in low tones. 'Doesn't look quite right in the head to me.'

Once back in his bedroom, Frederic checked that the door was firmly shut and then sat on his unmade bed and shuffled his feet on the floor. What had he done and what was yet to be done? His brain failed to grasp the action to be taken now, just as it had failed him when he was meant to read the piece of paper. He heard muffled thumps and bangs and cheery shouts from the men as they heaved the tea chests and the few pieces of furniture to the door. He had not yet felt the crippling distress (a black glimpse of which had entered his mind as he thought of Coombe without Elise) that he knew was to come. He knew that he was in a state of shock and that the real horror would come when the nerve endings were working properly again, free from the numbing effects. The pain was there, to be borne later.

Automatically, he stood up to get dressed, and as he did so he thought that his bedclothes too must be packed. So he shovelled them into another black plastic bag and pulled on his clothes, tossing his pyjamas and slippers in as an afterthought. He could not stop himself from turning to the trunk which was now parallel with the two beds. He tried to shift it back to its original place, but the strength was not in him. He thought with stabbing urgency of the untidy bundle that was Elise, shut in the dark trunk, folded up like a ventriloquist's dummy, stiffening and awkward. He felt that there must be something, anything, more that he could do for her and that there was still so much more to say. After forty years their long and hitherto uninterrupted conversation could not be silenced like this. The thought of that blankness was so appalling that Frederic fell to the floor, alongside the trunk, pushing his body against it like a prisoner huddling up to his cell wall, trying to derive some comfort from the knowledge that another human being lies on the other side.

Then there was a banging on the bedroom door and Frederic jumped up, hitting his head on the iron frame of his bed. A red line traced itself across his temples and he reeled and winced with the pain as he went across to open the door.

''Ere, you all right, guv?' The chubby young removal man peered suspiciously at Frederic and then round him, into the bedroom. 'You all right?' he repeated as Frederic leant, dazed, on the door jamb.

'Where's your missus?' he asked, remembering that the job docket had said that a Dr and Mrs Mann would travel in the van down to Somerset. Frederic did not answer. He felt his head, which hurt where a large swelling was developing underneath his probing fingers. The removal man, alarmed by the strange atmosphere and the quiet withdrawal of Frederic, went to look for his mate. They both came back a few minutes later with a mug of tea.

'Been having a brew-up,' said the taller, thinner man. 'Here, this'll make you feel better. Banged your head did you? Can be nasty, that! 'Course, you'd know, being a doctor an' that.' Frederic, pulling himself together (he must not think of Elise, crumpled inside the dark trunk), managed a smile, which seemed to relieve both the men, whose faces relaxed from wary concern into hearty smiles of their own once more.

'That's better, then,' said the short, dark one. 'Now, where's the missus? She can tell us where to pack the kettle and that.'

Frederic was shocked into saying: 'She's gone!'

'Gone? Oh, you mean gone on . . . gone on ahead? Oh, I

143

see. Oh, well, no wonder you find all this a bit strange. The ladies are always better at moving, we find. Now, you stop worrying, guv. We'll sort out the kettle and things in 'ere – just the beds and the trunk and those bags and suitcases, is it? I must say this is one of the easiest jobs we done, not much to move like some . . .' The young man prattled on as he gathered up the rubbish bags and moved around the room, checking that there was nothing he had overlooked. He went out into the kitchen and Frederic heard him say to his mate: 'Poor old sod. Don't think he's got a clue what's going on really. Hope he behaves himself in the van.'

Frederic moved warily away from the door, backing into the room until he reached the window which overlooked a tarmacked courtyard at the rear of the building. The other tenants kept their cars in here, in neat garages with the kind of doors which swung outwards and then slid neatly back inside. Each door seemed to be painted a different colour by the tenants, who bought a tin of red or green or blue paint for the front doors of their flats and then used up the rest of the paint to brighten up the garages.

Frederic, still worrying at the sore lump on his brow, gazed out at these doors, bright splashes of colour in the grey-brick dullness of the yard. The two removal men were now in the room with him, hauling out the beds. They took no notice of Frederic, nor he of them. He watched a young woman, with a baby in her arms and a young child clutching at her skirt, open one of the garages and disappear inside with her children. Soon afterwards, a red car backed out and he could see that the baby was lying in a carrycot on the back seat, whilst the toddler was strapped into some sort of a child seat, next to the cot. He took the whole scene in, sharply and slowly, moving his head, painfully, from side to side, carefully at first and then with mechanical regularity, so that the bright colours of the garage doors and the car blurred into each other like a child's spinning top, which goes slowly at first and then with a solid blur as the reality of the separate shades becomes an illusion, an impression of colour which cannot be defined.

He thrust his hands deeply into the pockets of the shabby

144

tweed jacket which Elise had decreed that he should wear today for the journey. How cold he felt, how cold his fingers were. The white dead tips of his fingers jammed up against a pen in his pocket and he pulled it out, together with a piece of crumpled paper which he found in the breast pocket. He looked at the paper. 'Eggs, cucumber, bread', was written there in Elise's large round regular hand. She often jotted down a few things for him to buy on his way home from the hospital. That piece of paper must have lain in his pocket for some time. He smoothed out the crumples and folded it the other way, so that the neat little list was on the inside, and leaning on the narrow, white-painted window sill, he began to write.

Behind him the removal men had bent their backs to the trunk. The smaller one straightened up with a grunt of surprise. 'Blimey! That's a weight! Got books in 'ere, have you, guv?'

'What! Don't touch that!' Frederic leapt over to the trunk, his eyes wide and straining, his face red and his long fingers spread wide, tendons and muscles taut. The men gaped at him. The ballpoint pen had fallen from his hand and lay on the floor under the window, but the piece of white paper upon which he had written 'My darling Elise' stayed on the sill.

''Ere! What's the matter with you, guv? The trunk's got to go in't it? I only said wot you got in 'ere, because it's bleeding heavy and I thought it might be books, and they're always heavy, books and papers. That's all.' The two men, one short and tubby, the other tall and thin, stood, blue overalled arms hanging by their sides, staring accusingly at Frederic, who wearily wiped his fingers across his eyes.

'Oh, yes. Books. Of course,' he said. 'My . . . precious . . . books. I am so sorry. I was not thinking. Of course the trunk is to go.' He screwed up his eyes with the effort of talking and he tried to think. The everyday grasp that he knew he ought to have was becoming harder to keep and this morning's tragedy seeped like a dark stain through his whole being, gradually eclipsing all else.

'Is that all?' he said, at length. 'I mean, when you have taken that trunk, are you ready?' The men, only slightly mollified and foreseeing trouble on the journey, nodded silently.

'Wait, then, in the van,' said Frederic. They exchanged glances which confirmed the dark thoughts of the old man's mental condition.

'I will join you, in one moment. I have only to say goodbye. You understand?' Frederic, who did not care if they understood or not, watched anxiously as they lugged and heaved at the trunk and, when they reached the hallway with it, he ran first to the door of the living room to watch them take it to the lift, into which it only just fitted, and then he bounded to the big plate glass window in time to see them tug it onto a little contraption with wheels and thus push it up to the lowered ramp and into the waiting van. He watched still, hands pressed against the cold glass of the large window, as the two men came out of the darkness of the inside of the van. They stood, talking earnestly, for a minute and one then pulled out a large white handkerchief from his overalls and slowly and thoroughly blew his nose.

As if at a signal, both men suddenly looked up at the flats and saw him, his face pressed against the window. He stepped back quickly as the short man and the tall man exchanged that private glance, each shaking his head, before they began the business of securing the back of the van.

Frederic ran back into the bedroom and fumbled on the floor for his pen. 'My darling Elise,' he had written. How long ago had he put those words down? He must explain to her, let her know that he would still treasure her in his heart, hold her dear above all else. To write it down was the only way he could marshal his thoughts, and he felt that she must understand once he had committed it to paper. As he tried to write of his love and his guilt, he heard the deep urgent noise of a motor horn. Twice, three times, louder it seemed at each sounding, and Frederic knew that it must be for him and he must go. Tenderly he folded the scrap of paper and tucked it safely inside the inside pocket of his jacket. The only thing left now in the room was the small document case containing all their papers – his chequebook, naturalization papers, marriage certificate, savings account books, investments, solicitor's letters concerning their new home. Elise had put it all ready by his bed, last night. That reminded him that, as he left the flat, he was to post the key back through the letter box for the agent, who would use his duplicate to come in and reclaim possession. He left the flat, shutting the door, and then stood irresolutely at the top of the stairs, torn between the safety of his old home and the pull it exerted, because of his life there with Elise, and the lure of the wooden bungalow in the countryside, where he and Elise had so often walked and where she had sat on the steps in the warm afternoon, watching him learn to handle the bees.

Harold, the short dark removal man, found him there and gently steered him to the lift and out of the building, helping him up the steps to the wide seat in the front of the van. He exchanged significant glances once again with Cecil, his mate, as he strapped the poor old bugger in and switched the radio on loudly, to give the old boy something to think about. Not that you could think much with some of that rubbish they played on Radio One these days, thought Harold, who much preferred modern jazz, but there you were, it would keep the old sod quiet.

Frederic did not hear the music. No more than a drowning man hears the sound of the waves washing on the beach. He sat there, eyes half closed, head lolling to one side, allowing himself to be driven to his new solitude.

He was still in shock, numbed. With a small piece of his mind he knew that days of awful blinding desolation and unbearable solitude lay ahead. But he could feel none of that now. He wanted, more than anything, to see Elise again. To see her and tell her that, for her sake, he could manage, he would manage, wanted to manage and to make the life they would have had together. He wanted to give her his note, his love and reassurance, and above all he wanted her to be settled, and at peace.

Frederic was in sole possession of his new domain by early evening. The late spring weather had turned bitingly cold and rain threatened. It was still light enough to see quite clearly and he wandered around the garden, noting that little had changed since he and Elise had last been here.

Half an hour earlier, Harold and Cecil had driven away, with their minds changed about the old man. As they had arrived, coming up the lane through the village, past the cricket pitch to the wooden bungalow, Frederic sat up, his head straight, and became alert, decisive. His eyes dried to a sparkling blue and his fingers no longer trembled. Elise had told him, he remembered, that the key was to be left under a green plastic tub, by the door. He jumped nimbly down the steps from the cab, recovered the key and let himself in. The two men already had the trunk out of the van and Frederic watched, resolved to act as soon as possible as they hauled it in.

'Over there!' he ordered, pointing to the back door. 'Leave it there and I shall unpack it later.' And so the afternoon wore on. Frederic tireless, running hither and thither, commanding, counter-commanding, organizing – even finding the kettle and ordering Cecil to make some tea. Neither of the men, overawed by the old man's authority and change of attitude, thought to ask about the wife who was meant to be here already. Each perhaps thought that he had got it wrong and there was no one after all. But, as they drove away with ten pounds between them, thrust into blue overall pockets, Frederic's sparkle faded, his steps flagged and he walked, as he knew he must, over to the trunk. As he struggled with the tight leather straps which encircled the domed lid, he felt a growing dread of what was inside. Not Elise, not Elise, he said to himself. She had gone and what was left was just the rubbery flesh, the chemicals, the minerals, the human building materials. Not Elise. And he was right. He turned away before he forced himself to look more closely. Only her hair, the hair (he could not see her dear face because of the way the body was folded), was real to him. Dark brown and curly and still alive. Her hair. He stood there and cried for her hair, large tears dropping into the gaping trunk.

Still later, after his walk around the garden, Frederic, who was after all a capable man, if unworldly, sat and pondered upon his future. Solitude was uppermost in his mind and, as a concept, that did not frighten him. He was used, after all, to a kind of solitude, an exclusiveness, containing only the life that he and Elise had been prepared to lead together. Now that would, in practical terms, have to be halved. But, in emotional terms, the portion left to Frederic for his spiritual nourishment would be small indeed, and he was aware of this. Solitude meant that those thoughts, those feelings and observations which had been the common property of the two of them, became his alone; it meant that there would be no return, no interest on the things that sprang from his mind, and they would always come back fruitless and unenriched. Even while he thought grimly of this barren future, his lips moved slowly, pouring out a silent litany, telling Elise the way the oil lamps cast a shadow on the beams and the wooden ceiling, how the kitchen window looked out over the beehive part of the garden and how the rain was pouring down, lashing against the uncurtained windows.

Frederic knew that he would not be able to sleep now. He went to find the black plastic bags and, from the one which contained the sheets and blankets from Elise's deathbed, he gingerly pulled out the embroidered coverlet. It was un-stained, fresh still, and he tenderly laid it across the bare bed, which was next to his own. Then, taking an oil lamp, he went out into the garden with the sack which held the rest of the sheets and blankets, before returning for Elise.

Many hours later, he staggered indoors, feverish, wet through and exhausted.

The rain, which from the inside of the bungalow had sounded like tiny lumps of gravel sprayed against the windows, was not too bad once he was thoroughly wet and he had grown used to it. It had filled his eyes and ears and his thin hair had stuck to his bony scalp in flat, dripping strands. He found a strong wide spade in the garden shed and, by the light of his oil lantern, which he kept dry by propping it up inside a large box, he started to dig out the soft earth of the bank.

He was careful to take out the top and sides in flat slabs, to be replaced in such a way that the roots of the growing stuff should take hold again. Then he burrowed and tunnelled in, scooping out the earth. There was so much to come out and the mounting heap on the grass alongside seemed enormous. He wondered if it would all pack back in again. He tunnelled in and lengthwise and, at one point, he became worried that the whole bank was going to collapse; remembering stories of wartime escape tunnels, he wondered if he should somehow shore it up. But he dug on, gingerly now, and the space at last looked as though it might be roomy enough. His hands slipped on the wet spade and water ran in rivulets down his face and neck; he stopped and rested for a moment, his racing mind overcoming all the physical exhaustion. The chamber which he had excavated glowed in the yellow light reflected from his oil lantern and it seemed cosy and warm, inviting.

He shook out Elise's blankets and sheets and laid them in the chamber, slapping at them with his spade, so that they lined the soft walls and the floor. Elise, who lay on the ground behind the mound of earth, was dark and cold and wet. Slippery from hours of pelting rain, her body, still in its cotton nightdress, was an awkward burden. But he bore it, stumbling and sliding, until he ceremoniously pitched it into the burial chamber he had made. He was hot and tingling now from the great exertion of the digging. He had not eaten all day and he felt light-headed, other-worldly and, strangely, elated. Elise lay with her back to him, her face against the wall of earth and small stones, and he knew now that he must cover her up with cold wet earth. With each shovelful his euphoria lessened and weakened, the muscles in his arms and legs becoming liquid, as if they were about to dissolve. But, grimly now, he carried on until there were only the thin slices of turf, the chunks of earthy rooted herbs to be put back, and he picked these up with his hands and put them roughly into position, until he could come out in the daylight and plant them properly.

Now he was cold and wet and he shivered as he stood and gazed at the dark outline that was the burial mound. His eyes prickled with fatigue and deep sorrow and little sore spasms ran up and down his back and over the tops of his arms. He ached all over from the hours of digging and the lower half of his back felt as if it would never straighten out again. Wearily, he pulled himself indoors, reaching the top step of the bungalow just as the oil in his lantern ran out. His exhausted body and mind could not work out how to make more light – there was no electricity – so he crawled into the bedroom, inching his way around the unfamiliar angles, until he encountered the rustling black sack which contained his own bedclothes.

He rubbed his wet face and hair with weary fingers and then made the long journey back, across the smooth wooden floor to his bed. Before pulling himself upright and peeling off the sopping wet clothes which clung to his exhausted body, he took the scrap of paper, the letter to Elise, out of his jacket pocket. It was soggy and wet, but he clutched at it. He was shivering violently and his feet ached with the cold. He wrapped himself awkwardly in the sheets, the blankets and the embroidered coverlet and lay down, drained and ill, on the cold mattress, to face the rest of the night.

Chapter Nine

'Did you say beef ?'

'Yes – in brown bread, please.'

'Mustard?'

'What dear?'

'On your sandwiches – would you like some mustard in them?'

'Oh, yes please, of course.'

M sat back, pleased with herself for having grabbed a seat at the small table for two at the Jubilee, which was a comfortable and obviously popular pub just a little way off the motorway. Petra, fighting her way to the small bar for food and drink, was not so sure.

'Two glasses of red wine, please, and two rounds of beef sandwiches on brown bread – yes – with mustard. Yes – English mustard.' The barmaid was young and seemed very anxious to please, which made Petra wonder if she was competent enough to ensure the safe arrival of the sandwiches. But thoughts of food and wine were not uppermost in her mind. Petra had never visited Caroline's house in Chelsea since her stay there with Henry, fourteen years before. She could remember each room and the layout of the place and even the feel of it, the town house atmosphere, but the details of the surroundings were hazy in her mind. M, presumably, had been there many times to see Caroline, but she did not know that Petra had even seen the house. Petra had often wondered uneasily if Caroline had told M but when, just after setting out this morning, her mother started to describe the place to her, she knew that the silly little secret had been kept. Petra listened to M's rambling description for a minute or two and then, feeling guilty and unable to explain, she changed the subject.

She rubbed idly at a drop of beer on the polished wood of the bar counter while she was waiting for the wine, dipping her finger in it and smearing the liquid in little circles. The barmaid turned round with two full glasses and Petra hastily rubbed at the smears she had made with a blue and yellow towelling mat which was on the bar. Was it going to be difficult to keep up the pretence that she had never been to Caroline's home? Did it really matter now, anyway? The real problem was how M was going to react once she had stepped inside the door and climbed the stairs. What sort of memories did Caroline's house hold for her, Petra wondered, as she paid for the wine.

M picked up her blue knitted jersey jacket from the other chair. She had put it there whilst Petra was at the bar just in case someone else had come along and had tried to sit down or to take the chair away. She hated any sort of misunderstanding and she sighed with relief as Petra sat down.

'Sandwiches are coming in a minute.'

'Do they know where we're sitting, dear?'

'I suppose they just come and yell,' said Petra. She looked around the pub with satisfaction which soon turned into a feeble sense of despair. The bits and pieces of brass shone from the ceiling or from deep shelves, and fresh flowers made splashes of light and colour in their vases on the windowsills and deeply polished wood tables. The window seats and some of the chairs were covered with cushions made of a thick linen material which showed hunting scenes in faded pinks and greens and blues. Magazines, copies of *Country Life* and the *Shooting Times*, lay in neat heaps on some of the tables and there was a deep fireplace with a glossy black-leaded plate at the back and large iron fire dogs, supporting long logs ready for next winter's blaze. Sunlight poured in through the small-paned windows, catching the head of the Greek goddess on the fire back and making the well polished glasses behind the bar shine and twinkle.

Petra felt satisfied because it was all so cosy and comfortable but she despaired because she knew that she was incapable of creating this type of homely atmosphere in her own house. M echoed her thoughts.

'Such a nice cosy pub, dear. I don't know why but this sort of old-fashioned furniture is always such a comfort. Caroline had one or two nice bits and pieces in her house. I thought you might like them.' She looked at Petra as she spoke in a level, normal voice.

Petra started to speak and couldn't, and then managed: 'Oh, but I don't remember them – what sort of furniture?'

'Two rounds of beef on brown bread!' brayed a large woman who came tripping out of the kitchen with a laden tray.

'Here,' said Petra.

'But you've never been to her house, dear, you can't know what she had,' said M.

'Hell,' thought Petra, 'I'll have to tell her.'

But M was not taking what Petra had said seriously. 'Oh dear,' she was thinking. 'That awful time. I don't think I can go there again but I've got to. We've got to get things sorted out, can't leave it all for another eight weeks.' She concentrated hard on her sandwich and screwed up her eyes as she thought: 'Caroline was so blank, so empty. She said she didn't want to live. What nonsense. Then this had to happen. But she didn't mean it, she couldn't, it was just depression, everyone gets that sometimes . . . I'm sorry dear, what did you say?' M's bright smile lit up her silver-blue eyes with customary ease and her little white teeth showed at the corners of her mouth.

'I just said, did Caroline leave a will?' Petra mumbled, and then swigged the last of her wine, feeling ashamed of the question.

'A will! Do you know, dear, Dad has never mentioned it.'

'But shouldn't we look for one? I mean, she had quite a few things to leave, after all. We shouldn't just assume that there was no will, should we?'

154

M was shocked. 'But who would she leave her things to – and the house – apart from her family? Really Petra, I think Caroline was a little young to have made a will. Have you made one – you're older than her, you know.' She was beginning to sound a little waspish now.

'Well, no, actually . . .'

'There you are then!'

'No, I haven't but I don't really have anything to leave. I mean the things that are mine are Philip's too. Caroline had her own house and car and lots of expensive clothes and I expect there's some jewellery. And we don't know that she didn't have a . . . well, a friend.' Petra found it hard to look at M and she felt the word 'friend' seemed far too coy, but she really wasn't sure what she was trying to imply.

M seemed insulted. 'I'm sure she had lots of friends – but you don't go leaving your house and your car to mere friends!'

'Well, a special boyfriend, then?' Petra persisted.

'Oh, no – no, there was no one like that. Caroline was a career girl, you know. She never let boyfriends interfere with that. Anyway, she wouldn't leave her clothes to a boyfriend.'

The tone of M's voice told Petra quite clearly that that was that and the discussion should now be closed, yet she tried once more. 'Well, we ought to look for one. Did she have a solicitor?'

'Your father knows about all that, dear, and he would have said if there was one. Now listen, Petra.' M leant forward and her neatly waved hair shook in stiff little ridges as she bobbed her head earnestly up and down. 'Dad and I have talked about this and we want you to have the car and her clothes and furniture if you'd like that as well.' Petra started to protest but M shook her head. 'Please, dear, you are her sister. Caroline would have wanted that.'

Petra had her doubts but she could not hurt M by voicing them. 'All right then.' She wanted to touch her mother's hand, to reassure her, but M had gathered herself together again, pulling her jacket and handbag into her control, nodding her head slightly as she fixed on her smile, standing up and taking brisk charge.

155

The cobbled mews was exactly as Petra had remembered it but much brighter. Tubs and troughs of pink and red pelargoniums, hanging baskets of nasturtiums and trailing catmint made the old yard look like a holiday place, somewhere abroad. Whitewashed walls and their pale pink and green neighbours gleamed in the sunshine and the place had a quaintness about it that Petra found endearing. She wondered if Caroline had noticed it. 'Of course,' she thought, 'it was winter when I was here and years and years ago, anyway.'

'Oh look, M, isn't it pretty, what are those flowers?' she asked, pointing at an exotic climbing shrub with felty heart-shaped leaves and large bell-like flowers in a shade between pink and soft orange. Like a ripe apricot, Petra thought. The artificiality of the scene appealed to her and she wanted to exclaim and admire for a bit longer.

M appeared not to have heard her. 'We go in,' she was thinking. 'In and up the stairs, that's right, and then I think we must make an inventory of all of the things. Yes, we'll write them down and then Petra can take what she wants. I do wish she'd be a bit more help, suggest something. Why docs she keep talking about a will, girls of thirty don't make wills, she had no one to leave it to except us. You don't expect to, to . . . to not be here at that age, you don't think about death then. No, we must go in.'

'Come along, dear, we must get started,' said M. As they walked up the stairs ('Why are they so dusty when no one's been here for six months?' thought Petra. 'Where does dust come from?') M was thinking about self-deception. At the little landing which opened out into the large living and dining area ('Mustn't forget to check the downstairs living room,' she thought automatically) she tried to blank out the images which were racing into her mind. Images from last year when Caroline had, for the only time in her life (apart from her behaviour at Petra's wedding and that, even M admitted, was wilful rather than weak), shown a bleak, despairing face to her mother. M had stood, just here, wringing her hands, whilst Caroline, face blank and dead, had said that she saw no point in living, that she wished she were dead, and what did people go and have children for but to bring a lot more emptiness into the world. M, who knew that there were terrible black, gaping voids in life, also knew that she could not face their dark emptiness, could never do anything but turn her mind away from them. She could not understand why Caroline had brought herself to look into their horror, and wondered what, if anything, had brought on this crisis.

'Don't, dear, oh, please, please don't,' she had almost wailed. 'You've got so much to live for. Your own house, a car, a wonderful job, travel, money. You could marry anyone you chose, tomorrow, I'm sure . . .' At the look of pure disdain, the snarl of horror on Caroline's beautiful face, she had faltered into silence. She changed tack. 'Why did you telephone me, Caroline? Do you want some help with decorating – the downstairs curtains?' M was an adept at changing the subject but this sounded silly even to her, and anyway Caroline was not listening. She just stood there, unblinking, gazing with dull, dark eyes past her mother, down into the black well of the stairs.

M knew all about horror. That was why she always turned the pages of the newspaper quickly if there were reports of massacres or of babies being ill-treated or starved to death. She did not like to hear about famine or people perishing helplessly and unhelped through disease. She would switch off the television or leave the room when war refugees were shown, lost and bleeding, and she always made sure that she had a nice safe library of books to read, or ones that had the nasty bits in predictable, skippable, places. What horror had Caroline ever seen, ever read about, come to that? What blank, black places was she gazing at and refusing to live with? M knew that she would not be told and she was glad. She was desperate to get Caroline onto a safe subject, to think of something that would shake her out of this silly mood.

'Please tell me what's upset you, dear,' she said, bravely, trying to hold her hands steady. They were like two little animals with life of their own, creeping and twisting, one over the other. She clenched the fingers of her left hand over those of her right, so that the nails dug hard into the palm, leaving red crescent-shaped marks.

'Nothing has upset me. Nothing special. I just don't see the point of living,' spat out Caroline, panting with the effort of keeping her voice at a controllable pitch and thinking what a silly cow M was really. What did she know or rather, what did she care about anything? She wished she had not telephoned her but it was done in a moment of weakness. Normally Henry would have come but he was in America just now, with Peter. Henry would have understood; he would have pretended that it did not matter, called her a silly bitch, shouted at her, taken her out for a walk, a drink, talked to her. He was a real person, Caroline thought. M was not and Daddy was not. They both lived narrow, blinkered lives, refusing to accept that anyone else's feelings were valid or even permissible. Why the hell had she telephoned M and let her see her in this state? It was the sort of thing that Petra would have done – and spent days apologizing for. Well, she was not going to apologize. She would switch it all off now.

'Why the hell don't you stop wringing your hands?' she said abruptly. 'You look like a deserted wife.' And she strode into her bedroom, slamming the door.

M was still standing there, guiltily (just like Petra, thought Caroline with some measure of irritation), when she came out ten minutes later with not a trace of the black despair on her face. 'You'll stay the night?' asked Caroline – meaning, you *will* stay the night – and M, bewildered, nodded her head.

'The spare room bed is made up – I'll switch the electric blanket on just to air it. I'll take you out to dinner.' M started to protest, but Caroline turned her back on her mother and disappeared into the bathroom, so there was no point in arguing.

Hours later, M tried hard to keep awake as she sat at a metal-topped table in a café that aroused disturbing feelings in her. The lights were hard and bright, big overhead lamps with curled plastic shades, while the walls and floor of the huge room were both tiled with diamond-shaped brown and white chequers giving a strange effect of curved space. The little round tables were spaced far apart and eight or ten people clustered precariously around each with just enough room for a hand or an arm each to rest on the surface, which was made of some curiously soft metal. Waitresses, skimpily dressed in black outfits with starched white collars and little caps and aprons, ran to take orders as coins were rapped on the table tops, and at the far end of the room – M squinted to see just how far – a band was playing, she supposed, some sort of modern jazz. A bar, metal-covered, just like the tables, ran the length of the room; behind part of it, white-hatted chefs wearing swathing white aprons cooked steaks and fish and ladled steaming pieces of meat out of large casseroles. In the middle of the bar, drinks were served, and at the far end, near the band or group or whatever they were called these days, more chefs were busily chopping vegetables, slicing salads, mixing dressings and arranging piles of fruit in baskets. M stared at the blackness along the other side of the café where a plate glass window stood uncovered and unseeing. Her eyes smarted and hurt, tired by the bright lights of the long room.

She and Caroline had a table to themselves when they got there. Caroline had ordered a starter of deep fried vegetables, each piece crisp and still untouched by the cooking in the middle, and they had dipped the cauliflower sprigs, the mushrooms, bits of pepper in different sauces which were set before them.

Then came a rack of lamb, juicily pink inside and deliciously charred on the surface. M caught sight of the menu and raised a mental eyebrow when she saw the prices, but she did not want to antagonize Caroline so she said nothing and enjoyed her food. Caroline said very little and, when they had finished eating and the gazelle-like waitresses had bounded over and taken away their plates, people who knew Caroline drifted over and settled down, occasionally rapping pieces of silver on the table, ordering glasses of wine, brandy, mineral water, coffee.

Caroline sat back in her cane-bottomed chair, her eyes half closed, a sleepy smile on her face, nodding slightly when someone spoke to her. M felt very tense. No one seemed to acknowledge her and Caroline did not bother to introduce her to anyone. In fact, although at times there were ten or twelve people clustered round the zinc-topped table, not many words were spoken. People came and went and stayed and to M it was all like a bad dream. She could not tell the sex of some of Caroline's friends. Men with ear-rings, girls with orange hair, boys wearing tights, people with shaved heads, long hair, junk shop clothes. No wonder Caroline felt so strange if these were her friends, M thought, indignant, imagining the innocent pleasures Caroline and Petra should have had as teenagers and somehow had not. There should have been parties with fruit punch, nicely organized dances, trips to the theatre with children of their friends, hers and Tom's. Caroline should not be sitting here now with all these freaks. M felt like bursting into tears, the dreamlike atmosphere of the place upsetting and disturbing her more than Caroline's outburst that afternoon.

Just as she felt that she could not stand it any more, she was going to have to say something, to get up and go, there was a light touch on her arm, a feather stroke. What beautiful eyes, M thought, what a lovely girl.

'Is this yours? I think it must have fallen out of your bag.' M gazed at the brightly coloured silk square in the girl's hand. 'Oh, no – that's not mine,' she started to say and then realized that it did belong to her; she had tied it round the strap of her bag in case she needed a scarf. Her nervous laugh jarred the soft, pliant atmosphere and a couple of Caroline's friends winced painfully, rather dramatically. Caroline did not stir. 'Oh look, yes. It is mine. How clever of you. Thank you.' M took the scarf, the shocking pink and green square, from the outstretched hand and tucked it, fussily, in her bag.

'I think it's just lovely!'

'What – sorry?'

'Just lovely, that scarf of yours.' The voice was very deep and rather hesitant and M looked closely at the slim young thing dressed all in black: black tunic over black tights which ended at the ankle, leaving the feet bare, and a black and silver band threaded through spikily cut, dark hair.

160

'But you don't wear anything coloured,' she protested.

The creature with the doe eyes and pink and white complexion and the big white hands, laughed. 'Oh, but I do – I do often. I'm in mourning tonight, aren't I, Caro?' The last words – an appeal to Caroline who, leaning back in her chair, looked as if she were holding court – held a certain stress, a caress.

Caroline smiled again, lazily, wickedly. 'That's my mother, Joey – not your style at all, naughty boy.'

M was horrified; she gaped at the vacant-eyed girl (boy?) with the pale face and the thick dark wings of hair and then at Caroline, who was challenging her to complain, to make a scene. Joey – was she really a boy, M wondered – patted her on the arm and then leant forward, swinging one leg (the trousers which ended at mid-calf did not reveal hairy legs, M noticed). 'Isn't Caro awful? – she's always having a go at me.' There was a catchy little laugh in the husky breathless voice. 'But I do adore her – she's so good to me, you know. Are you really her mama?' M found this last word more offensive than anything. Its very old-fashioned gentility, its evocation of trouble-free country house days, contrasted so strangely and so strongly with the harsh white light in this weird café and the odd people gathered around her, that she felt like choking. She could not reply and Joey laughed and pinched her arm. 'Don't you worry about Caroline. We all take care of her.'

'Caroline.' M pulled her arm away and stood up briskly to cover her shakiness. Caroline raised one eyebrow and someone giggled. 'Caroline, I'm very tired. I'm going back to bed now. No, don't get up. Have you a spare key? I'll get a taxi.' Caroline, without a word, handed over a key and M, feeling that her back was being pierced by a thousand cynical eyes, made her way to the plate glass door knowing that time was out of joint and the structure of Caroline's life would always be an unacceptable puzzle to her.

Now, back at the house with Petra, she felt again that sense of loneliness, that rejection of any width of vision and feeling that may have been offered to her that night at the café. She had been shown everything in the glare of that cold white light

161

but had tightened up inside and had refused to have anything to do with it. Caroline had offered her her own way of life and she had turned her back on it and had not even tried to understand.

'Oh dear,' said M quietly. 'Oh dear.' She wasn't sure if she had spoken aloud or not and she felt rooted to the spot, unable to walk to the bedroom, to the kitchen. All her determination, all her strength of purpose, had been channelled into this trip to pack up what was left to her of her younger daughter, to tidy things up as some measure of compensation for the burial that would never take place. But now her strength was failing her, the blackness was widening and all the nice warm light thoughts with their sense of order and routine were falling prey to the dark chaos that she hated to think Caroline had been predisposed to.

'M, come on. It's not going to be that bad.' Petra spoke softly but firmly. She knew that her mother dreaded breaking down (she had been so cross last night to be discovered in a moment of weakness), and she was not sure if she could deal with the situation. 'Look, what we both need is some tea, or coffee. I expect there's some in the kitchen – probably a bit stale but it will do. You go and put the kettle on and I'll see if I can find some milk.'

M nodded, tugging at the curtains in her mind; tea and coffee were familiar parts of this routine. She walked forward into the kitchen whilst Petra went back down the stairs. There was plenty of tea in a big black canister. M eased off the lid and sniffed at it. A strange sweet slightly scented smell told her that it was a speciality tea of some sort – jasmine perhaps. She boiled the kettle, put out cups and saucers and automatically opened the fridge door. Petra came back without any milk ('The only bottles I saw were on someone else's doorstep and I didn't feel I ought to steal it,' she said, hoping the feeble little joke would lighten the atmosphere), to find M walking briskly round the kitchen peering into cupboards.

'Just look at this, dear.' She held up a dishcloth. 'That has been here since Caroline's accident – it's quite fresh, and damp. And there are eggs in the fridge.'

162

'Oh, M, I'm sure you're wrong. Who on earth is going to bring a dishcloth in here?'

'Well, all I can say dear is that something is very odd.' M had a gleam in her eye, like a dog sniffing down the wind, questing for a scent. 'The house doesn't feel as if it's been empty for the last six months. I'm going to have a look in all the other rooms.'

They found a toothbrush and a half-used tube of toothpaste in the bathroom ('That could have been Caroline's spare one,' said Petra) and there was a razor and some shaving foam in the bathroom cabinet. Petra could not resist the urge to open the airing cupboard door, but when she saw M gazing mournfully at the big photograph, yellow now and torn and crinkled at the edges, she wished that she had not. The small bedroom was just as inconclusive in its half evidence that someone was using the house. The bed was made up but the sheets, which smelled faintly of some sort of musky perfume, were only a little crumpled. There were clothes in the cupboards but they might have been Caroline's own. Slim trousers, T-shirts, jerseys and tunic-style tops. There was nothing that could force one to say 'Someone slept here last night.'

'What about the eggs, though?' said M triumphantly. 'The eggs and the dishcloth!'

'Eggs keep for ever and you could have been mistaken about the cloth. It seemed pretty dry to me,' said Petra. 'You might have splashed it when you filled the kettle.'

'The kettle!' shrieked M, and they charged back to the kitchen to make the tea which they drank weak and without milk.

'I don't quite see what we are going to do with everything,' said Petra after she had wandered, tea cup in hand, in and out of every room in the little house, trying to see what changes had been made since she had stayed there, years before.

'Well, I thought we'd make a list of everything and take the smaller stuff with us today – trinkets and jewellery and little ornaments. Is there anything you'd particularly like, dear?' Petra instantly thought of the photograph, the small framed one of the two children, herself and Caroline, dressed up for a winter ride on their ponies. But she shook her head. 'Well' – M was determined to press her point home now – 'I want you to take the car. I expect the keys are still in Caroline's desk. It probably won't start after all this time, in which case we'll have to telephone a garage.'

Petra struggled with a desire for a car of her own and her reluctance to take Caroline's. She wished she could really feel her sister's death, be able to weep freely over Caroline, to say 'I wish you were back with us.' But that had not happened at all in the weeks since the dreadful accident, and all she had felt was shock at the drama of the news and a terrible pity for M and Daddy, who grieved so quietly for their younger daughter. Why therefore should she not have the car? It was, presumably, just sitting in a garage and might just as well be put to use. It was not like wearing Caroline's clothes. That she knew would make her feel inexpressibly uneasy and guilty at fortune so negatively won. M told her the lock-up garage was at the end of the mews, and they found a small bunch of car keys in Caroline's desk.

'Jolly lucky there hasn't been a burglary in here,' Petra muttered as she made once more for the stairs.

'Oh no dear! Such a nice area.' M was shocked and Petra did not feel like arguing with her.

There were six garages which looked as if they had been converted from old loose boxes – an appropriate mark of the change of the times thought Petra as she started fitting the smallest of the three keys into the locks to try to discover which was Caroline's.

'I say, are you new here?' A pretty, loose-limbed, delicate-looking girl with big brown eyes and flat locks of shiny dark brown hair which fell thickly around her face stood smiling at her. Petra jumped, guiltily aware that it looked as if she was trying to break into the garages.

'Well no – that is I'm trying to work out which garage belonged to my sister. Caroline Appleton. I've come up to try to sort out her things – she lived in that house there.' Petra pointed back at the white house with the green shutters. 'And now we're looking for her car.'

164

'We?'

The girl was thickly made up, Petra realized, disliking the twisted smile on her thick loose lips. She replied a little curtly, resenting the explanation: 'Yes. My mother and I. We've both come up to sort out Caroline's things. Look, I'm sorry – did you know her?'

'Know Caro? Oh yes!' The girl was still smiling strangely and Petra started to feel a little flustered. She even wondered if this girl with her slow deep voice and overstated features was perhaps a little touched, a bit mentally disturbed. She stood there, still smiling directly at Petra, head on one side and a bright hard look in her eyes.

'Well, could you tell me which is her garage?'

The girl said nothing, and Petra realized that perhaps she knew nothing of Caroline's death. All Caroline's friends, and she supposed this creature must have been one, were presumably used to long periods of absence when she was away on jobs for weeks at a time. So she said a little more gently: 'Look, Caroline was killed nine weeks ago when she went to India. There was an accident. Did you know?'

'Oh, yes.'

Petra stared hard at the smiling girl who stood with awkward grace; one long leg loosely stuck out at an angle with the heel of her rather large foot, shod in flat black pumps, resting on the cobbles, toes pointing away from the ground. One arm was curved across her body, the broad hand with its delicately polished fingernails tapping the opposite thigh while her left hand was pushed into her waist so that her elbow stuck out in a sharp point. Her big bony wrist pushed below the cuff of the loose tunic top which she wore.

Suddenly the creature laughed and Petra jumped. 'Look, there's Caro's garage – at the end there. See it's got a three on it, same as her front door. What are you doing with her house? Did she leave it to you?'

Petra's first reaction to this question was that it was certainly not this girl's business to be asking about family affairs, but it reminded her of her own doubts about M's firm assumption that there was no will. She decided to have a good look

165

through the desk when she had found the car. So she just said: 'Oh, there's a lot to sort out, yet.'

'And the car! Do tell, are you having the car?' The girl struck an absurd pose, giving a sort of coy skip and a jump, still with that stupid smile on her face, and Petra began to feel angry.

'Look, I don't know yet. I said that there is a lot to be sorted out. Did you say it was in that garage. Are you sure?'

'Oh yes, quite sure,' said Joey, who had earlier that morning backed the car into the garage and locked the door with the set of duplicate keys that he had found in Caroline's bedroom. Petra was now busily fitting the key into the lock and he stood there trying hard to remember if he had left any sign in the house of his occupation. He thought not. He had known that his precarious ownership could not last and it seemed now that it must be over. 'Ah well,' he thought and he turned abruptly on his heel and walked, whistling loudly through his teeth, out of the mews.

Petra had swung the door up and over and she turned round just as he was disappearing through the arched entrance. She shrugged and turned back to the car, a dusky blue one-year-old MG Midget. She thought of the old Hillman that she and Philip shared and she knew that she would be too weak to refuse this little sports car. She opened the driver's door, stepped in and turned the ignition key. It started first go and she carefully drove it out and parked it by Caroline's front door. She sat there for a minute or two, fiddling with the switches, testing the lights, the indicators, not wanting to go back into the house and upstairs to M. For some reason she felt an urgent desire to confess, to tell M about the three days she had spent here with Henry, fourteen years ago. Entering her dead sister's house was like going into church. Petra felt it had become hallowed, a sort of shrine to Caroline (was this because she had never seen her sister there, yet was conscious the whole time of Caroline's dominating presence?). She felt she dare not go in without making a clean breast of things. She had left the front door on the latch and she made up her mind, rushed in and bounded up the stairs, leaping three steps at a time.

166

'M!' she shouted. 'All right?'

M was sitting at Caroline's desk in the dining room, sorting through a small heap of papers with her right hand. Her left fist was tightly clenched and held firmly on top of a large glossy, coloured booklet. She turned round and Petra failed to notice the distress in her eyes.

'M, look, I want to tell you something.' Petra was flushed and felt near to tears. 'This isn't the first time I've been here, in Caroline's house. I stayed here once when she was away. When I left university. I stayed here for three days before I came home. Henry, Caroline's friend, was here too. He often stayed here.' Petra stood in front of her mother, panting a little because of her frantic dash up the stairs and because of the burden of the confession. M still looked vague.

'Oh, really dear? Well, that was a long time ago now, wasn't it? I expect the break did you good. You weren't very well then, were you, if I remember.'

Petra felt silly and crestfallen. M was quite right; it did not matter at all, and yet the weight of the deception had been with her since they had set out for London that morning. What on earth did it matter?

'I'll go and make some more tea,' she said quietly, and was about to walk through to the kitchen when she saw a tear fall onto M's clenched left fist. Petra knew that this was nothing to do with her silly confession. M had been sitting here, at Caroline's desk, looking at little personal things – restaurant bills, notes with times and addresses jotted down, theatre programmes, perhaps even letters – and it was more than she could bear. Petra put her hands onto M's dejected shoulders and felt her mother's already tense muscles tighten up still more against the touch.

'Look, M,' she said gently, 'it's no good bottling it all up – you must cry for Caroline. It's no good being business like and pretending that it hasn't happened, because it has. She wouldn't want to see you all screwed up because of her.'

M, who was crying now, weeping silently and copiously, nodded and sniffed. Petra rushed into the bathroom and came back with a box of tissues. She pulled a chair out from the dining table and sat down by her mother, offering the tissues awkwardly. M took one and blew her nose. It was terrible to see her cry – Petra could not remember seeing her in this sort of distress ever before. Through the sobs, which were now audible, M was trying to speak. Petra squeezed her wet hand and listened.

'She was . . . what you said . . . all screwed up. Caroline.'

'Oh no, M.' Petra was shocked. 'I'm sure you're wrong.'

'You didn't know her, Petra.' The words were tumbling out quickly now. 'You didn't know her at all. She was very lonely, I'm sure she was, and she felt that no one loved her, only us and I don't think we counted. She had such peculiar friends.' M sobbed loudly now, thinking of the odd people who had clustered around Caroline's table in that horrible restaurant.

'She had Henry,' Petra told her.

'Henry?'

'Yes. You remember – he came to us with Caroline that Christmas. He was a special friend and they were very fond of each other. I'm sure they always stayed in touch. He had a key to the flat, at least he used to, and he used to look after Caroline.' (At this moment Henry was confronting a worried and bewildered Philip on the village playing fields in Coombe, but Petra fixed him, in her mind, somewhere in an apartment in New York.)

'Oh him!' M's distress could not disguise her scorn. 'I know who you mean. But Petra, he was no good. He was a – well, he was a homosexual, you know.'

'I know all that!' Petra remembered fancying herself in love with Henry and the awful desolation when Caroline had mocked her with his homosexuality. 'But they were still very good friends. I wonder where he is now. Funny he never wrote when Caroline was killed.'

M's fists started to clench and unclench as she thought of the circumstances of her younger daughter's death. The glossy travel brochure under her left fist fell to the floor and Petra bent to pick it up. She glanced at the picture of snowy cloud swathed mountain peaks, blue-white in the reflected sunlight, and she knew that it was this picture that had released M's long overdue tears.

M's hands lay helplessly on the desk; they were soft and white and a little plump, the creased flesh on her pointed fingers just bulging over the thin gold wedding ring on her left hand. Each oval nail was rounded to the same length so that M's fingers were tipped with perfect white crescents. Petra put one of her own hands over M's. It felt like holding a captive animal, shaking, but submissive and passive.

'Look, M.' She was trying to choose her words carefully. 'I think that Caroline wouldn't have lived any other way. I never saw her much after we left school but she was just the same when we were young. Don't you remember? She would always do exactly as she wanted and that's how she carried on. Even if she was wrong about things you always felt she'd got it right because she was so certain. I don't suppose she would have married and had children if that's what you are worried about; she just wasn't that sort of a person.'

'But that doesn't mean that she had to die like that!' M's hand was fluttering now, agitated. 'If only there was something left. We haven't even a grave to visit, we can't take flowers. There's just nothing.'

Petra did not know what to say to this. The part of the Himalayas in which the little aeroplane taking Caroline and a party of thirty-two other tourists on a sightseeing trip had come down was a wild and inaccessible region, desolate and remote even in that strange, high place. No one knew, and there was no reason why they should ever discover, what had really happened. There had been a garbled distress call back to the airfield where the twin-engined propeller-driven plane was based and from where it flew its daily complement of tourists, and that was that. No one had been able to pinpoint the site of the crash and no wreckage or bodies had been found. Caroline had been wiped out by a whim of the weather or by mechanical failure or a terrible mistake on the part of the pilot, and her body was probably lying in some frozen rocky valley, or buried deep beneath the ever-changing drifts of snow which washed over the unexplored mountainsides. Perhaps

169

one day her bones would be found by some mountaineer or explorer, but that was unlikely. M and Daddy had at first wanted to rush out to Nepal to glean some clues, to pay some sort of hopeless tribute to their younger daughter, but in the end they both decided it would be far too upsetting and could serve no useful purpose.

The most terrible thing about the whole business, in their eyes, had been the fact that they had not known until the day after the plane crash that Caroline had even left London. The news of the little aeroplane's failure to return to base (with thirty-three British tourists on board, the television news-caster had said) had been transmitted one evening in early May. How dreadful, poor things, M had said, wishing she had managed to leave the room before it came on. She thought, guiltily and happily, of those bare rocky frozen mountains with the constant whistling of the thin wind and of her own nice warm bed. The next morning she was confounded by a postcard from Caroline, postmarked Delhi and showing a picture of a white tiger nursing its cubs. 'Having holiday of a lifetime here in India. All rather a rush, didn't have time to inform,' it said in an uncharacteristic mixture of gushing prose and curt telegraph language. M and Daddy exclaimed over the card and changed Caroline's location in their minds from London to India, surrounding her with exotic temples and street bazaars instead of parking meters and London stone. M rang Petra to say, what do you think, what next, Caroline's gone off to India without telling us. When she put down the receiver she thought, with a fear that chilled every bit of her, of the bodies lying lost on the icy mountainside.

'Don't be so silly, dear,' said Tom at lunchtime when she told her fear. 'That card was from Delhi. The plane crashed in the Himalayas. There cannot possibly be any connection.' M rushed to get the card and tried to read the postmark, but could not. She went to all the travel agents that afternoon and spent the evening studying brochures about trips to India. Nearly all of them included a visit to the Himalayas. M knew with a certainty that would listen to no reason that Caroline had been on the aeroplane that had burst itself open on the jagged,

170

unforgiving rock. When the telephone call came through from some official in London, two evenings after the fatal television broadcast and one day after Caroline's postcard, M took it quite calmly. She had prepared herself for it.

Now the picture on this brochure, the one that Caroline must have studied before she left the safety of her house in London, showed the mountains, smiling and sun-tipped, soft snow cushioning the hard rock and gentle green valleys promising happy landings. M, who always tried to see life in these terms, as coloured pictures in glossy brochures, was feeling the darkness and the pain hidden by the smiling sun and concealed by the soft snow and welcoming greenery. Petra could not comfort her now, she knew that M must be left alone, so she picked up the notepad and pencil lying on the desk top and went downstairs to the little-used sitting room to start her inventory.

Petra, carefully driving back from London in the small blue sports car that had been Caroline's and now belonged to her, was wondering if she should be glad that she had the car, or guilty because there was still no aching void where Caroline should have been. She shuddered and closed her eyes wincingly hard, as she thought of M's desolation in the cold house. There was M now, in front, driving as efficiently as usual, steering her red car through the London traffic, making for the motorway with Petra following close behind, concentrating hard on not getting lost, and still wondering how M could cope the way she did – with all her doing rather than feeling. Or did she feel just as much as everyone else, controlling herself so well that the action, the doing, came naturally as a cover for the suppressed feeling? Petra, herself so floored by any emotional upset that she was incapable of carrying out the simplest action that involved anyone but herself, marvelled at her mother's strength of will, at the same time despising her for it, looking at the resolution as some kind of spiritual weakness.

As she compared her own weaknesses with those that she suspected her mother possessed, she lost her concentration on the road, and the little red car in front nipped smartly onto the first exit of a roundabout where cars converged from all directions, jockeying for position. Petra, realizing that she was now in the wrong lane to follow, was swept away and had to drive right round. By the time she took the correct exit, M was out of sight.

'Damn!' shouted Petra, furiously, out loud, for some curious reason feeling extremely sorry for herself. 'Damn, damn, DAMN!' and she burst into tears of self-pity, driving ferociously, squinting through tear-blurred eyes, steering her sister's car onto the motorway.

Later, when she was safely out of London and back on the road in the blue sports car, she wondered why Caroline had gone off to India in such a hurry. It suddenly occurred to her that her sister would not have been alone. If she had wanted a relaxing holiday she would have taken a properly planned cruise or booked in at some luxury hotel in a sunny part of the world. Not even Caroline would have gone to India, a place for sightseeing and storing up images, on her own. She must have gone with a friend. Petra's mind raced over the possibilities and she thought that Caroline must have fallen in love with someone. Deciding on the spur of the moment to go to India, not telling anyone, that was the sort of thing you did when you were in love. She wondered if this theory would make M feel any better.

When she pulled into the gravelled driveway M's car was already there, parked neatly by the wall of the house. Petra reached over to the little shelf behind the front seats and picked up her handbag. There was a small plaid travelling rug in the back and she straightened this and pulled up a box of tissues which had fallen behind the passenger seat. She reached across and felt in the pocket of the passenger door and found an A to Z of London and a couple of maps of East Anglia. In the pocket of her door, the driver's door, was a long white envelope, thick and expensive paper, fresh-looking. It had Caroline's name typed on the outside and was sealed. Petra held it for a minute and then looked up towards the house to see if she was being watched from the windows. There was no sign of M or Daddy so she slowly opened the flap and pulled

172

out a document. When she had unfolded the long piece of paper, which was a photocopy of the original, she sat very still as she carefully read through the long-winded legal phrases. Then she folded it up again and slowly got out of the car, carefully locking the door.

What on earth was Daddy going to say when she showed him Caroline's will and told him that everything had been left to Henry?

Chapter Ten

Henry rolled over in bed and felt for his watch on the little table. He held it close to his short sighted eyes and worked out that he had slept for nearly ten hours. The thick curtains cut out the mid-morning light so he clicked the switch on the bedside lamp before remembering that there was no bulb in it. Slowly he moved his tongue round the inside of his mouth. It felt thick and furry and stuck to the roof with an unpleasant metallic taste. He groaned slightly in anticipation of what was to come and raised his head from the pillow, shaking it cautiously from side to side. Not too bad he thought. The back of his neck felt rather stiff but there was no serious ache in his temples. He still felt heavy and drowsy but he knew that he would have to get up soon to go to the lavatory. He wondered if the whole household was asleep (not the children surely?) or if they were considerately letting him stay in bed as long as possible. The bed was warm, comfortable, and he drifted in and out of waking images as he decided to get up and dress himself before looking for the bathroom.

He was used to waking early in his bright, east-facing New York apartment where he and Peter had had adjoining rooms. The strong light filtered through the thin blinds and he had known instantly on waking where he was, what he was to do that day and how their life, his and Peter's, was to be structured over the next few hours. But now hazy images chained him to his soft pillow. Philip carrying the sleeping Fiona upstairs last night; Peter carrying Caroline, also sleeping, tenderly from one room to another until she giggled and woke properly and they both looked with love and guilty tenderness at Henry, who was standing alone. He wondered if Caroline had ever stayed in this room in her sister's house. He guessed not; she had never mentioned a visit to Somerset. Then he remembered Philip's story of the night before, of Caroline and the witch, and he laughed to himself. Caroline must have been totally out of her depth, as she always was when any show of emotion was made and offered to her. She always coped, though, by being rude or overbearing, arrogant or indifferent, giving an impression of strength and complete superiority. But she suffered all the same and, Henry thought sadly, she had surrendered these ridiculous defences to Peter.

M, unable to face the dreadful fact of Caroline's death, squeezed her eyes tightly shut, shook her head and thought desperately about anything and everything else until the rhythm of her everyday life was restored. She could not overcome her grief by facing it. Henry, on the other hand, had done the opposite. He had been in America when the telephone call came and, after sitting and thinking for an hour or two, had packed a small suitcase and driven to a place of retreat; a large house in the middle of empty, fertile country. Inside the men led an orderly holy life of prayer and contemplation. One of Henry's boyhood friends had joined this order some years before and although he was no longer there, Henry still paid occasional visits to the old house. Now he was welcomed gravely and courteously and with total lack of curiosity. He was assigned a wooden cubicle in a room which contained three similar divisions. The room itself was made from a much larger area by means of a flimsy partition, yet despite the thin quality of the walls and the lack of carpets and rugs to muffle the noise of feet on the bare floors, there was no sense of intrusion. The people who visited this house did so to help themselves; to look for the cause of their sorrow within themselves.

Henry found a printed sheet bearing times of the offices of prayer and of meals, pinned squarely to the back of his cubicle door. A plain wooden cabinet stood by the bed and on it was a copy of the New Testament, but no reading lamp. Henry did not worry about this. No one asked him questions, no one attempted to preach to him. He spent hours sitting in his wooden stall, on his hard bed with its flat mattress and its plain white linen cover onto which was woven a complicated green cross. He sat there and opened his mind completely to his grief and to the memory of Peter, who had become lost to him not when the aeroplane crashed but when they both went to stay with Caroline at her house in London.

Henry went, at the appointed times, to the chapel, to pray with the brothers, but he prayed to Peter, not to God. He ate in the bare, echoing dining room because it was courteous to do so, and at the correct hours for exercise he walked in the grassy, tree-lined grounds. After two days the place became impregnated with his memory of Peter. The thin wooden walls of his cubicle, the long uncomfortable benches in the little chapel with its rough stone walls, the big hand-hewn wooden tables in the dining room, even the avenues of lime trees outside, all absorbed something of the intensity of Henry's contemplation, and they retained it so that he felt the breath of it everywhere, as he entered his bedroom-cubicle, the chapel and the refectory. He realized that he was trying to come to terms with the first loss, with the Peter who had left him for Caroline, and, once he knew this, the images started coming. Images of Caroline and Peter, side by side in that aeroplane, excited by the stupendous views of the mountains, the frozen valleys, the jagged icy pinnacles of forsaken rock, pointing to Heaven, the roof of the world. Caroline would have sat by the window and Peter would have leant across her to point at the blue shadow cast on the snow by a towering peak, a black rent in the empty land where a great chasm lurked.

Click! The images, Caroline laughing, Peter with a steady smile on his good-looking face, their cheeks just brushing so they tingled together as they bent their heads close to each other to look out of the little round window, came whole into Henry's mind and fixed themselves, frozen, there. The stewardess hurrying down the central aisle of the small plane

176

in response to a call from the pilot's cabin and the quick expression of unease on the two faces, still close together. Click! Henry saw them clearly, framed in his mental lens. He saw their hands twine; Caroline's long slim, ringless fingers with their short very white, rounded nails curling round Peter's brown, carefully manicured hands, tightening, tightening as the plane began its crazy plummet. Click! Those hands were frozen, fixed for ever in Henry's mind. And the last image was one that Henry saw the most clearly, even with his eyes wide open. It was of Peter's face, blue eyes resolute and steady, gazing ahead, accepting what fate was throwing at him whilst all around people screamed and wept and tore their clothes. Peter still holding tightly onto Caroline's hand, gazing ahead, smiling very faintly, blue eyes open wide. Henry accepted this last image of Peter as his own.

He could not see Caroline's face in the same clear way. Caroline who had been his friend, his partner in adversity, the person with whom he was wise against the rest of the world, had been completely lost to him when she fell in love. Henry had learnt to face Peter's death, guided by that image of a calm, wide-eyed smiling man facing the plummet to the hard ground. But the other still hurt, still bit into his soul. He felt the pain coming now and forced his head into the pillow while he looked at it until it passed.

'Come over with me this trip,' he had said to Peter that January morning in New York. 'I'll wire Caroline – she'll be happy to put you up, too.'

'I might just do that, Henry.' Peter had seemed slow and tired since Christmas. 'It's years since I was in England and I guess Caroline owes me a bit of hospitality.' Caroline had stayed with them several times on her visits to New York and the three of them had gone out, happy and uncomplicated, to bars, shows and restaurants. Peter, who was a partner in his father's real estate business, could afford a long holiday starting in February.

Henry normally travelled light. His heavy gear went on

ahead and he followed and caught up with it. He kept a wardrobe in New York but he bought clothes in all the countries he visited, which may have accounted for the eccentricities of his dress. But Peter, who liked formal arrangements, and whose life was ordered and meticulous and who could never wear brown suede shoes with a blue suit, or not open a door for a woman or refuse to say 'excuse me' if someone walked into him on the sidewalk, could not be so casual. So they decided to make a junket of it and travel by sea on a cruise liner with all the appropriate deck gear and cabin trunks.

Henry, normally as prosaic about travel as about all the mechanical functions of life, the process of getting from A to B, of performing the necessary rituals in order to make or do, found that he was enjoying the trip enormously and without reserve. Used to travelling swiftly, alone, glancing at sunsets only to assess their photographic qualities, swimming because he needed the exercise, eating with a book or a work schedule or a costing sheet on the table in front of him, he was at first amused at the pleasure Peter found in life on deck. But very soon he discovered the same intense enjoyment in the rituals of travel; at the steward's concern over their welfare, at the cups of hot soup brought out to them when they sat wrapped in plaid rugs on the chilly deck, at the stupendous beauty of the ever-changing patterns of sea and sky. Normally impatient to get the journey over and done with, so he could act on his arrival, he found that sharing the trip with Peter, making a ceremony out of the simplest parts of it, laughing at some of the passengers, making brief friendships with others, gave that voyage a special significance, took it out of ordinary time, made it into a fused sequence of days and nights that were precious and special and happy. He and Peter had lived together for many years and this holiday was a renewal, a complete episode for both of them, without any pressure or any suggestion that each was less than perfectly happy with himself and with the other.

Henry had telephoned Caroline from New York and she was expecting them both to stay. She also knew that Henry would be away for most of the first week or so, visiting historic houses and castles in the North.

Caroline opened the door when he pressed the bell. Peter was paying the taxi off and Henry, about to give her his usual friendly kiss on the cheek, was taken aback when she made a grimace and turned to race back up the stairs, shouting 'Come in!' as she did so. He assumed that she must have been speaking on the telephone or that the kettle was about to boil, but when he reached the living room she was pacing around with a tense little smile on her face.

'What's the trouble, Caro?' he said quickly. He recognized this mood, the restless dissatisfaction, the uneasy refusal to settle to anything. 'Are you working?' he asked when she appeared not to have heard his first question.

'Finished this morning,' she said without looking at him. 'They want me to do a job in Paris next week. Jewellery. Gold. I can't face it.'

Just then Peter's footsteps could be heard coming steadily up the stairs and Caroline made a tragic face at Henry, took two quick steps into her bedroom and shut the door firmly after her.

'Where's Caroline?' Peter, pleasant, friendly, open as always, grinned at Henry as he reached the top step.

'In there.' Henry indicated the bedroom. 'Her room. She's a bit out of sorts, it seems.'

'Oh dear!' Peter was genuinely concerned; he had an immense capacity for being sensitive about other people's feelings. He hated to make a nuisance of himself (he is, thought Henry, the only really self-effacing man I know). Now he was trying to pin down Caroline's malaise. 'You mean she's not well? She's sick? Because if that's so she's not going to want us around, or me, anyway. I'll go find another cab and check in at some hotel until she feels fit again. You stay and keep an eye on her and let me know when she's OK.'

Peter was already stooping to pick up his suitcase but Henry laid a hand on his arm. 'Hey, steady on. Don't be silly – she's only got a mood on. Happens all the time with Caroline. She'll shake out of it any time and I know she'd be very upset if you

179

left. Look.' Henry threw open the door of the spare room and guided Peter towards it. 'Both beds made up and ready for us.'

Peter carried his smart pigskin case with the gold initials P de B embossed on each side into the room and looked for a chair to lay it on. He still seemed worried.

'I didn't think that Caroline was the moody sort because she's always been such good fun. Are you sure she's happy about us both staying here? I mean, Henry, I'd hate to intrude.'

Henry laughed. 'If you could only see your face. Don't look so worried – Caroline won't turn nasty and start biting you if that's what is freaking you out. Tell you what, I'll treat us all to dinner out tonight and we can talk her out of it.'

The dining room at Isaac's was designed to give the impression that you were the guest of honour at a private dinner party in a very wealthy London mansion. Caroline, who had been there before, refused to be impressed but Peter found the contrast hard to assimilate, between the understated elegance of the room with its period furniture, its thick carpets and heavy curtains, spotless table linen and polished wood which reflected the dully gleaming silver, and his favourite (also expensive) New York restaurants.

'But it's so small Henry,' he kept protesting. 'And I can't tell the difference between the guests and the waitresses. They can't serve more than thirty people in an evening. Where's their profit?'

Henry looked at Caroline, who laughed for the first time that evening. She patted Peter on the hand. 'Does your menu have any prices marked on it, Peter? No, neither has mine. Henry's worrying about that – he's treating us tonight. I only hope his expense account will take the strain.'

They had finished their soup and Caroline cut into the glistening mound of thick white turbot which had just been set in front of her. She smiled again at Peter, a brilliant, flawless smile. 'I shouldn't imagine, though, that you've ever had to worry that much about the size of the bill, Peter – like most of the people here. Have you noticed how young we all are?' Still smiling, challenging Henry, she cut through the glazed, prawn and parsley scattered sauce into the close-grained white flesh of her fish.

It never occurred to Henry that Caroline was being rude to him. He inclined to her judgement. 'Yes, the young can make money quickly these days. You do, Caroline, you must admit; Peter's always had money, it's in the family. As for me, well, I spend other people's money.'

Peter was growing distressed at Henry's easy analysis of their financial standings. 'But really, Henry,' he protested. 'You can't say you don't know where your next meal is coming from and I'm sure that Caroline works very hard for her money. I do, too,' he added lamely. Then, before they could start to tease him about his wealth, a subject which never failed to embarrass him, he looked round curiously at the people sitting soberly at the polished silver-laden tables. 'Why are all these people rich – what do they do?'

Caroline shrugged. 'Media, advertising, television mostly. Some inherited wealth. See that girl over there with the blonde hair? The well-bred looking one? Well that dress didn't leave any change from five or six hundred quid – it's a one-off design. Kantos, I'd say. She's got a very wealthy father and her mother is now married to an even richer man. She's playing at being a journalist because she wants to feel experienced. The chap with her, the curly-haired one with the purple bow-tie, he looks a lot older wouldn't you say? He's on his third divorce, is in debt up to his eyeballs but still sponsors a motor racing team.'

Caroline bowed her head slightly as the man in question looked up and caught her eye and raised a hand in greeting. 'Did some work for him, once,' she muttered.

Henry, toying with his own bow-tie (how he enjoyed dressing up in a dinner jacket when he felt like it and he thought that his grey and shocking pink, hand-made silk bow-tie struck just the right, slightly bizarre note), was at first interested and then slightly alarmed to see the expression in Peter's clear grey eyes. He was staring at Caroline as though he had never seen her before. What was in that look? Admiration, yes (for what? – her undoubted beauty perhaps: Peter always

admired the flawless and most men gazed like this at Caroline);
but there was more than that. There was a question in the look;
an expression of interest, of wanting to know more, to be
given more. Henry had never seen Peter's expression so
animated and he thought that it suited him, cancelling out the
chinless, slightly vacant look that he was inclined to assume.

'Well tell me what you enjoy most about having money,'
Peter said to Caroline.

'Oh but I don't,' she replied, frowning a little. 'I mean I
don't have that much money, not in your league anyway.
What I have is invested well, I hope. My accountant sees to
that – early training paying off I suppose. You see in this
business you only have so many years before your earnings
start dwindling rather alarmingly. Only the young are
beautiful these days.' Peter started to protest but she went on
quickly: 'I started to earn my own living very young – I was
just sixteen when the first cheque came in and I thought it was
all a big joke. I never thought much about my career as such. It
just happened you see. It hadn't occurred to me I might be a
model, but when the offers came in it didn't occur to me to
turn them down. I couldn't wait to get away from my family,
to be completely independent and free from my parents and
my sister.

'I thought Petra might assert herself once. Remember,
Henry?' Caroline grinned at Henry, who was looking
thoughtful. She poured some mineral water into her glass.
'But she settled for the safe way, too. They don't like to think
too much about things, my family. Do you know I
remember, when I was about fourteen I suppose it was, we
had guests to dinner – someone they didn't know too well, a
friend of a friend – and it turned out that he did some voluntary
work for one of the children's societies. He started to talk
about some of the things he had seen. Not very pleasant dinner
conversation, I must admit. Slums with rats in the hall and shit
on the floor. Starving, neglected children with sores on their
faces, that sort of thing. No one said a word. M, that's my
mother, rushed out to the kitchen to check on the pudding and
my father simply looked at his plate and turned to Petra to ask

her what she'd been doing in school that afternoon. I don't know what the man thought. He got no response at all from us. That's the sort of family we are. Comfortable.'

She put down her knife and fork and sat back in her chair before looking carefully around the room; then she turned back to Peter. 'I'm sorry Peter, you were asking me about money. Well, I make enough for me. I don't depend at all on my family. I suppose I'm comfortable, too.'

Peter's cheeks were bright pink with excitement after Caroline had given so much of herself away. Henry, who had never heard her speak so positively of her family, was taken aback. Peter spoke first.

'But you're not comfortable Caroline. Not in the way you say your family is. You get depressed – thinking and worrying about things. Henry told me that you felt depressed earlier today, when we arrived. Caroline's blackness, he called it.'

Henry waited for the quick flash of Caroline's anger but she smiled instead. 'Why do you suppose that is?' she said. 'I sometimes wonder if it's because I have tried to struggle out of the mould and it doesn't suit me. I haven't achieved anything important or worthy with my lifestyle, any more than my family has with theirs. It's just a different sort of complacency, you see.'

'But what do you want to do about it?' Peter looked worried. 'Go out to Africa or India and look after starving children? Become a charity worker and visit old people? That sort of thing?'

Caroline lost her smile and her face set in stony lines. 'Don't be silly, Peter,' she said sharply. 'Even I'm not arrogant enough to think I could cope with that sort of life. What I'm trying to say is that I thought I had broken out of the family pattern by escaping from their house and doing this sort of work, but I find that I didn't escape or rather I didn't discover my own niche, the things I should have done. I don't suppose I ever will now. You don't know Petra, my sister. Henry does. She solved the problem by marrying and having children. I wonder if she feels that she's wasting her life.'

'She was certainly looking for something when I knew her,'

Henry interrupted. 'She didn't know what she wanted and I wonder if she would have recognized it if she'd found it. Perhaps it's a family trait, Caroline, like short sight and bad teeth – it's inherent in you girls to spend your whole life searching for fulfilment. Mind you, I think you are being extremely naïve if you think that no one else suffers in the same way. Most of the human race is infected with it.'

'But there are degrees, Henry,' Caroline replied carefully. 'Anyway, it can't be inherited. My parents are the most self-satisfied people I've ever met.'

'Perhaps you're reading them wrongly – or maybe it's slipped a generation. Genetics is a funny business,' Henry replied calmly.

Peter still seemed worried. 'I can't say that I've ever seen life in those terms, you know. If I'm right you are looking for a role, or even for a whole identity, and it seems to me that that kind of uncertainty comes from lack of confidence. If you're the kind of person who knows what he wants and where he's going, you don't need to look for something that you feel will protect you because you make your own protection. I don't see that you should feel like that, Caroline.'

Caroline laughed and put her hand over one of Peter's. Her fingers, long and slender, curled slowly round his square brown hand and she felt his knuckles tighten and then relax. She laughed again.

'You are nice, Peter. I don't feel like this all the time you know. Comes of living on my own I expect, and I'm probably talking rubbish. Do you know London?'

Peter shook his head, his hand still captive. 'No, not well.'

'I'm going to turn down this Paris job. I need a rest anyway. While Henry is poking around his old castles or whatever it is this time, I'll be your guide to the sights of the big city. We'll be tourists for a few days. Yes?'

Henry and Peter in the course of their long-standing relationship had had few arguments and there had been little sexual jealousy; they were used to being apart for long periods because of Henry's job and it seemed that they were set to march steadily forward into middle age, the respectability of

184

their liaison undiminished by its basis. So it was that Henry left London the following day in his blue, hired Audi quite relieved that Caroline and Peter seemed happy at being thrown into each other's company for the next three or four days. Caroline had shaken out of her black mood and seemed childishly pleased at the prospect of a few days 'on the loose', as she put it, in London with Peter.

Peter slapped Henry on the back as he climbed into the car. 'Take care, fellah!' he said, heartily and uncharacteristically.

When he returned to London the evening before he was due back, he let himself into the house with the key he always carried. As he reached the top of the stairs he dumped his small overnight case on the floor and, assuming that Caroline and Peter were out, he marched on through the dining area to his bedroom. The door of Caroline's bedroom was wide open and he came to a sudden halt as he glanced in and saw the two of them, Peter and Caroline, sitting up in bed, naked with only a very thin sheet covering very little of either of them. They looked at him with twin stares of apprehension mingled, he could see, with some sort of triumphant, rueful joy.

Henry, now out of bed in Petra's home at Coombe, bent over the little white washbasin on its old-fashioned pedestal and spat toothpaste water at the plughole.

'It doesn't signify,' he said aloud, and as he stared at himself in the spotted mirror his short-sighted eyes somehow transmuted his bleary reflection into that double image of happiness and love. And friendship. Caroline and Peter, she who had never been able to love and he who had never loved a woman since his mother's death, had, by some strange process, each recognized that bond and, in breaking it, had achieved a unity and strength together. That much was indisputable and he could find no way of denying it. And they had been so desperate that he should not feel excluded.

185

Perhaps that was why he had felt great sadness rather than jealousy.

Standing in his underpants at the basin with its crazed surface where the old glaze had cracked, Henry could shut his eyes and see the way that Caroline and Peter had both looked at him that evening. He had been shocked, knocked out of joint by the totally unexpected, looking for an obscure explanation when the simple, the obvious, was there in front of him. Then, just as he felt his knees buckle and he knew that he was about to sink to the floor, as his mind and body refused to tackle what he saw, both Caroline and Peter, sitting straight up in bed, eyes shining, stretched out their right hands to him in a single act. They pulled him towards them into that room by sheer strength of will and love and overflowing happiness which had to be shared. He tottered forward and sat weakly and primly on the foot of the bed, finding himself unable to look at either of them, shielding his eyes with the back of his hand as he did when the sun was too bright. They were both protected from his gaze by some sort of golden warmth, a radiance of love and strength which he felt made them powerful and more than human.

'Oh, Henry!' was all that Caroline could say, with a tenderness in her voice that he had never heard before, her eyes glowing and her hand reaching out to him. His brain refused to accept what his eyes had registered. Peter would not be in bed with any woman. Peter could not feel that sort of tenderness with a woman. The whole scene was so impossible, the obvious could not enter into it. Caroline's 'Oh, Henry' echoed through his slowly working mind until suddenly he knew he had to accept what he saw or lose everything. He felt himself becoming defensive, as if he had been used (although he could not work out in what way this was so), but he could not bring himself to appear mean, petulant, to these two who clearly wanted to include him in their radiant circle of warmth. He smiled at the wall behind their heads and staggered out of the room to pick up his bag, which was lying at the top of the stairs. Henry stared at it in a daze. It seemed incredible that it should still be there in the same state – was it five minutes before that he had carelessly dropped it on the floor, or several hours? He could not tell. It was as if he had stepped in and out of another dimension and life should not be the same. Then he bent to the bag and started frantically to pull at the thick white zip fastener. He must get back to that room, to that dimension. The feelings that were on a high plateau now must be nourished and sustained. He pulled an almost-full bottle of twelve-year-old malt whisky out of the middle of the bag and carried it back in triumph to the bedroom-shrine.

In their New York home Henry and Peter lived equably, but if it had come to any sort of a showdown Peter would have admitted that Henry was the senior partner in the arrangement. It is a fact that there generally is a senior partner, although a reluctance always to admit this cloaks the truth. But now Henry knew that the position had changed and Peter was radiantly and indisputably in charge. He accepted the tribute of the bottle with a modesty that Henry knew was akin to the action of a king or a president accepting gifts from a subject. Caroline, who hated whisky, was gracious enough too to take a sip, and Henry, when the bottle reached him, took an enormous gulp and another, so that the thin amber liquid gurgled down his throat and some dribbled onto his chin. It occurred to him that apart from Caroline's 'Oh, Henry!' not a word had been spoken. How long had he been in this room? – his sense of time was still confused, hazy. He did not know. He looked at Peter, smiling, in control, upright, fingering the bottle gently before he took his third or fourth swig, he gazed at Caroline's dark hair draped like black silk over her shoulders, her breasts so perfect that they seemed entirely unremarkable (or perhaps it's because I'm a bloody queer I don't feel startled by the sight of Caroline with nothing on, thought Henry gloomily). Caroline just sniffed at the whisky now when it was passed to her, a long, deep, sensuous testing of the liquid, and she turned to smile at Peter before passing the bottle on to Henry, who took another long rippling gulp, tipping his head back, noting with surprise that the bottle was almost empty.

Suddenly Henry the upright, Henry the arbiter, had felt that his friends, righteous and perfect in the shell of their new love, were about to stand up and judge him. What was worse, they were going to find him wanting, find him far less than perfect. As the unworthy cannot bear the gaze of God, as the human eye cannot look into the eye of the sun, Henry could no longer face this tremendous force. In his dazed state emotion overcame all reason and, while Peter and Caroline grew to giant size to occupy his mind, he, Henry, dwindled to nothing. He couldn't bear it. He thrust the bottle at Peter, pointing at the last eighth of an inch, making false smiles with his mouth and deprecating gestures with his hands. He could not stand judgement and he thought as he left the room that he could hear ringing laughter, the sort of laughter that comes from a clear conscience and a supreme confidence, the laughter of gods – but he could have been mistaken.

Now, as he pulled his clothes on (blue canvas trousers and a dark blue and white striped sailor's top today), he wondered again about his memory of those last days at the flat. Had he and Peter spoken together alone after the scene in Caroline's bedroom? He could not remember. Surely they must have done, but what had they said? He could invent conversations but none of them rang true. He remembered Caroline, excited, telling him that she and Peter were going to India and he remembered Peter coming into the room and walking over to Caroline, siding with her. 'Come with us, Henry,' he had said (had challenged?), and the three of them had laughed.

Henry prepared to go downstairs and he decided, for the thousandth time, that none of this mattered, this could not have been what hurt him, none of these memories haunted him. But he closed his eyes and shuddered as he saw again, frame by frame and in slow motion, in clear photographic detail, the tiny porthole window of the aeroplane with the images outside, the snow and the rock and the sky, becoming crazily jumbled and blurred as the frail machine spun towards the heavy earth. He saw Peter, strong and smiling, and he saw Caroline wide-eyed and scared. He saw their hands, clasping, closing together, joined in death. That was the image which persisted.

Chapter Eleven

'I'm sorry, Philip, I didn't hear that – what on earth do you mean? Please just listen for a minute, please. I'm trying to tell you about yesterday. The most incredible thing – but that was at the end of it all. M and I went up to the house just as we planned except M kept nearly getting into a state – you know – which isn't like her at all. She nearly broke down at one point. What? Yes, but she was OK. It's very pretty you know, a mews house, and when we got inside she had the feeling that there was someone else living there. It was all rather weird. Of course there wasn't.'

Philip, still in his pyjamas and dressing gown, scratched his head, which hurt, and sighed. He wondered if Henry was awake yet and if he had a hangover too.

'Did you say there was someone else there?'

'No – this line's very bad. Of course there wasn't. At least I don't think so.'

'Perhaps someone had been in – burglars. After all it's been shut up for months now, it's an obvious target.'

'Oh no – it was all too tidy. It doesn't look as if anything's been taken, although I suppose we've got no idea of what was there. But there was no mess, nothing forced. Burglars generally leave the place in a mess, don't they? But that's not the point, Philip. You know M and Daddy want to give me most of Caroline's stuff? Well she's gone and left it all to someone else!'

'Really?' Philip stopped scratching and yawning. It had not occurred to him that there might be a will. He had not made one himself; in fact he had not even thought about it. Perhaps he ought to, but surely it was not the sort of thing that someone like Caroline would have done?

'You mean she left a will? You found it?'

'Yes, in her car. I drove it back from London yesterday and when I'd got to M's and I was getting out of the car I found this long white envelope in the door pocket. Her will. She's left everything to Henry Sicardi and M and Daddy are furious.'

'What! Henry who?' Philip wished his head would stop hurting and tried to sort this out. He didn't think for a moment of the Henry who was cleaning his teeth and staring at the cracked glaze in the basin upstairs.

'Henry Sicardi – he's a photographer but you don't know him and I can hardly believe it and it took me some time to work out that it was Henry because I didn't know his surname before. But Caroline brought him home once or twice and then I met him again when I left university.'

Petra was just going to tell Philip more about Henry but he had suddenly made the connection. 'But he's here! Henry Sicardi is upstairs in the spare room. He met us at the cricket match yesterday and he stayed here last night.'

'Can't be him. You don't know him. I'm talking about one of Caroline's friends. Who's staying with you – what do you mean?'

'I just told you.' Philip was now aware of Henry moving about upstairs so he automatically lowered his voice. 'That bloke Henry. He is here. Bald chap, tall, with odd clothes and little gold-rimmed glasses. Sounds a bit American and he talks in a finicky sort of way. He said he knew you.'

'A long time ago.' Petra was trying to gather her thoughts into some sort of coherent order. 'That does sound like Henry. Funny, I never knew his surname before, but Caroline makes it quite clear in her will that it's him.'

'Was he her boyfriend? I thought so you know – something he said last night about losing someone and he tried to pretend it wasn't Caroline, because we were talking about her, but I thought aha! There's something here.'

Petra did not know what to say. Philip sounded, for him,

very animated. 'No, you've got it wrong. They were just very good friends, really.'

'Oh?'

Philip clearly did not believe her, but she could not go into the true nature of the friendship and of Henry's homosexuality, not on the telephone. 'Look, Philip – don't, whatever you do, say anything to him, will you. Please. I'll be home this afternoon, or early evening anyway, and we can discuss it then.'

When Petra put the telephone down, she realized that she had not asked Philip why Henry was at Coombe or how he had discovered her address. But she accepted it. Caroline's death, the journey to London with M, her conversation with the bony, big-limbed girl and the discovery of Caroline's will, all seemed part of some plan, a corner of some gigantic jigsaw puzzle which was slowly being fitted together. Daddy was still sulking over the will, and Petra realized that the main part of the upset was that he had not included it in his calculations, had not reckoned on it. He pretended that he could not remember Henry at all, and she could see that he was already thinking of contesting the document. M still could not believe in it. Although she and Petra both felt wrung out on Saturday night, she had prepared a proper evening meal which they ate at the polished dining table. Petra and M cleared away afterwards while Daddy disappeared into his study to take a proper look at the will – which seemed, to his disappointment, to be properly drawn up by what appeared to be a respectable firm of solicitors. He supposed that they held the original.

'You know, dear, I shouldn't be at all surprised if she was influenced in some way to make this will,' said M darkly as she handed Petra a plate to dry. 'We don't know anything about this man, after all. I can't see why she should leave her house – and all those clothes for goodness sake – to someone we don't know. And your car.'

Petra, carefully drying a glass, found herself smiling. 'Well, it's not my car now, I know, but I think I'll use it to get myself home tomorrow. After all, nothing's really been sorted out and I don't suppose Henry would mind. He's got his own car

192

anyway, I should think.' She had told M earlier what she knew of Henry, but M had refused to listen, preferring to think of him as an adventurer, a villain who had forced Caroline to sign the will.

Now, as she drove back to Coombe, feeling strangely lighthearted, she tried to imagine the circumstances of Caroline drawing up the will. She must have made an appointment to see a solicitor, have turned up at his office with a briefcase full of documents, deeds, details of her investments and assets. There was no doubt that her life had been well ordered in that respect; even Daddy had grunted approvingly when he saw from the will how her affairs were arranged. He had stopped handling Caroline's money himself several years before, as they had both felt it would be more convenient if another firm, a London company used to dealing with tax problems, was used.

So Caroline, smartly dressed no doubt, had turned up at the lawyer's office – alone or with Henry? Petra found herself wondering yet again if Henry knew of the will. Surely Caroline must have told him. Or did you not tell people? Petra did not know, and she could see that it could be an embarrassing point. She pictured Henry at home and wondered what she would say to him and how she would tell him. Philip had seemed to think Henry was all right, which was strange as he was usually very suspicious of anyone who was out of the ordinary. She tried to imagine the Henry she remembered, sitting down at the pub with Philip, side by side, drinking beer and discussing the sports pages of the newspaper, but she could not concentrate on the image.

She swung the wheel to turn the car up a long sweeping bend which fringed a steep meadow pasture, dotted with huge oak trees and tiny black blobs which she decided were sheep. The road straightened along a ridge crowned with a semicircle of fine trees in full summer leaf – beech, she thought. The sight of the sheep and the trees, the hot sun and the speed of the car filled her with exhilaration, and she suddenly burst out singing at the top of her voice, tapping her fingers on the steering wheel. Old hymns, which she used to sing in assembly at school, half-remembered with their stirring rhythmic tunes, came pouring out. She felt elated, capable of doing anything. Plans, projects for the future, came rushing and tumbling through her mind.

'Onward Christian soldiers,' she bellowed, thinking about the heap of old bits of patchwork she would sort out and assemble into a quilt for Fiona's bed. Perhaps she would book a holiday in France next year. A family holiday and they would save up hard for it. They would rent a *gîte* in Brittany or even in the South where it was hot, and she would enrol in French conversation classes during the winter evenings so that she would be fairly fluent by the time they went. 'I was always quite good at French at school,' she thought. She changed down to persuade the car to speed up a steepish hill. The meadows on either side had not been cut or grazed and the yellow-green grass was studded and starred with the blue and pink and orange and white of midsummer flowers all gently bending together as a ripple of wind pressed against them like the brush of an invisible hand.

'With the cross of Jeeeeesus, going on before,' she concluded triumphantly, her foot hard on the accelerator, thinking of the books that she must sit down and read – a planned programme of reading perhaps, like the one Scott Fitzgerald drew up for Sheila Graham. She felt excited as she thought of the difficulty of some of the books which would be on her list, of their importance.

And there was the garden – that needed a lot of work. Visions of the pictures she had seen of gardens in magazines and books grew in her mind. She would dig and plant and weed and know the names of the plants and the varieties. She would help William with his reading, teach him his letters, and she and Dan would go out looking for wild flowers together. Petra drove on fast and happily as the hot afternoon sun gave a still radiance to the rolling landscape and made the inside of the little blue sports car bright with its warm promise.

'You look like a sailor.'

'No, I don't. Sailors walk like this.' Henry speeded up his walk along the wide grassy verge by the playing field to a ridiculous rolling gait which made him feel dizzy.

'Do they really?' Dan sounded doubtful, but then he shrieked with laughter. 'Oh, I see! I see. You mean they get used to balancing at sea when it's all rough and then they can't walk straight when they get home. I don't think I've ever met a sailor. There's a picture of one in my history book and he's wearing a jersey like yours. Did you buy it from a sailor?'

'No, I'm afraid not. But I came over from America earlier this year in a boat, a liner, and there were lots of sailors on that. But the passengers wore stripy jumpers and the sailors didn't.' Henry could not work out if Dan was just being polite or if he was genuinely interested in him. He had agreed to walk down to Frederic's house with the child with the news that the flower was a musk mallow.

'Do you know my Mummy?'

'Well, I used to know her, a long time ago.'

'She's coming home this afternoon, Daddy says. Does she know you're here?'

'I don't think so.' Philip, puzzled and a little suspicious now about Henry and the reasons for his visit, had not mentioned the phone call from Petra earlier in the morning. Henry surprised himself by looking forward with a great deal of pleasure to Petra's homecoming. He wondered if she had found any clue at the house to Caroline's love affair with Peter. He had not been near the place since he had learnt of the deaths, although he still kept his key.

'You knew my Aunty Caroline didn't you?' Dan, used to going for walks with adults, took hold of Henry's hand as they stepped off the verge to walk past a gateway. 'Was she a friend of yours? Mummy says she was killed in an accident but I know she was in a plane crash. I heard Daddy say so. Does it hurt to be killed in a plane crash?'

'No, no. I don't think so.' Henry tried to sound soothing but he knew that the images, never very far away, were there again.

'If you get killed in a plane crash do you get all smashed up like the plane?'

Dan was clearly not a bloodthirsty or ghoulish child by nature, and Henry took a deep breath as he tried to understand that the boy had probably been worrying a great deal over the accident. He had possibly formed a very clear picture in his mind of the crash and of Caroline's death. Henry remembered that when, as a child, he had heard his parents talk of a relative who had broken her leg he had had an unshakeable mental image of a leg snapped cleanly in two, with a shining white bone surrounded by neatly cut purple red flesh, ringed like the inside of a tree trunk.

'I'm sure your Aunt Caroline didn't feel any hurt,' he lied to the child, wondering, as always, if any of the passengers had survived for minutes, hours, days even, before they died of their injuries and of the appalling cold.

'I've never known a dead person before,' said Dan, complacent now. 'I hope the bee man is in because he might show you his bees – oh look Henry, do you know what that is – do you know?'

Henry gaped as Dan pointed in a frenzy of excitement to a large black homogeneous mass stuck crazily to the branches of a tree in the front of Frederic's garden. He gazed in amazement at the thing, which seemed alive and was continually moving while retaining the same oval shape. It was like some overblown exotic fruit dangling grotesquely among the swelling green apples on the tree.

'I know – I know! We saw one the other day. We helped him with it. It's a swarm! His bees. Mummy helped him and they stung her on her knee. Henry, we must go and tell him because he said that you mustn't lose a swarm. Come on, let's go and find him!'

Henry stared uneasily at the moving crawling mass of bees in incongruous collaboration with the apple tree. What, he wondered, was it like to be an insect at the centre of that swarm? But Dan, so excited that all his previous worries about Caroline and her death were clearly forgotten, was tugging at his hand, pulling him through the gate, into the garden, round the side of the house.

'Hang on Dan! I guess we'd better knock at the door first.'

'No – he's always round the back. By the bees. Come on.'

But Henry, who had already had some feeling about Frederic's eccentricity planted in his mind by Dan's chatter about him, insisted on knocking first of all at the wooden front door of the bungalow. No one came so there was nothing for it but to follow Dan, who was still clutching his wilting mallow, round to the little garden at the back.

The first thing that struck Henry was the peace and stillness. Moving forwards where the place was overhung with green leafy branches and drenched with the scent of flowers was like stepping into a green sacred square. Dan, awed by the sense of quiet and by the dim, tree-filtered light, was standing by the row of hives, looking towards the grassy bank at the other side of the square. He turned and looked back at Henry and then pointed, unsure of himself, at the bank.

'He's there, Henry,' he whispered. 'The bee man. But I think he's asleep.'

Henry, his mind still full of death, of Caroline's death and of Peter's, knew almost before he had looked, that Frederic was not asleep. He did not stop to think but, holding firmly onto Dan's hand, he walked steadily, the boy beside him, up to the long rope-like body which embraced the grass and the earth. Dan was silent, still in awe of the place and overcome by the solemnity of Henry's manner. Henry dropped the child's hand and, stooping carefully and precisely, he lifted Frederic's bony awkward arm from its curious cradling position on the mound. It was cold and felt like thick rubber. Just as carefully, he allowed it to drop, and then he ran his hand down the back of the old man's head and neck.

Frederic's face, buried in the dark grass, was not visible and the limp body seemed at one with the peace and other-worldliness of the place. Henry thought of his first instinct to call the garden a shrine and he shrugged mentally. He turned to Dan, who was standing like a ramrod, very upright,

197

breathing quickly, his mouth open and his hands balled into tight fists.

'He's dead isn't he, Henry?' said the boy. 'I thought he was asleep. Why is he dead?'

'He was an old man. We all have to die you know, Dan,' said Henry gently, worried now about exposing the child to the most inevitable and the most frightening of all human experiences. 'Wasn't this his favourite place?'

'Like Aunty Caroline – is this what happened to Aunty Caroline?' said Dan, ignoring the observation and pointing now at Frederic, whose thin body was fused with the earth.

'Oh yes. Yes, he's dead like Caroline,' said Henry, in pain and relief. Dan unclenched his left fist and the crumpled mallow, withered to a tired pink and green scrap, fell unnoticed to the ground. He gave a gulp and a sob and pointed to a patch of flowers a few feet away from Frederic's head.

'Look – those are the flowers, Henry, see, those pink ones. I never told him what they were.' Henry said nothing but suddenly Dan's expression changed.

'The bees!' he shouted. 'We've got to get those bees down for him. It's very important – he said it was, last time. We must do it for him, Henry, we must.' Dan's face was dark and closed and urgent and he stared intently at Henry, who shuddered with horror at the thought of the swarming, crawling mass, units of thoughtless life making a terrifying whole. He could not do it. Then he looked again at the child.

'How old are you, Dan?' he asked gently.

'I'm nearly seven. I shall be seven in two weeks and three days. I know how to get the bees. He showed us before and Mummy helped. We need a basket thing to catch them in. We must do it, Henry – you can reach the branch. They'd be lost otherwise. He said so. He said that when they swarm they rest for a little while and then they fly off to look for a new home. We must save them.'

Henry marvelled at the child's resolution. He grasped at a straw, though. Perhaps what Dan said was right – perhaps they had rested long enough and had disappeared already.

'The old man is dead you know, he won't worry about his

bees any more,' he said feebly, but the child looked at him with such incredulity that he stepped back. Recognizing the tension in Dan's face, he became resolute himself. He pushed away the creeping horror that the thought of the swarm inculcated in him and he tried to smile.

'OK Dan, what do we do?'

Two minutes later Dan and Henry were standing at the foot of the apple tree, gazing at the black swarm. It reminded Henry of a picture in a book that he must have read as a child, a version of 'Aladdin', with a smoky indistinct black mass wisping its way out of the lamp and about to resolve itself into something large and terrible.

Dan, trusting now, his confidence in Henry restored, held the oddly shaped wicker basket which they had found in the shed by the side of the house.

'You just hold this underneath them and shake them down from the branch. He said they can stay in the basket. We could put it down by the hives. That's what he does.'

The swarm was at the upper end of the branch near the tree. Henry, cautiously and with a shaking hand and dry mouth, stepped forward and gave the end of the dropping branch a gentle twitch to test the bees' reaction. It was worse than he expected. A deep resonant angry buzz which echoed round his head came from the very heart of the swarm, which shimmered at the edges as those clinging to the outside became dislodged and buzzed around to orient themselves again. Henry could not believe that the murmur was the joint voice of the bees and could not rid himself of the idea that in the middle of that heaving, crawling mass was one large and fearsome entity, directing the others with her angry voice and her terrible powers, commanding them above all to resist any attempts at capture. Blind panic weakened his legs as a couple of the dislodged bees hissed their way crazily around his head, and he dashed back a few paces, watched with amazement by Dan.

'Are you frightened, Henry? Of the bees?'

'Yes,' said Henry humbly. 'Yes, I'm afraid that I am.'

'They won't hurt you. He said that they won't hurt. They

only sting when they're frightened. Shall I stay here with them while you go and get Daddy? He won't be frightened and he's got a book about bees. He brought it home for Mummy.'

'No!' Henry was cross, not with the child but with the stupid irrational fear that was paralysing his legs, making his heart pound and his stomach flutter in sickening lurches. People were stung to death by bees sometimes, or was that hornets? Death by aeroplane, death by bees. He gave a short laugh and Dan looked worried.

'No, don't get your Dad. Of course we can do it, but I think we ought to wear some gloves, and perhaps something on our heads.'

'I think there were some in the shed.'

The bee veil, attached to an old hat and made of meshy black netting which swung around his face and down to his shoulders, made him feel better, because it looked professional, the thing to wear. There had been two of these, carefully folded, in the shed and Henry made Dan put one on as well as a pair of soft long white gloves which were much too big for the boy. Henry could not find another pair for himself, but there was a thick pair of old gardener's gloves which he pulled on and fastened at the wrist with some rubber bands he found in a tin on the shelf. The thought of getting stung on his fingers or his face made him prickle with fear.

They marched back to the tree, feeling very solemn. A clear duty, a ritual act, lay ahead and Henry felt that the robing, the dressing for the occasion, heightened the ceremony. He tried to be sensible and work out the logistics of the exercise, but Dan had clearly got it all sorted out.

'I can't knock them off, Henry because I can't reach, but if I hold the basket underneath like this it touches the bottom of the swarm. You just shake the branch and push them in – use that bit of wood there.'

Henry obediently bent to pick up the broad piece of wood and marvelled at the confidence with which Dan clutched the skep and held it up trustingly under the swarm, which had by now recovered from its earlier disturbance and was humming quietly, a self-contained world. Henry took a deep breath, feeling the trickles of sweat beginning to irritate his neck. If he knocked too hard those bees could fall on the child's head. On the other hand he might just frighten them, and they would whirl away from the central force which held them and become a terrifying, stinging crowd.

He spoke quietly to Dan. 'How do we keep them in that basket?'

'Piece of cardboard – look.' Dan had it all ready on the ground beside him.

'Now listen to me, Dan. If those bees miss your basket, you are not to try to scoop them up. You move away, fast. Understand?'

Dan, impressed by the low urgency in Henry's voice which suddenly gave him authority, moved his head in a solemn nod and heaved the basket up to within an inch of the swarm. Then he pushed it up further so that it just touched the pendulous tip of the vibrating mass of bees. The intensity of the buzzing increased once more and Henry knew that he must move now. In a state of abject terror he stepped forward, blinking as salty sweat ran into his eyes. He grasped the end of the branch and using an instinctive scooping movement, twisted the thick piece of wood to persuade the whole mass into Dan's basket. At the same time he gave the branch a sharp shake and gazed in amazement, his fear forgotten, as the mass of the swarm, still buzzing, fell neatly into the skep. Dan staggered a little as they subsided, but with great presence of mind he put it gently on the ground, covered it with the carboard and straightened himself to stand and grin at Henry. Henry, weak with relief, grinned back, and they both stood in silence watching the dozen or so escapees spiralling up and up, circling through the branches of the trees seeking their lost home.

Henry sighed and bent to pick up the skep. Holding the cardboard lid firmly on with his thumbs, he carried it round to the back of the house and placed it gently on the ground near the hives. He turned to go and, with a sense of shock, suddenly remembered the reality which had been driven from his mind by the collection of the swarm.

'We must go and tell someone about the old man,' he said, but Dan was not listening.

'Were you really frightened of the bees, Henry?' he asked.

Henry could not answer. He had no distinct memory of the horrors of his childhood, but shapes and forms came into his mind – things connected with the dark. The dark, darkness, death. He stooped and picked a handful of flowers, pink and blue, and held them out to Dan, who took them gravely. Henry caught his breath as he watched Dan trot steadily across the grassy patch which separated them from the sleeping dead man on the bank. He took off his spectacles and wiped them on his stripy shirt as the boy strewed the flowers gently over Frederic's head and back.

'Herring boxes without topses, Sandals were for Clementine,' sang Petra at the top of her voice as she flicked at the indicator switch on the dashboard before turning left off the main road. She slowed down for the junction and manoeuvred a double bend before straightening up along a low flat stretch of road bordered on the left-hand side by a leafy crowning of beech trees. The land at the right was divided at right-angles to the road by wire fences which separated long grassy meadows stretching away into a blue haze of distance. All along the fences at regular intervals were large black dots which Petra took to be some kind of post or support, but as she slowed down she realized that they were birds, rooks, sitting evenly spaced out along the lines of the wires.

Petra, who had been focusing on the broad sweep of life which had suddenly opened up before her, the chance of fulfilment, with French lessons, pottery classes, an ideal home and garden, an Open University course with a job to follow, retracted her vision to adjust to the odd sight of the rooks, hundreds and hundreds of them, all striking the same attitude, poised on the rim, on an edge, waiting for a signal, looking for a direction. It was just as well that as she spotted the waiting rooks she slowed down to see them more clearly for, with her head full of plans for the future, she did not notice the enormous sheet of dark water spread over the left hand side of the road. Suddenly the little MG was floundering and swerving. Petra gasped as the narrow windscreen blurred with streaks and drops of muddy water and she prayed that nothing was coming the other way as she fought to keep the car on what she hoped was a proper course. Where the hell was the wiper switch? She flicked wildly at the dashboard, knocking the indicator on before the wipers began their rhythmic sweep across her clouded vision.

All at once she was soaking wet. Mud and water, separating out, were dripping down her face, soaking her hair, slipping down her neck and soaking her clothes. It took her some time to understand what had happened and why a narrow band of daylight had appeared between the top of the windscreen and the soft hood. By the time she was able to stop, when the road had become a clear passageway once again with the past behind and the way ahead visible, she saw that the fabric of the hood of the car had sagged under the weight of the water which was forced upwards as she sped through it. The metal clip on the front had given way under the strain and pints of water had poured through the gap. She was shaking when she got out of the car and refixed the hood, and she sat quite still in the driver's seat for a few minutes before driving on. Home was only an hour or so away now.

'Oh Jesus,' said Henry vehemently, hopping awkwardly on one foot and shaking his right leg violently. Philip gazed at him in astonishment and tried, at the same time, to make sense of Dan's garbled story. Henry flapped his hands at Philip, who had been half-heartedly pushing an old lawnmower round and through the overgrown grass between the apple trees in the garden. A searing pain, growing in intensity, speared his leg just above and inside his knee. He knew what had happened – one of those appalling little bees had crawled up inside his trouser leg and had bided its time before administering its vicious sting. The pain was unbelievable and Henry could feel the colour draining from his face.

203

'You all right?' Philip asked doubtfully, looking suspiciously at the pale and swaying Henry, who was moaning softly and flapping the widest part of his trouser leg.

'Bee sting – knew I should have worn my tracksuit today, it couldn't have crawled up those trousers,' Henry groaned.

'What, on your leg? You should put some vinegar on it, I think.' Philip was trying to remember what it said in that little manual on beekeeping that he had edited recently at work. There must have been something in it about the treatment of stings. Dan was hopping from foot to foot and seemed likely to burst into tears, but Philip, unable to break into the necessary area of communication and feeling his inadequacy keenly, just looked helplessly from his son to Henry, who was rolling his trouser leg up and looking at the little red mark with its dead-white halo.

'That'll be swollen out here by this evening,' Henry said at last. 'Look Philip, can you call out an ambulance or the police or whatever. I'm afraid that the old man down the road is dead. No, it's all right. Dan understands – he's seen him too.'

'Dad! Dad!' Fiona came running out of the house and gave Henry's bare leg a contemptuous glance as she rushed up to Philip. 'Mummy's just rung up – from a phone box. She says she'll be here in about half an hour. Oh, and William's crying – I think he's bumped himself.'

The family group pulled apart and reassembled itself. Philip walked resolutely into the house with Dan and Fiona in tow. Henry's leg, now mercifully pain-free for a while, was still bared. He stood alone under the apple tree marvelling at the ways in which the mind adjusted itself to deal with any situation, letting action be the panacea until the emotions took over.

Chapter Twelve

'No! I don't believe it! Philip, can you come here a minute?' Petra, sitting uncomfortably on the side of her bed, skimmed quickly through the letter in her hand. It was postmarked London and she had recognized Henry's precise handwriting on the envelope when Dan had brought the post up to her earlier. In the six months since Henry had stayed with them at Coombe, recovering from his bee sting, there had been three other letters and a few postcards, from India, from France and from Sweden. She tried to see the date of the postmark and sighed – it had been written and sent from London, three days ago. So Henry was by now in Sri Lanka. He had said he was going tomorrow in the letter.

'Philip,' she shouted again, and winced as she felt the tenderness in her right breast. There were still a couple of pages of the letter unread, but she could not get past the fact that he had decided to go to Asia to become a Buddhist.

'Are you all right, love?' Philip's face was habitually creased into a heavy, anxious look, these days, since the evening, three weeks ago, when Petra had found a little hard foreign lump in the soft flesh of her breast. A pea-sized lump which shook the level tenor of their lives and frightened Philip into a knowledge of uncertainty. Through the visits to the doctor, to the specialist and the hospital, through the operation, even the reassurance that it was benign, just a little lump of harmless tissue, he had been shaken. Petra found his depression hard to accept. Caroline's dreadful death, the discovery by Dan and

Henry of the old man's body – neither of these events had tugged at his existence. Their impact had been that of excitement: he was a spectator outside their horror. But his routine, his comfortable regular way of living, had been broken into, not only by Petra's forced withdrawal from household affairs for a few days, but also by this new vision of what the future could hold, his first glimpse of the darkness.

Petra herself had not been worried at all. She knew it was just a harmless nothing, a freak invasion, and she submitted to the examinations, the hospital routine and the discomfort of the operation. She was distressed, not for herself but for the sake of some of the old women, many of them obviously suffering from terminal cancer, who were living their last weeks and days in the big surgical ward. She could not understand how they could still worry over the common-place, over a plant not being watered back at home, a cat being fed or the difficulties encountered by the men who would not be able to get in to read the gas or electricity meters. How could they fret about the everyday details of their lives and occupy themselves with the small, familiar things when they faced the biggest, and most awesome mystery of all? One old lady, thin and frail and desperately distressed over the indignities she had suffered over the course of her treatment for bowel cancer, but too polite, too bewildered and too used to being bossed around to do anything but apologize and thank the nurses when they were being impatient with her, turned to Petra one day, thin wisps of grey hair hanging scraggily down the sides of her wrinkle-etched face, and started to talk. She outlined in great detail the layout of the little kitchenette in her one-bedroomed old people's flat. She talked of the special little cupboard above the boiler, where she kept a store of tins of soup and fish and meat.

'You see, dear, there's always something there then if I can't somehow feel like proper cooking. Tomato soup's the one I like best, that's my favourite, but I keep lentil too, and if I'm feeling a bit off-colour it's an easy meal, you see.' And she rambled on while Petra listened with a growing sense of

206

horror at the old lady's determined clutch on some sort of stability in her diminishing life.

Philip must have felt the same sort of horror when Petra discovered her lump. The knowledge made him shrink inside and become helpless and a little in awe of her. She had found this touching and rather amusing at first, but it was now beginning to irritate her, and she spoke more sharply than she meant to as he asked her again now, how she felt, if she was all right.

'Yes, of course, I'm fine. Philip, did you hear what I said?'

'About what?'

'Henry – Henry Sicardi. Look, he wrote this letter from London, three days ago. He says he's going out to Sri Lanka to join a Buddhist monastery. In fact he should be there by now because he says he was going to post the letter on the way to Heathrow. I wonder if he's going . . .' Petra's voice tailed off doubtfully, but Philip picked up the thread of her thoughts and knew what she meant.

'No one ever found any wreckage, you know. Henry would have no chance of discovering anything, and what would be the point if he did? If he says he's going to become a Buddhist, I imagine that's exactly what he is going to do. But what about all the money and stuff he was left?'

'Oh. I don't know. He might say. There's a couple of pages I haven't read yet.'

Henry, sitting uncomfortably on a low table in a cold bare little reception room of the vast solid monastery built like a small town into the rock and earth of eternal mountains, thought of his letter to Petra and wondered what her reaction to it had been. He coughed dryly and winced as his back and chest ached. His eyes felt sore and gritty and he carefully and absently poked a long finger behind his spectacles and gently rubbed at his half-closed eyelid. He was trying to be still, to be at peace, to find that within himself which he was sure was there somehow, but lost. But the long wait to see the priest was making him tense and edgy. He fidgeted, trying to ignore the growing ache in his crossed legs and to blank out all thoughts which distracted his mind from communicating with his inner self. But he kept thinking about the wills. Had Caroline and Peter agreed together to leave all their possessions to him in some sort of pact born of guilt? He remembered, Peter's will was dated two years before Caroline's. Had they discussed their intentions, perhaps feeling a certain responsibility towards him, an urge to protect him against the emotional deprivation that their liaison undoubtedly brought him? He sighed and eased his cramped muscles, rubbing his ankle and tensing and untensing his thighs. Death, the reality of death, must have been a long way from their minds. There could have been no premonition which sent Caroline to her solicitor to draw up the document. It had even occurred to Henry that neither Caroline nor Peter knew the right thing to do, the right way to dispose of their goods, and each had left everything to him so that he could sort it all out. He always managed to sort things out. He breathed deeply and slowly as he had been taught, losing himself for an instant in the concentration on the one action, but the noise of his efforts disturbed the stillness of that room which seemed to Henry to reject him, to suppress quietly the grossness of a breathing, sweating physical being. He felt as if the air in the room was moving at his intrusion, distressed at his presence and his lack of spiritual peace.

He thought of the articles he had read in newspapers and magazines, of the pieces he had cut out about the holy men in their saffron robes. In his small case he had cuttings from a Sunday newspaper, including an account of the existence of one of these men, a meditator and a recluse who was able, at will, to raise his body temperature to cope with the freezing weather conditions in the wild area in which he lived bare-foot and bare-chested. His mind had become a mystical power-house controlling his bodily needs automatically, while it transcended the physical and concentrated on the eternal. Henry knew that this was the ultimate, the goal. A sudden sense of panic constricted his throat and squeezed at his heart. Sitting uncomfortably, his thighs aching, his head hurting and his eyes sore and dry, he looked around for a way to escape but just as he was gathering himself together to tiptoe to the arched doorway, a grave figure, robed and with downcast eyes and folded hands, glided in to motion him courteously onwards and inwards to another still stone room.

Petra, her little face sharp and pink, hair tucked neatly behind her small ears, sat still on the edge of her bed, her right breast throbbing and aching, reading her letter while Philip stared moodily out of the window seeing nothing. Petra then looked up at him and wished he would cheer up a little bit. 'Trust Henry to do the right thing!' she said.

'What's so right about becoming a Buddhist? Bloody silly to go all that way, I think. If he felt so strongly about it surely he could have joined a monastery or something here, or in America. He is American, isn't he?'

'Canadian, I think. Don't know really. He lived in New York but he doesn't seem to belong anywhere. But I'm not talking about him becoming a monk. I must say I think he's very brave doing that, because it does seem pretty drastic and perhaps he won't stick it. I'm talking about the wills. He says in this letter that Peter left him a lot of money. Doesn't say how much but he's given it all back to the family. Peter's family in New York. Seems they were going to fight the will, anyway.'

'Probably the easiest thing to do, then,' said Philip grudgingly. 'He doesn't need it anyway from what I'd gathered.'

Petra tried to assess her husband's mood. She looked at him warily, thinking that he had never made any positive statement about Henry and she was not sure whether he actively disliked him or just could not make up his mind. It had been hard for Philip, she knew, to adjust his ideas when Henry had told them about Peter. He had been delicate about the precise nature of his relationship with Peter, but Petra knew and Philip thought that he did.

The hot spell was just beginning to break when Petra had drawn up outside her house in Coombe in Caroline's blue car. Thick black clouds gathered themselves slowly together behind the tall trees at the back of the fields, and the brilliant light created by the conflict between the substance of the clouds and the brightness of the sun made those trees stand out, more green and more real than they had ever been. Petra stood and gazed at them for a minute before she reached in the car for her overnight bag and went on into the house.

'Hello Petra,' said Henry weakly from his position full-length on the sofa, which was too short for his lanky legs, one of which flopped onto the floor while the other stretched carefully up and over the arm.

'Hello Henry.' Petra stooped and kissed his forehead, while Philip and the children gaped at her.

'You've got mud on your face, Petra.'

'Mummy, the bee man's dead, lying in his garden.'

Petra did not hear her son. She was still looking at Henry. 'Whatever happened to your leg, Henry? You haven't changed a bit.'

'I think I must react a bit to bee stings. I feel rather odd.'

Petra gazed at his leg as he pulled up his trousers to show her the enormous hot red swollen patch. She said nothing but left the room to get the stuff for bee stings which she thought must be in the bathroom cabinet. When she returned with it, Philip told her again about the mud on her face.

'I know. I drove through a puddle. I hope you don't mind, Henry – keep still while I put this on, although I don't suppose it will do much good now. Henry, that car I'm driving – the blue one outside the window – that's yours I'm afraid. We found Caroline's will in it and she's left everything to you.'

Henry glanced out of the window, peering through his tiny gold-rimmed spectacles at the car and then looking curiously at his deformed leg. He lay back on the cushions, squeezing his eyelids shut.

'Is he all right?' Fiona was awed by this performance.

Petra sent all the children out of the room. 'How long has he been like this?' she asked Philip, who had gone across to the window to look at the car.

'He hasn't – only just before you got here. It's not the sting, or not just the sting. I think it's what you just told him. How did you get your face all muddy like that by driving through a puddle?'

Petra looked in the mirror which hung by the door and tried to dab at some of the dried mud with a shredded piece of tissue which she found in her pocket, but she only made the patches streakier.

'Philip's right. It's not my leg. Do you think we should call a doctor, though?' Henry, who could cope with most situations, now discovered that he had a morbid fear of insect bites and stings.

'No. It's only a sting. They always go like that. Has Caroline's will surprised you?'

'Yes. No. I mean I say yes because it hadn't occurred to me that there might be a will, and then it's not really surprising because I suppose she did it to make it up to me. Although she couldn't possibly have known that they were going to die.'

'They? Make what up?' Petra frowned at Henry and then she caught Philip's eye. He was pursing his lips and shaking his head slightly. Petra thought he looked ridiculous with that thick piece of hair flopping over one eye and she nearly burst out laughing. But when she turned back to Henry she saw a look of intense concentration on his face. His eyes behind those small round lenses seemed reduced and blank; blue points focused inwardly.

'Caroline wasn't alone when she died in that aeroplane. She was with Peter. Peter was my friend, too. My flat-mate from New York. You understand, Petra?' Petra nodded. 'They were in love, had been together for some weeks, and slipped off to India, just the two of them for a holiday. They were both in that aeroplane when it crashed. They died together.'

Philip shook his head. He assumed that Peter had cut Henry out, had taken Caroline from him, but he failed to see why they should both will their estates to him.

211

Petra understood instantly. 'So you lost them both, Henry. I'm sorry. You lost them both before the crash. Caroline never told anyone that she had Peter you know. She certainly didn't tell M. We didn't even know that she had gone to India until a day or so after she died. That's what upset M so much, you see, that Caroline didn't even tell them that she was going. It seemed so unlike her to do things on impulse. She always did what she wanted, but it was carefully planned. It was the suddenness of everything that shocked my parents.'

'Oh my damned leg!' moaned Henry, gently stroking the shiny red swelling with a fingertip. 'Are you sure it's going to be all right, Petra? What if it carries on spreading at this rate? You read of people going into shock and dying of bee stings.'

'It will be all right. I had one like that last week on my knee. It's gone now.'

'Oh my God!' Philip hit the side of his head with his palm. 'The old chap! Petra, the old bee man in that wooden bungalow down the road, well he's dead. Dan and Henry found him this morning lying in his garden.'

'Dan did?'

'Yes, but don't worry, he seems OK. He thought that the old man was just asleep apparently, although he does realize that he is dead.'

'Caroline,' said Henry. 'He related it to Caroline's death. Did you tell the children how Caroline had died?'

Petra looked shame-faced. 'Well, no. Not really. It was rather difficult. Children and death. It's like talking about God or sex with them. We just told them as little as possible. I don't understand what you mean about him relating the old man to Caroline. How did he die anyway?'

'I don't know, but he must have just had a heart attack or something. Dan was talking to me about Caroline as we walked down there. He was taking a pink flower to the old man. He wanted to know how she died – I think it was just the state of death that puzzled him. He couldn't relate it to anyone who was alive. But then he saw someone in that state and he just accepted it. That's all you can do, really, isn't it?'

212

Petra couldn't meet Henry's bright, blank stare. 'When did all this happen?' she asked.

'About an hour ago,' said Philip. 'We called an ambulance and rang up the police and I expect they'll be round any minute to take statements or whatever it is they do. I hope they won't want to talk to Dan about it.'

The light was slowly draining out of the room as the dark clouds drew themselves slowly up and together. Outside the window the green leaves were lush against the heavy purple of the sky, whilst the big white daisies that scrambled un-hindered in the untidy flower beds gleamed with an intense luminosity in the gathering dark stillness. The three of them stared out of the window. Petra felt oppressed by the weather as much as by the unasked questions, but just as she was about to speak again there was a loud knock at the door and the first heavy drops of thundery rain splattered plumply onto the nodding daisy heads.

When the inquest came it was an odd experience for Petra, especially as it turned out that she had been the last adult to talk to old Doctor Mann, on that day – only just over a week before – when she had helped him with his swarm. In fact the Coroner made great play of the fact that Doctor Mann was a recluse and that it seemed no one else had ever spoken to him, or seemed to know anything about him at all. Petra felt ashamed as he looked steadily round the village hall at the jurors, all local people, at her and Henry and Philip, and at the few curious souls and the local press sitting uncomfortably on hard chairs. She felt condemned for not looking after the elderly and lonely people although, as the Coroner himself later remarked, there was no sign at all of any physical neglect on Frederic's body.

Henry, his bee sting by now much less swollen, gave evidence of his discovery of the body and the Coroner seemed to find the fact that he and Dan had occupied themselves with collecting the swarm significant. (It turned out that the swarm itself made its way out of the makeshift shelter of the skep and disappeared without trace.)

'But I don't quite understand why you found it imperative to collect this swarm after you knew Doctor Mann was dead,' he insisted, looking at Henry with raised eyebrows, taking in the pink silk shirt, open at the neck, and the loose white suit.

'It was because he was dead that we did it,' replied Henry, and by the end of his evidence it was clear that the Coroner and the members of his hastily convened jury regarded Henry as a highly suspicious character.

But, as Philip had remarked beforehand, it seemed that there was no real need for an inquest at all. Surely the cause of his death must have been natural – an old man dying in his sleep, in his garden. But the doctor who carried out the post-mortem could find nothing organically wrong. His heart was still healthy – it had simply stopped beating. And there were the letters.

Petra, in giving her evidence, had mentioned that she thought that the old man had muttered something about writing to his wife. That released the floodgates of zeal on behalf of the local police, who had been sifting through the hundreds and hundreds of notes and letters stuffed into the old trunk. None of them thought to examine the trunk more closely or they might have found more interesting evidence. But they had been busy. They even managed to produce the letter which Frederic had written on the day that the bees first swarmed.

'Darling Elise,' read out the pale-faced solid young police-man in his Somerset accent. 'Today I find that they have settled well in their new homes. I have added some more frames to two of the other hives, as the nectar is flowing well this year. I picked some of the little wild roses for you today but the petals fall so quickly. I cannot describe the beauty of these lanes at this time of year, but you will know what I mean when I say that they are full of the luxury of June – as you love them. I will try to tell you about them tomorrow.'

There was a hush in the court after this was read out and Petra saw that the young policeman, sweating in the heat of

the room, was now rosy-red about the face with embarrassment. The police had deduced from the state of the ink and the
glue on the envelope that this letter was a very recent one, and
they linked it with Petra's evidence. But who was Elise?

There were nearly two thousand of these letters, some long
and rambling, others short and poignant. All were written to
Elise – to 'My dearest Elise' or 'My darling'.

Petra wondered if the Coroner was going to order some
investigation into Frederic's background – after all he had only
been in the village for five years or so. But the doctor said he
could find no evidence that the old man had committed
suicide. He could not really say how Doctor Mann had died,
and no one seemed to think that the letters presented any sort
of evidence that he was about to take his own life. The
Coroner gave Henry a stern glance as an 'Open' verdict was
brought in by the bewildered jurors, and thus was Elise
allowed to rest in peace beneath her bank.

Henry left Coombe the day after the inquest, and Philip
grumbled because they had not discussed Caroline's will. But
Petra pointed out that such a discussion would be fruitless
anyway, because the person who had had the document
drawn up was dead and no one could ask her why she had done
it. 'Does it really matter, anyway?' she had asked him, secretly
glad that Henry had begged her to keep the car, which he said
would just be a nuisance to him.

The excitement and the activity left Petra still full of plans
for her new and fulfilling life. She felt invigorated, high-
powered. She did enrol for the French conversation class
which was to start in September and she took some very thick
volumes out of the library and even went so far as to ask Philip
to buy her *War and Peace* for her birthday, not because she
wanted to read that particular work but because she could not
think of anything else as important. Philip warned her that this
would be a waste of time, and so it proved.

Around the end of July a thick letter arrived from a firm of
solicitors in London, advising her that Caroline's will had
been proved and that Henry had made over the house and its
contents to her. Daddy immediately told her to sell it and to

invest the money, as its upkeep would be nothing but trouble (he proved to be right, too), but she made arrangements with a firm of estate agents to let it. She felt that if it did not hold any sentimental memories for her, it ought to.

By September she had forgotten all about the French classes, although she did start to go swimming regularly once a week at the Sports Centre in a nearby town.

Then came the lump and its removal and now that was over and Henry was being a Buddhist and M and Daddy were coming to stay for Christmas. Petra wished she could work up some enthusiasm for getting things done once more. She gazed across her bedroom floor at the shabby rug which had once been soft sheepskin and she looked at the dressing table which she knew had woodworm and should be treated. There was a small heap of children's clothes on the floor, all of which needed buttons sewing on or zips mending or hems fixing. She would do those tomorrow. And the magazines – she would buy a scrapbook tomorrow and cut out all those recipes and gardening hints and the pictures she liked.

Putting on a dressing gown and easing her toes into soft slippers was a positive action in a life which branched out in front of her in a bewildering network of paths and dead-ends, none of which was labelled clearly enough to lead her anywhere. She walked out of her bedroom and pushed Henry and his Buddhism out of her mind. Caroline's death and Frederic's fading away upset her too much these days. She went into the bathroom, and the slow thunder of the hot water and the heady rise of steam scented with rose-coloured foam was a balm which soothed her body and mind.

Easing herself into the hot water she closed her eyes and breathed in the steam. Henry had made his choice. Was it that she had none to make? Caroline and Peter had picked a path that led to oblivion. It is too easy to go through the habit of living, thought Petra, rolling the soap to a smooth oval, until you realize that the only person with the key to the code of directions is yourself, and you have never properly under-stood how to use it.